RUSTLER MOON

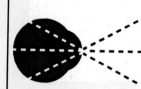

This Large Print Book carries the
Seal of Approval of N.A.V.H.

A JARED DELANEY WESTERN

RUSTLER'S MOON

JIM JONES

WHEELER PUBLISHING
A part of Gale, Cengage Learning

GALE
CENGAGE Learning·

Farmington Hills, Mich • San Francisco • New York • Waterville, Maine
Meriden, Conn • Mason, Ohio • Chicago

GALE
CENGAGE Learning·

LIBRARY OF CONGRESS CATALOGING-IN-PUBLICATION DATA

Jones, Jim, 1950–
    Rustler's moon / Jim Jones.
        pages cm. - (Wheeler publishing large print hardcover) (A Jared Delaney
    western)
        ISBN 978-1-4104-8168-9 (paperback) — ISBN 1-4104-8168-9 (softcover) 1.
    Cowboys—Fiction. 2. Children of murder victims—Fiction. 3.
    Rangelands—Fiction. 4. Cattlemen—Fiction. 5. Ranchers—Fiction. 6.
    Violence—Fiction. 7. Large type books. 8. New Mexico—Fiction. I. Title.
    PS3610.O62572R87 2015
    813'.6—dc23   2015013916

Published in 2015 by arrangement with Cherry Weiner Literary Agency

Printed in the United States of America
1 2 3 4 5   19 18 17 16 15

ACKNOWLEDGEMENTS

I would like to graciously acknowledge the assistance and encouragement of the following people: Ramblin' Ralph Estes, Ranger Rick Huff, Sheriff Jim Wilson and the lovely and talented Kip Calahan, for reviewing various drafts of the manuscript and offering invaluable feedback. Melody Groves for technical help as well as professional advice and friendship. Paul Hutton for support, encouragement and professional guidance. Most especially, to my lovely wife, Ann, for all her love, support and encouragement. You make it all possible and worthwhile.

This book is loosely based in historical fact (that means it's a pack of lies that I made up). As the cowboy says, never let the truth get in the way of a good story!

PROLOGUE

Mama wakes me up in the middle of the night and I can tell she's scared out of her skin even though I'm still half asleep. She says, "Git up the hill and hide in the underbrush. You don't come out until me or Pa comes for you. Nobody else, you hear!" I start to say, "What is it, Mama?" but before the words are even out of my mouth, she says in a hoarse voice I've never heard before, "Now, Jared! Your life depends on it!"

With my heart poundin', I do as I'm told, scootin' out the back door in my long underwear, the rocks and dried grass pokin' my feet as I go. As I run up the hill, I hear horses approachin' at a gallop and men hollerin', though they're still a distance away and I can't make out what they're sayin'. Somethin' in the sound causes a chill to creep up my back and I get that funny, prickly feelin' in my stomach that sometimes comes when you're excited about somethin', but also comes when you're scared. I'm almost to the thick underbrush near the top of the hill when the first shots ring out, startlin' me so bad I nearly trip. I stagger down beneath some mesquite and wiggle in a little farther, bein' careful not to snag myself on the branches. I'm just turnin' around and tryin' to catch a glimpse of what's goin' on below when Pa yells out a curse and I hear his old Henry rifle discharge, followed by Mama's scream. I hear more shots and angry voices that I don't recognize. They sound more like a pack of wolves on the hunt than humans and I must admit I'm purely terrified. I know I need to go down to help my parents. I tell myself to get up and run back to the cabin. I'm nine years old. I have my own rifle. I know how to use it. There's no excuse. Somehow, my legs won't move, no matter how many times I tell'em to, no matter how many times I curse myself for not actin' like the man my Pa would have me be. All the while, the shoutin' and shootin' continues. It seems like it goes on for hours, though it had to have been only a matter of minutes.

All of a sudden, it's quiet, the kind of quiet that spooks you when you're out huntin' and the birds quit singin', like maybe there's a mountain lion around just waitin' to pounce. Again, the silence prob'ly doesn't last but a few seconds, but with me holdin' my breath and havin' my heart in my throat, it seems a lot longer. Then I hear a voice that chills me to the marrow. It's sort of soft and hard at the same time and I don't know how a voice can feel cold, but it does. The voice says, "All right, boys, fan out and see what else you find. From the looks of it, this old dirt farmer and his woman's all that's here, but let's just be sure."

If I was ashamed before, I'm mortified now. I know somethin' awful has happened to Mama and Pa, I can tell by the way their voices aren't among the ones I hear, but I can't move. I guess I know how the field mouse feels when the owl is circlin'. You sense it even if you can't see it and you know if you budge, you're dead, but you can't stop shakin' even so. A part of my mind keeps thinkin' Pa would turn away in disgust if he could see what I was doin', while another part, kind of way in the back of my mind, says, "Jared, you ain't never gonna have to worry about facin' your Pa cause he's moved on to another world." I know that means my Mama has passed, too, and I can feel the tears start to well up in my eyes. I shudder and a sob starts to work its way up from my guts when I hear boot-steps crunchin' in the dirt about twenty feet down the hill. I don't rightly know how you stop a sob, but I do, right in its tracks, if a sob has tracks.

I try not to breathe as I wait to see who's comin' up the hill. I realize that if I hold my breath, it'll all come out in a rush and I'll be like that field mouse with the owl. I try real shallow breaths, sure whoever's comin' up the hill will be bound to notice. He walks on past me, though and goes on up to the top of the hill where he's silhouetted by the light of the quarter moon, the one they call the rustler's moon. Up above me like that, he looks about ten times larger than life with his big hat and a rifle that he carries with one hand as if it weighs nothin'. As long as I live, that image will be burned into my mind like some kind of brand. I know the man is the owner of the voice I heard, don't ask me how, but I know it as well as I know my own name. Then he speaks and at first, I think he's talkin' to me, which causes me to wet my pants and adds further shame to my predicament. Then it seems like maybe he's just talkin' to the air or the spirits or something, cause he speaks like he's havin' a personal chat with someone.

"Well, we have us an interesting situation here, don't we. I purely enjoy these times when I get to make some kind of choice that'll come back to roost way on down the line. I could have the boys burn this place to the ground and clean up all the mess that's left hanging around so I'd be shed of it all from now on. On the other hand, we could grab what was worth taking and leave that old man and his woman lying there. If we do that, it could get interesting in a few years as things develop, don't you reckon?"

All this is said in a conversational tone that's chillin' nonetheless, and I feel again that he's talkin' both to me and about me. That doesn't make sense to me, though, cause I figure if he knows I'm here, he'd just shoot me or haul me out for somethin' worse. While I ponder the question, he starts walkin' back down the hill. Just as he gets even with my hidin' place, he stops, turns and looks down to where I hide, quiverin'. I find myself lookin' into the coldest, bluest eyes I've ever seen then or now and no doubt, forever. He lets out a little chuckle and says, "Yep, it could get interesting in a few years as things develop, I reckon." Right then, that rustler's moon goes behind a cloud and it seems like my life slips into a fog.

CHAPTER 1

It was mid-afternoon of a hot summer day when Jared Delaney rode into the New Mexico town of Cimarron. It didn't look much different from all the other little towns he'd ridden into over the past several years as he'd rambled around Texas and the New Mexico territory. A bank, a Western Union office, some buildings with false fronts and some honest to goodness wooden structures aged to a gray color by the wind and weather. Hand-lettered signs indicated the mercantile and the office of the town doctor. A stone building looked like a courthouse but it seemed to be abandoned. People walked along the boardwalks as he rode through and of course, they glanced his way, as folks will do when a stranger rides into town. Nothing unusual about that but at the same time, Jared had a funny feeling he was scrutinized more carefully and with more suspicion than he was ac-

15

customed to in previous times when he'd crossed over that invisible barrier separating "in-town" from "out of town."

His perception of being closely scrutinized was not far off the mark. At first glance, there was nothing remarkable about the young man, yet there was something that called out for a second glance. A shock of black hair peeked out from under his Stetson and if you got close enough, you'd see he had blue eyes. Not a bad-looking fella, all in all, if that mattered to you. Judging from the length of his stirrup, he might be on the tall side, which would turn out to be the case if you stood up next to him. A shade over six feet was a fair guess. Appeared as if he should be happy-go-lucky. Had the look of a cowboy, which he was, but there was something else, too, a sort of haunted quality that didn't quite fit with the rest of him. Hard to put your finger on but it left you feeling a bit uneasy. A sense of unpredictability, maybe, which as it turns out, was not an especially good characteristic to have in this town at this time.

Jared was looking for work, a place to stay and a drink, not neccesarily in that order, and the heat won out, so he stopped at the only watering hole he saw. The sign said

"Colfax Tavern" and printed underneath it in big letters were the words "cold beer." Cold and wet sounded just fine to Jared, so he hitched his horse and walked inside. It was the middle of the afternoon, but there were a fair number of customers. Jared looked the crowd over, noticing that while some of the men looked at him with curiosity, others stared at him with outright hostility. He had a notion that if he said or did the slightest thing out of line, he'd find himself in a serious bar fight at the drop of a hat. Avoiding the hostile stares, he walked up to a space at the end of the bar and waited to get the bartender's attention. The bartender, a burly fella, was in a conversation with some rough looking cowboys at the other end of the bar and didn't seem to be in a big hurry to serve anyone, but Jared curbed his impatience, not wanting to do anything to spark the tinderbox of tension in the bar. Finally, the bartender noticed him and sauntered down to the end of the bar where Jared stood. Jared judged him to be a bit of a dandy with his handlebar mustache and braces. "What'll you have, stranger?" asked the bartender.

Jared replied, "I'll have one of those cold beers you were advertisin' out front on your sign." The bartender walked down the bar and reached underneath in the cool shadows, pulled out a bottle and returned to where Jared was. Jared slipped several coins across the bar and the bartender took them, keeping the change for himself without asking. Again, Jared overlooked the impertinence and took a long draw off of his not-so-cold beer. He set it down and asked the bartender, "Where might a workin' cowboy find employment around here?"

"Depends on what all he's accomplished and whose side he's on," responded the bartender, somewhat sassily, Jared thought. The response more puzzled than annoyed Jared. He thought maybe he ought to introduce himself and find out more about the situation.

He said, "Well, I just rode into town and the only side I'm on right now is my own. Name's Jared Delaney and I last worked for Mister Goodnight at the JA ranch in the Palo Duro Canyon. I was with his outfit for three years." Jared stopped there, figuring anyone who knew about Charlie Goodnight would know he wouldn't put up with a cowboy for three minutes, let alone three years, if he didn't know his stuff.

The bartender addressed Jared with a little more respect and a hint of friendliness. "I'm

Heck Roberts. I bartend and manage this lovely establishment you're standing in. If you worked for old Charlie, I expect you know what you're doing which gives you a little more leeway in deciding whose side you take." Jared noticed out of the corner of his eye that the cowboys who had been staring at him with fire in their eyes seemed to have heard the change in the bartender's tone of voice as their attention was now directed back to their card game. Roberts continued. "What brings you to our fair little community?"

Jared thought the bartender's reference to Goodnight as "old Charlie" was disrespectful. He said, a bit curtly, "I left Mr. Goodnight about nine months ago cause I was ready for a change. I'd never been in this neck of the woods so I drifted out this direction. Heard it was good cattle country."

"Nine months is a lot of drifting, boy," Roberts said. "Makes me curious about what you were up to on your way out here."

Jared thought the bartender was more than curious, in fact, moving into nosey territory, but since he was ready to take a break from his rambling ways and figured the man was a potential source of information, he again chose to overlook the lack of manners. "I stopped off for the last six months in Lincoln and worked as a deputy for Sheriff Mills. Steady work and I got to sleep inside most of the time, but as borin' a job as I ever had. Mostly gettin' paid to nose into other people's business, which ain't really my style." Jared arched an eyebrow at the bartender, hoping he would take the hint. Apparently it went right over his head.

"I've heard about Sheriff Mills and Lincoln," Roberts said. "Sounds interesting to me."

Jared shook his head and said, "Well, maybe to you but not to me. Sheriff Mills spent most of his time kissin' up to the folks that had money so he could get re-elected. Seemed to me it interfered with his real job of keepin' the peace."

Roberts chuckled and said, "Maybe he thought his 'real job' was getting re-elected."

"Could be," Jared replied. "Anyhow, I drew my wages three weeks ago and wandered up this direction. It's pretty country and I hear there's quite a few cattle ranches around where a man of my skills could get work."

"Aren't you the interesting fella," Heck said. "Things have been a little dull around here lately but maybe you can liven them up. First thing you're going to want is another beer on the house, then a place to stay for the night and some advice on who to talk to about your plans."

A young woman who obviously worked for Roberts swished over and stepped up beside Jared. Her honey brown hair was done up in ringlets with bows and she was wearing a pink dress that looked sort of puffy and frilly to Jared. Like all the other girls in the place, she was painted with rouge and smelled of cheap perfume, yet there was something about her that was appealing in an almost innocent way. "Funny word to apply to a working girl," Jared thought as he tipped his Stetson in acknowledgement of her presence.

"Howdy, handsome, welcome to the Colfax Tavern. What's your name?"

Jared blushed and looked at Roberts, who just laughed. He then turned back to the woman and said, "Why, I'm Jared Delaney from Texas, m'am."

"Glad to meet you, Jared Delaney from Texas, name's Christie Quick and I ain't a m'am. That ain't my real name either, just a nickname. I got it a few years back in a place that wasn't near as fancy as this one," she said with a nod and smile at Heck. "I'd go upstairs with some cowboy to take care of business and the bartender would holler at me, 'Christie . . . quick!' The name stuck.

21

Care to join me for a drink, Jared Delaney from Texas?"

Jared was a bit befuddled. Meeting up with a calico queen hadn't been on his list of things to do when he rode into town. He had business to take care of first. In addition, he'd never felt comfortable around women, having lost his mother early, and he tended to say things he later regretted. He blushed some more. "Thank you kindly, m'am, but I gotta find a place to stay and I need to rinse the trail dust off the outside as well as the inside. Maybe I could come back later and take you up on your kind offer."

Christie laughed and said, "You ain't only handsome, you're polite, too. That ain't somethin' girls see around here too often. Any time you want to come back, look me up. If you don't see me around, I'm probably upstairs, but don't worry, I'll be quick." Laughing, she turned with another swish of her dress and walked over to a group of cowboys and gamblers who were deeply involved in a poker game.

"She's something else," said Heck, following her with his eyes before turning back to Jared. It seemed to Jared that Roberts had a malicious glint in those eyes as he watched the young woman walk away and he wasn't sure what to make of that. Lust he would have understood, even as green as he was with the ladies, for the woman was the most attractive girl in the place, hands down. He mentally tallied the incident up as another slightly odd characteristic of this town.

"You'll need a place to stay," Roberts said, interrupting his reverie. "The St. James Hotel has fairly clean beds, you can get a bath, and their steaks are as good as you'll get in town. I also recommend you make your next stop the Sheriff's office. Nathan Averill likes to keep tabs on new folks in town and he might even have some tips on where you could find work. He'll want to know what direction you might be leaning, too." Jared noticed that this last bit of news was delivered with much less enthusiasm than the rest and wondered about the significance of that. "When you take care of all that business," Roberts continued, "come on back. I think Christie likes you and there's some other folks you should meet so you can get the lay of the land, if you know what I mean."

Jared wondered what all the talk about taking sides meant. He knew all towns had their factions, both political and social but he'd never been confronted with it so quickly or openly as he had upon entering

Cimarron. He was tired and dusty, though and figured he'd find out soon enough. At the moment, he needed to know how to get to the sheriff's office, so he asked the now-friendly bartender for directions. Roberts said, "Head south when you walk out of here, go past the school and look to your right. You'll see a sign."

Jared said, "Thanks Mr. Roberts, I'll prob'ly be back later this evening."

Heck said, "You'll have to get over those manners if you're going to last around here. Call me Heck!"

Jared grinned and said, "All right, Heck, I appreciate your advice and the beer." As he walked out, he noticed the same bunch that had eyed him with hostility were watching him closely as he left the bar.

Jared followed Heck Roberts' directions and headed down Main Street. As he passed the school, he heard a bell being rung. Next thing he knew, he was engulfed in a small sea of youngsters ranging in age from about five to fifteen. As they streamed past him, a striking young woman with a mass of raven hair tied up in a bun stepped out of the door and hollered, "Look out, don't trample innocent bystanders, you aren't stampeding cattle!" Several children looked back at her and waved with smiles on their faces. She waved back and shook her head. She nodded to Jared, who tipped his hat and nodded a bit awkwardly, then she walked back inside the schoolhouse. It seemed to Jared that her piercing green eyes took in everything about him in that brief encounter. He wondered uncomfortably what conclusions she had drawn. It occurred to him that he'd been in town less than an hour and had already seen two very attractive ladies, one a school teacher and the other a working girl in the bar. He had to laugh at himself as he realized that he was equally uncomfortable with both. "You're a real lady's man, ain't you, Delaney?" he thought ruefully.

Breaking free of the stampeding students, Jared saw the sheriff's office across the street and crossed over to knock on the door. A gruff voice from inside replied, "Come on in, it ain't locked." Jared entered and saw a man whom he assumed to be the sheriff sitting at a desk, cleaning a Colt revolver. The man looked to be getting along in years but just how old he was, Jared couldn't tell. His hair was iron-gray and his skin was weather-beaten and browned by the sun. He could have been forty, sixty or anything in between. He didn't appear to have an ounce of fat on his body and looked like he was strung together with barbed wire and leather. As Jared walked in, the sheriff looked him over with steel gray eyes that revealed nothing . . . neither friendliness nor suspicion. On second thought, perhaps they revealed caution and a watchful neutrality, which was next to nothing. Finally, he rose, extended his hand and said evenly, "Afternoon, my name is Nathan Averill. I'm the sheriff. Who might you be?"

"Name's Delaney, Jared Delaney. I just rode into town. I stopped in the tavern down the street and the bartender informed me I oughta check in with you. I'm lookin' for work."

"Heck Roberts sent you over, did he?" the sheriff responded with a hint of a twinkle in those gray eyes. "Did he turn a little green when he told you about me? Never mind, you don't need to answer. I probably ought not to start teasin' you until I get to know you, if you do stick around. You look like a cowboy, son. Is that the sort of work you're lookin' for?"

"Yes sir, it is. I've got considerable experience in the saddle and was told you might point me in the direction of a ranch that's in need of a hand," Jared answered.

"I might be of assistance," the sheriff

replied. "Tell me about yourself."

Jared told his story like he'd told it to Heck Roberts, telling about his years on the Goodnight ranch and describing his brief stint as a lawman in Lincoln county. At the mention of Sheriff Mills, Averill made a face and laughed when Jared explained his distaste for what he called "kissin' up." He said, "Yeah, if old Ham Mills was as good with his sixgun as he is with his mouth, he might get re-elected for cleanin' up the riff-raff. He'd rather get his mouth dirty than his hands, if you know what I mean."

Jared gave a chuckle and said, "Looks like you've made the acquaintance of Sheriff Mills. Anyway, I lost my taste for bein' a lawman and drifted up this direction." Jared paused, then said, "Speakin' of politicians, I ain't familiar with your local politics, maybe you could educate me. The bartender asked me a couple of times in about ten minutes what side I was on. All I knew was that I was on the west side of the street, which I'm pretty sure wasn't what he was referrin' to. Have I wandered into a hornet's nest?"

Sheriff Averill got a grave look on his face. "I reckon that does describe the situation. If you're gonna stick around, you oughta know what you're gettin' into. Let me fill you in."

"I'd appreciate that, Sheriff," Jared said.

"Well, son, most of the folks in this town and the surroundin' countryside are law-abidin' citizens who're just tryin' to scratch out a livin'. Like most barrels, though, I guess we got a few bad apples. There's a group of men connected with some fellas up in the capitol, they're called the Santa Fe Ring, and between'em, they carry a lot of weight here in Colfax County. They're the ones that got the district court moved to Taos, which accounts for our abandoned courthouse. They bully people around election time, they use scare tactics to get some of the smaller ranchers to sell'em land and they've been known to come up with entirely new herds of cattle overnight."

"No offense, Sheriff," Jared interjected, "but that don't sound all that different from any number of other towns I've been through here in New Mexico and in Texas, too. What is it that makes your town such an all-fired hornet's nest?"

"Well, there's a man you'll hear about quite a bit if you stick around, a fella named Morgan O'Bannon. Along with his two brothers, he owns the biggest spread around here. He also owns that tavern you were just in, which is why it's the only one of its kind in town. Some folks'll tell you O'Bannon is

28

a real gentleman, while other folks will get real quiet and change the subject." He picked up the Colt he'd been cleaning, sighted down the barrel and then, apparently satisfied with what he saw, set it back down. "My personal opinion is that Morgan is a very dangerous man. Chances are when he hears you're in town, which he will soon enough since you just shared a beer with one of his minions, he'll offer you a job. I don't know you well enough to start givin' you advice, yet I'm gonna advise you not to take that job. You seem like a decent young fella. If you join up with that outfit, you'll be headin' for trouble."

Jared considered what the sheriff had said. "Thanks for the advice, Sheriff, I expect I'll follow it, at least until I have a chance to size things up myself."

Sheriff Averill took a long look at Jared and seemed to be doing some sizing up of his own. "You know, with your experience, you might consider becomin' my deputy. The last fella I had workin' for me left me about the same time you left Lincoln, though for very different reasons. I got a pretty good feel for people. I got a feelin' you got some strength inside you, a little bit of granite, as they say."

Jared was taken aback that the Sheriff had

offered him a job on the spot and wasn't sure how to respond without offending him. He said, "Sheriff, that's a mighty flatterin' offer, considerin' you don't know me. If I accepted, though, I'd be pickin' a side first crack out of the gate and I don't even know who's who yet. I think I'll take that good advice you just gave me about not joinin' up with anyone yet. Right now, I'm just a cowboy lookin' for work."

The sheriff smiled and said, "All right, son, I can respect that. Stick around long enough, you'll have to make a choice whether you like it or not. For now, I understand your wantin' to see how the wind's blowin'."

"Thanks," Jared said, "I meant no disrespect."

"None taken, son," the sheriff replied.

Jared said, "Besides lookin' for work, I'm also lookin' for the St. James Hotel. Could I trouble you for directions?"

"The St. James is north of the tavern where you started this afternoon, on the same side of the street, just past the old courthouse," the sheriff said. "Tell'em I sent you and said they should give you a room on the west side so you don't have to wake up with the sun. Also, tell'em I said to change the sheets." The sheriff rose and walked toward the door with Jared. "I'll give some thought to the job possibilities for an experienced cowboy and meet you at the St. James in the mornin' to let you know what I come up with. They serve a breakfast that'll stick with you most of the day."

Jared thanked the sheriff, shook his hand and headed out the door, back in the direction of the St. James. As he walked away, Nathan Averill came to the door and studied him, pondering the conversation they'd just had. On the surface, it hung together pretty well. Delaney seemed like he'd make a good hand, having some pretty fair experience that would stand him in good stead with any rancher looking for help. There was something likeable about him, as well. His recounting of his time spent with Sheriff Mills suggested he shared Averill's low tolerance for blarney and he struck the sheriff as an honest and direct fella. There was that other quality, though, the same one that had made people on the street take that second, uneasy glance in his direction. Averill wasn't sure what to make of it but he had enough faith in his gut reactions to know it warranted further investigation. He was a firm believer that if you dug deep enough for information, you could figure out what made a person tick. Once you knew, you'd know what category to put'em in . . . friend or foe. Right now, Jared Delaney was in Sheriff Averill's third category . . . unknown.

Stopping outside the Colfax Tavern to collect his horse, Jared headed on to the St. James. When he checked in and mentioned Sheriff Averill's name, the clerk gave him a big smile and took special care to get him situated in a clean, reasonably-priced room, on the west side of the hotel. He told Jared where he could get a hot bath and suggested the beefsteak in the dining room. Jared accepted this special treatment gratefully and after a big dinner capped off by a large serving of apple pie, he went to his room for the first night's sleep indoors he'd had in weeks. The feather bed was so comfortable that at first, he couldn't fall asleep. After considering the events of the day for a while, he dozed off.

Jared woke himself up with his cries and saw a little bit of light from the quarter moon seeping in through the crack in the curtains. Sweating, trembling, and disoriented, it took him a moment to recall where he was. During that long moment, it felt like his life was hanging by a thread. Gradually, he collected his wits and came back into the present where, as best he could tell, there was no immediate threat. His breathing and heartbeat slowed down to something like a normal rate as he looked around the room dimly lit by moonlight and established that he was safe, at least for the moment. As usual, he couldn't really remember much of the dream, which troubled him no end. It was like a fog had set in and his mind's eye could see only a few steps ahead. He saw snatches of images . . . his Pa lying on the ground, his eyes begging him to help. There was an image of another man with cold, blue eyes, laughing at both him and his Pa. He taunted, "C'mon, sonny, show me what kind of man you are," as if he expected Jared to do something but Jared felt like he was frozen in place. He tried to will his arms and legs to move so he could save his Pa but nothing happened. Jared was left with a cold sweat and the same old feeling of shame that he couldn't explain.

CHAPTER 2

"Mornin', sheriff," Jared said as he walked into the dining room. "If the breakfast is half as good as the supper was, I might just retire here."

Nathan Averill was already seated, drinking a cup of steaming hot black coffee. Looking over the rim of his coffee cup at Jared, he thought that for all his apparent good spirits, he looked tired. "How'd you sleep, son?" Averill asked.

Jared experienced a brief moment of discomfort as he recalled snatches of his dream. Sitting down, he said, "Just fine, sheriff, once I got use to sleepin' on somethin' a little softer than rocks."

Averill laughed. "Ain't it funny what a man can get used to when he has to. Sometimes that's a good thing, sometimes not so good."

Jared smiled at the sheriff's observation. "Reckon you're right, sheriff. I don't know much about how the rest of the world works but that's how it is in a cowboy's life."

Averill nodded and said, "I had some thoughts about where you might start lookin' for work, but first, I wondered if you'd be willin' to tell me a little more about yourself. I hate to pry, but I'm afraid it comes with my job. I must admit, too, you got me curious. You always this cautious about committin' yourself to anything?" The sheriff had been watching Jared carefully as he spoke and noticed he was starting to look riled up. "Don't get me wrong, son, you seem like an upstandin' young man. I know you just rode into town but there's times a fella needs to make a decision on the fly or he'll get himself in a jam. Like we discussed, things are a bit dodgy around here and I'm responsible for tryin' to keep the lid on. That means I need to collect all the information I can so I can make sense out of what's happenin'."

Jared looked at the sheriff and said, "What sort of information are you lookin' for, Sheriff?"

"Pert near anythin' you want to tell me about your past," Averill replied. "I believe the things we live through mold us to be who we are. If you wouldn't mind, I'd like to understand the shape of your mold a little better."

Jared was a private individual. Usually when faced with such a request, he would've been offended. Although he'd initially felt put off by the interrogation, there was something about the sheriff's manner that seemed to draw him out. Jared got the feeling that he wasn't just doing his job but was genuinely interested in what he had to say. He hesitated, then began. "I was raised up in the panhandle of Texas. When I was a young boy, my parents were killed in a raid by some outlaws. I don't remember none of this, it's just what I was told later."

The sheriff nodded sympathetically. "Sorry for your loss, son. There was a lot of that sorta thing durin' that time." The sheriff paused, then continued, "You're sayin' you got no memory of what happened?"

"That's about the size of it. Hard to believe somethin' changed the course of my life and I can't even remember it but that's what happened." The sheriff could hear the exasperation in Jared's tone. "Anyway, John and Lucy Gilbertson, from a neighborin' ranch, found me wanderin' around on the prairie near 'bout starved and out of my head. I didn't talk for about six months. They took me in, fed me and gradually, I came around to where I'd speak a bit. I never asked'em any questions and they didn't offer much information, so I didn't know what happened to my parents until I was older." Jared paused as he thought back about all the times he'd wondered what happened to his parents but had been afraid to speak of it to the Gilbertsons. "Once I started talkin' a bit, they told me they'd keep me on and let me sleep in the barn if I'd do chores for'em. I had no place to go, so I took'em up on their offer. They worked me pretty hard but they didn't mistreat me. Lucy even taught me to read and write some." Jared stopped but the sheriff waited patiently so he continued with his tale. "When I got a little older, they let me start workin' their horses and turns out I had a knack for it. By the time I was sixteen, I was doin' the job of a foreman, though I didn't realize they weren't playin' me fair. That's why I left, cause I found out I could get paid a decent wage doin' what I'd been doin' for only room and board." A look of resentment crossed Jared's face but it vanished almost immediately. "Don't get me wrong, I appreciate the Gilbertsons. I expect I would of died if they hadn't taken me in, but I feel like I paid'em back in full with the work I did over the years."

The sheriff, who had been silent and attentive up to now, asked, "When did you find out about what happened to your parents?"

Jared thought for a moment and replied, "When I decided to leave, John took it personal. He got mad and told me I didn't appreciate all they'd done for me. He said they'd saved my life and then he told me about the outlaws that had been on a tear through the countryside at that time. He said if they hadn't taken me in, those outlaws would of got me like they did my Mama and Pa. I didn't know what to say to him since I couldn't remember what had happened. I just thanked him again for all he and Lucy had done and told him I still needed to go make my own way."

Nathan Averill leaned forward a bit and asked, "How old are you now, son?"

Jared replied, "Why, I just turned twenty-one this year. I don't know my birthday cause I don't remember anything before my folks died and the Gilbertsons didn't know anything but the year I was born."

The sheriff looked thoughtful and said, "So your parents were killed by outlaws back in about sixty-six, just after the war between the states, is that about right?"

"Well, I guess that'd be about the time.

Why do you ask?" Jared said, puzzled.

The sheriff shook his head and said, "No particular reason, I just know a little somethin' about the outlaws rampagin' through the Indian Territory and north Texas after the war and I had a hunch. You not bein' able to remember makes it of little matter since I don't expect you can recall any details that might help figure out who done the deed."

Jared thought about the man with the cold, blue eyes in his dreams but said nothing about that to the sheriff. Instead, he said, "You know, sheriff, I do remember missin' my Mama, which don't exactly seem manly to admit, but there you have it. I don't even remember what she looked like, there's just kind of a hole inside me where those memories should be. It's the same with my Pa. It seems to me he was big and strong, someone I'd be proud of and would want to make proud of me, too. Sometimes I feel like I don't measure up and I'd give just about anything to have my Mama and Pa here to talk it over with, just so I'd have a little more direction."

Jared stopped for a second, embarrassed at having been so open. "I said more than I intended and I don't even know if I answered your question."

Averill looked him over and said, "Son, you did fine. I reckon I got a better feel for what you lived through and how you got to be the man you are. As for the man you'll be, I expect that's square in your hands, no matter what happened to you before."

"I suppose you're right," Jared said, "but it don't make it easy when you don't even know what happened to you before."

"That's true enough, son, it ain't easy but that don't mean you can't do it. Anyhow, I want you to think about my job offer. I'll leave it on the table for now. In the meantime, I've done some thinkin' and I believe a good bet for you would be to go see Ned Kilpatrick. His ranch is just to the northeast of Cimarron and I know he's short a few hands. Since you're good with horses and cattle, you might inquire out there."

"Thanks, sheriff," Jared said, "I appreciate the tip."

"You might not thank me before all this is done," the sheriff replied. "The reason he's short-handed is due to outlaws . . . cattle rustlin' thieves and murderers. That's why Ned's lookin' for help, it's why I'm lookin' for help and it's why it'll be mighty hard for you to remain neutral if you stick around here for long."

As Jared contemplated what Nathan Averill had said, he heard footsteps approaching
and turned to look over his shoulder. He
saw the raven-haired young woman he had
seen the previous day at the school walking
toward them. As she came up to the table,
she said, "Mornin', Nathan. I see you've
already begun recruiting the new gentleman
in town without giving the rest of us a
chance." She said all this in a haughty,
imperious manner, but with the tiniest hint
of a smile on one side of her mouth so that
if you were paying attention, you could tell
that she was teasing. She also gave the
impression that if you weren't paying attention, she wouldn't really care what you
thought. "Who's your new friend, Nathan?"

Sheriff Averill rose and half-bowed to the
lady. He turned to Jared and said, "Jared,
I'd like to introduce Miss Eleanor Coulter,
our school marm. Eleanor, this is Jared
Delaney. I've offered him a job as my
deputy, but I have a feelin' he's more likely
to seek quieter employment as a cowboy,
likely at the Kilpatrick ranch."

As Jared tipped his hat to the school
marm, a look of concern clouded Eleanor's
blue eyes and she replied, "I'm not sure that
herding cattle is really all that quiet these
days, Nathan." Turning to Jared, who was

41

standing by watching the interplay between the young woman and the sheriff, she said, "Pleased to make your acquaintance, Mr. Delaney. Will we be seeing you in church tomorrow morning?"

Already uncomfortable in the presence of the appealing schoolteacher, Jared was caught off guard by the change in direction of the conversation and was momentarily flustered. "I'm really not much of a church-goer, Miss Coulter, I just never had the opportunity, workin' out on ranches for most of my life."

"Why, Mr. Delaney," Eleanor responded with the same hint of a smile he had seen earlier, "If you were a regular church-goer, I don't expect I would need to invite you. You probably wouldn't be sitting here with an old sinner like Nathan Averill and your first stop in town wouldn't have been the Colfax Tavern." Jared blushed as Eleanor continued. "It's because of these things that I took it as my duty to let you know we do, indeed, have two churches in this little community so that newcomers have a choice. We have our Methodist Church with the Reverend John Richardson and our Catholic Church with Father Antonio Baca."

"I reckon I don't even know much about the different ones," Jared replied with an

42

embarrassed look. "Which one's better?" After he said it, Jared realized from the look of amusement on Eleanor's face that he had probably just committed another blunder. He stammered, "I mean, do they get along?"

Eleanor laughed. "The Reverend and the Father are great friends as well as rivals and they have many a 'spirited' discussion, if you'll pardon the expression, over coffee at the Mares Cafe. So I repeat my question. Will we be seeing you in church tomorrow morning? And by the way, my personal preference is the Methodist church."

Jared glanced at Nathan for some sort of help but all the sheriff did was grin ruefully at him and shake his head. "Don't look at me, cowboy, you're on your own. I got no dog in this fight so I don't want no part of it, thank you!"

"It's 'I don't want any part of,' Nathan, and I thank you for your discretion," the schoolteacher said. "So, Mr. Delaney?"

Jared shook his head and grinned. "Miss Coulter, I can't think of anyplace I'd rather be tomorrow mornin' than church. I hope to see you there."

"Well, now, Mr. Delaney, that wasn't so painful, was it?" Eleanor said as she smiled a sunny smile. "I promise to sit beside you so if you start to nod off during Reverend

Richardson's very interesting sermon, I can give you a little nudge to keep you alert."

Jared replied, "I'll try to get a good night's sleep so it won't be necessary, Miss Coulter."

"If you really do show up and stay awake through the whole service, Mr. Delaney, I'll consider the possibility of your addressing me by my first name," Eleanor said with a twinkle in her eyes. "In the event that your eyes stay wide open throughout, you'll need to know that my given name is Eleanor."

"Well, then, I guess that gives me two good reasons to make it to church, Miss Coulter," Jared replied with an impish grin of his own. "I might learn somethin' from what the Reverend says and there's a chance we might get better acquainted, too." Eleanor smiled and nodded to Jared, then took the sheriff's hand and gave it an affectionate squeeze as she turned and walked away.

Jared was feeling good about how he had held his own in the unfamiliar territory of male-female interplay. He turned to Sheriff Averill and said, "She seems nice."

"As you can see, she loves to tease, which some people in town take the wrong way," Averill replied, "but she's as fine and decent a lady as you'll meet anywhere, son. If she's on your side and you ever get in trouble, she'll fight like a wildcat to help you out of a scrape. On the other hand, if she thinks you're a bully or troublemaker, you'd better look out!"

Jared was impressed with the strength of feeling in the sheriff's voice as he talked about the young woman. He wondered about their connection and thought about asking but then decided that unlike many of the folks he had encountered so far in Cimarron, he would mind his own business.

They sat quietly, finishing their coffee. The sheriff seemed comfortable with the silence and like many cowboys, Jared was used to going long periods without engaging in conversation. Finally, Averill broke the silence and said, "Let me give you directions out to the Kilpatrick ranch. Ned and Lizbeth Kilpatrick are solid folks and if you tell'em I sent you, they'll give you a fair shake. In the meantime, don't forget my offer to you is still on the table. The way things have been goin' lately, bein' a deputy ain't a lot more dangerous than bein' a cowhand." The sheriff gave Jared directions to the Kilpatrick's place and stood to walk him out of the dining room.

Jared rose also and shook the sheriff's hand. "Thanks for all your help, Sheriff Averill. I think I'll head on out to the Kilpatrick ranch right now and when I come in for my church-goin' experience tomorrow, I'll let you know how things went."

CHAPTER 3

As Jared rode out the trail northeast of town toward the Kilpatrick ranch, he tried to focus on his conversation with the sheriff, particularly what he had said about the dangers that seemed to be an everyday part of everyone's existence in Cimarron. However, his mind kept drifting back to Eleanor Coulter and his "deal" with her the next morning. He had not been lying when he told her he hadn't spent much time in church, so his stomach was tied in a square knot as he wondered what the experience would be like. He also was feeling skittish. He found himself attracted to Eleanor, but also felt intimidated by her sharp wit and forthright ways. He chuckled to himself, thinking the next day might be only a little less difficult than breaking a bronc. In fact, the more he thought about it, the more he thought the bronc might be the easier path. At least he had the experience and skills to deal with a snorty horse. He might be over his head trying to hold his own with an attractive young woman.

With his mind engaged in wrestling with the complexities of dealing with the fairer sex, Jared wasn't especially cautious as he rode up to the Kilpatrick's ranch house. He didn't see anyone and was just preparing to call out a greeting when a voice came from the shaded front porch saying, "Hold it right there, stranger. Stay on your horse and put your hands where I can see'em. I got a Henry rifle pointed at your chest and it'll blow a hole the size of a cabbage through you." A man on the porch stepped out into the sunlight. He was of medium height, appeared to be in his late thirties and was holding a Henry rifle just as he had said. "State your name and your business, and be careful that you don't move too fast, cause I don't mind shootin' first and talkin' about it later."

Jared waited a long moment, trying to get a handle on what was happening. It felt like his blood was running a couple of degrees colder. Finally, he sat up in his saddle and slowly raised his hands up even with his shoulders. "Name's Jared Delaney, sir. I'm new in these parts. I'm lookin' for work as a ranch hand and Sheriff Nathan Averill told me that you might be hirin'." The man didn't respond so Jared continued nervously. "If I caught you at a bad time, I'd be more than happy to turn around and ride right back into Cimarron. I ain't lookin' for trouble and I'd just as soon not have a hole as big as a cabbage in me." He smiled what he hoped was a friendly and non-threatening smile as he said the last part about the cabbage.

Ned Kilpatrick stepped further out in the sunlight toward Jared but he was having none of Jared's affability. He kept the Henry trained on his mid-section. "You say Nathan sent you out here?" Kilpatrick said. "Why should I be believin' you just cause you happen to know the name of our sheriff?"

At that moment, a lady, maybe a couple of years younger than the man, stepped out of the front door and said, "Ned, I doubt this young man would know the way out here and he prob'ly wouldn't know to use Nathan's name unless he had actually spoken with him. There ain't many people we trust these days, but if Nathan thinks this fella is worth talkin' to, that's good enough for me. Why don't you put that cannon of yours down and let's invite Mr. Delaney in for some lemonade."

Jared held his breath, waiting until the

man lowered his rifle, then dismounted slowly. He allowed himself to breathe then but kept himself ready to dive out of harm's way if the man decided to blaze away at him. He said, "Much obliged, m'am. I apologize to you folks for just ridin' in here like I owned the place, but like I said, I'm new in town and it's takin' a little time for me to get use to how jumpy everyone seems to be."

As Jared walked slowly toward Ned Kilpatrick with his hand outstretched, Ned appeared to relax somewhat and lowered his rifle. He said, "Sorry about the way I welcomed you, Delaney, but these days, a fella can't be too careful. As you prob'ly heard, there's some rough types around. You just never know when they're gonna show up which makes us a might cautious. Come on in and we'll talk about the job possibilities over a glass of lemonade, like Lizbeth said." Kilpatrick nodded toward the woman. "That's Lizbeth, my wife, by the way. As you prob'ly could tell, she's got the cooler head between the two of us." Jared tipped his hat to Lizbeth Kilpatrick, noting that she was almost as tall as her husband. She had brown hair with a touch of gray at the temples and he would have thought her rather plain in appearance under different circumstances. Seeing as how she had likely just saved his life, he thought she looked like an angel.

"Pleased to meet you, m'am, and thanks again for persuadin' your husband not to blow a hole in me," Jared said as he followed the Kilpatricks up the steps of the porch and into the house. Although the ranch house looked a bit rough from the outside, it was surprisingly neat on the inside. It was clear to Jared that Lizbeth Kilpatrick took pride in her home and wanted it to be presentable to company.

After they were seated around the oak table in the kitchen with glasses of fresh lemonade in front of them, Ned Kilpatrick said in a brusque manner, "Why don't you tell me what you've done in the way of bein' a cowboy. We're short-handed right now but we'd like to have someone who's had some experience."

Though taken aback by the rancher's abrupt manner, Jared kept his cool and replied, "I suppose I might do that, Mr. Kilpatrick."

Kilpatrick seemed to sense that Jared might have taken offense and smiled to try to ease the tension a bit. "Since I didn't shoot you, I reckon I wouldn't mind if you called me Ned and referred to my wife as

Lizbeth."

Jared responded to the change in tone and said, "Thanks, Ned. And you're welcome to call me Jared. I understand that you want a hand who's been around. I worked for three years for Charles Goodnight on the JA Ranch." Jared noticed Ned sitting up straighter in his chair as he heard the name of the legendary rancher. He continued, "I've been on two cattle drives up the Goodnight-Loving Trail and I've handled just about every chore there is on a ranch. I know horses and cattle as well as anyone you're gonna meet. I don't mean to brag, but I want to be square with you about my qualifications."

Kilpatrick nodded his head and said, "Charlie Goodnight's got the respect of anyone who ever worked a herd. If you worked for him for a few years, you do know your stuff."

"Well, I like to think so, Ned," Jared replied. "I don't mind hard work and I can take orders from a man I respect. As you prob'ly heard, you learn fast when you work for Mr. Goodnight or you don't work for long."

Ned nodded and said, "That's what I heard, all right." He paused and looked a little uncomfortable, then continued. "I guess I oughta ask whether you're handy with a Colt. These days, that's almost as important as knowin' how to rope and ride."

Frustrated, Jared shook his head and said, "Ned, I just rode into town yesterday and right away, people started urgin' me to take sides. I ain't even had a chance to figure out what sides there are. I can handle a six-shooter and a Winchester just fine, but I'd much prefer to never have to use'em on anything but game and rattlesnakes."

Ned looked serious and said, "That sounds real sensible, Jared, but it's easier said than done. There's snakes a lot more dangerous than the rattler . . . I'm talkin' about human snakes. Sometimes a man's gotta make a choice."

At this comment, Jared's temper flared and he stiffly said, "If you don't think I'm man enough to make the right choices, Mr. Kilpatrick, you don't have to hire me, but I aim to take my time and size up the situation before I decide about takin' anyone's side."

"Calm down, Jared," Kilpatrick said, "I didn't mean to offend you, I just want to make sure you know what you're gettin' into. I'd be happy to offer you a job and hope you'd be willin' to consider it."

Jared stared hard at the rancher for a moment but saw only concern in his eyes. He took a deep breath and said, "I appreciate your bein' honest with me, Ned. I'm sorry I got testy. It's just from the moment I came to town, people have been at me to jump right in the middle of somethin' and I don't even know what it's all about. I'm willin' to consider your job offer, but I'd like to hear more about what you're offerin'."

Kilpatrick thought for a minute, then said, "Standard cowboy wages up here in Northern New Mexico are twenty-five dollars and found. Since we got a little different situation here with these outlaws runnin' around makin' things dicey for a workin' cowboy, I'm willin' to go thirty-five dollars a month for you, particularly since you have the experience of workin' for Mr. Goodnight for several years. What do you think about that?"

Jared didn't have to think for long to know that it was a fine offer, much more than he could get on any of the ranches in Texas that he'd heard about. He figured the increased danger was something he could deal with by just staying out of the middle of things as much as possible.

"Ned, you got yourself a cowhand. If you don't mind, I'll spend tonight in town. I got me an appointment tomorrow at the church with the school teacher lady, Miss Eleanor Coulter."

Lizbeth Kilpatrick, who had been quiet, suddenly laughed out loud and said, "Ned, you may have to raise Jared's pay another ten dollars. His life just got a lot more dangerous!"

Ned laughed along with his wife and Jared shook his head. "Lizbeth, I've only met Miss Coulter the one time, but you may be right. I guess if you wanted proof I wasn't afraid to get involved in some kind of scuffle, you got it now."

Lizbeth shook her head and smiled, saying, "Eleanor's got one of the sharpest tongues around if she thinks you're bein' wrongheaded and she don't mind usin' it on anyone who crosses her path. Some think that ain't fittin' for a woman, but I'm not one of'em. I got nothin' but respect for Eleanor. If she's your friend, she's your friend for life as long as you uphold your end of the bargain."

"That's good to know," Jared said. "I reckon if I survive my church-goin' tomorrow, I'll be out here before dark with my gear and be ready to go to work Monday mornin'."

Ned gave Jared a pointed look. "Looks like you already figured out who's boss, clearin' your startin' times with my wife."

Jared was embarrassed until he realized that Kilpatrick was joshin' him. He said, "Well, you didn't shoot me when I rode up and you don't seem inclined to shoot me now, so I guess we'll get along. What I meant to say was that I hope it's all right with the both of you if I get started Monday mornin'."

"That's fine, Jared," Kilpatrick said. "Just get here tomorrow in plenty of time to get a good meal and a good night's sleep. Monday mornin', we'll see what you're really made of."

Jared shook hands with both the Kilpatricks and mounted up to head back into town. As he rode away from the ranch, he glanced over to a small rise just beyond the fence surrounding the ranch house and saw three small wooden crosses. The dirt looked fresh and as he rode south toward town, he wondered again what he'd gotten himself into.

CHAPTER 4

Jared stopped by the St. James when he got back to town and let the clerk know he'd be staying for one more night. He went upstairs and got his gear together, then spent a moment looking at his shabby wardrobe, thinking about what he would wear to church in the morning. He shook his head as he looked through his clothes and thought to himself that he wasn't going to make much of an impression on Miss Eleanor Coulter by his manner of dress. He picked out his cleanest dirty shirt, smoothed out a pair of pants before hanging them both over the chair that was the only furniture in the room other than the bed. He thought about wiping off his boots, then decided to wait until in the morning, since he figured he would be going out this evening and would run the chance of stepping in a mud puddle or worse somewhere along the way. Having prepared the best he could, he set out for what he figured would be his last night on the town for a while.

After another fine meal of steak and potatoes at the St. James, Jared wandered back up the street to the Colfax Tavern. This time, when he walked through the swinging doors, Heck Roberts looked up immediately from behind the bar and hailed him in a friendly manner. "Hey there, Jared, come on over and have a beer on the house."

Jared walked over and said, "Good evenin' Mr. Roberts, I mean Heck. I wouldn't mind that beer and I'll be happy to pay for a shot of whiskey to go with it. Since I'm gonna be a workin' cowboy again day after tomorrow, I reckon I can afford it."

Roberts gave Jared a surprised look and asked, "So who's the lucky rancher, cowboy? I know it isn't Morgan O'Bannon, since you haven't had the pleasure of meeting him yet." With some annoyance, Jared noticed a tone of disapproval in Roberts' voice as he continued to speak. "By the way, in my opinion, taking a job before you even got to hear Mr. O'Bannon's point of view wasn't the wisest decision you could have made."

"There you go again, Heck, like everybody else I've met in this town, goin' on about who I should take up with. I hired on with Ned Kilpatrick to do the job of a cowboy and that's the way I look at it . . . it's just a job. I ain't joinin' the army, like this was the War Between the States or somethin'." Jared tried to lighten his tone so the bartender wouldn't take him wrong, figuring that was a good start for staying out of the middle of things.

"I knew a gentleman once," Roberts said, "who couldn't decide which side of the street to walk down. He was afraid of offending the shop owners on one side if he walked down the other. So what he does is, he walks down the middle of the street and he keeps looking to either side to see how people are reacting. You know what happened?"

Jared shook his head and said, "No," thinking to himself that Roberts sure seemed to enjoy the sound of his own voice and wondering how long this tale would last. Not too long, he hoped, since Roberts hadn't served him his beer yet.

Roberts laughed and said, "He was so worried about offending someone that he stuck right in the middle of the road. Pretty soon a wagon comes tearing through the middle of town, but he's so busy looking to both sides that he doesn't see it and that wagon runs him over. You see, sometimes it's not any safer staying in the middle of the road because you're likely to get run over anyway."

Jared laughed politely along with the bartender and said, "Heck, that's a mighty funny story. I'll keep it in mind." His smile slowly faded as he said, "What I keep tryin' to tell everybody is I just took me a job as a cowboy. I don't know who stands for what in this fracas and to tell you the truth, I don't much care."

Roberts seemed to miss Jared's change in tone as he continued self-importantly, "Cowboys that ride with Morgan O'Bannon gets respect from everyone, plus there's the fringe benefits. You get to run a tab for your drinks, which Mr. O'Bannon picks up at the end of every month, and believe me, the ladies in here are a lot more free with their favors, too, if you know what I mean."

At that moment, Christie Quick came sashaying down the stairs and spying Jared, walked over to the bar. "Hey there, polite and handsome from Texas, I see you came back to see me."

As usual, Jared felt flustered and embarrassed as he tipped his hat. He said, "It's a pleasure to see you again, Miss Quick, but I really came in just to wet my whistle." Thinking that he might have insulted her by saying that he'd only come for a drink, he added, "No offense, m'am." She laughed at his apparent discomfort and if she was offended, he sure couldn't tell it. He continued on, saying, "I need to get a good night's sleep cause I'll be goin' out to the Kilpatrick ranch tomorrow, gettin' ready for a full day of work on Monday." Jared conveniently left out the news of his plan to attend church in the morning with Eleanor Coulter. "Maybe I can make it in next Saturday night and we could spend some time together." As Jared made the last statement, he blushed as he realized what it sounded like. He stammered for a second in an attempt to apologize, which Christie brushed off with a laugh and a wave of her hand.

"I think you're younger and greener than I realized, Jared Delaney. You don't need to apologize to me, you just need to come back when you grow up." She shook her head in disbelief. "I can't believe you already took a job without even meetin' Mr. O'Bannon. He's gonna be in later and if you want my advice, it'd be worth your while to stick around and say a friendly hello."

Jared shook his head at once again receiving more unsolicited advice, then said, "Thanks, Miss Quick, but like I said, I got a long week ahead of me. I'd best be gettin' a good night's sleep. Maybe I can meet Mr. O'Bannon next week if I come in on Saturday night."

Jared nodded to Christie and Heck Roberts, then walked out of the Colfax Tavern, not knowing it would be considerably longer than a week before he was to meet Morgan O'Bannon.

CHAPTER 5

Sunday morning, when Jared awoke, he didn't recall any nightmares during the night. It was a tremendous relief not to wake up in a sweat, trembling with fear of something he couldn't quite identify but which seemed all too real nonetheless. With trepidation, he got out of bed and began pulling on his clothes for church. While not as terrifying as his nightmares, the impending challenge of staying alert through a sermon and not committing any social gaffes was daunting. He dusted off his hat, made himself as presentable as he could and after several cups of coffee, walked over to the Methodist Church. He didn't see Miss Eleanor right away and stood around for a couple of uncomfortable minutes before he heard her voice call out, "Good morning, Mr. Delaney! If you stay awake throughout the sermon, perhaps we can address one another by first names."

Jared heard some snickers from several bystanders but when he looked around, he couldn't pinpoint the culprits. He decided he might as well get used to being the butt of Miss Coulter's humor, so he joined in and said, "I had three cups of joe this mornin', M'am. I think I might just make it." He was pleased that she laughed at his humor and felt a slight decrease in his level of discomfort. Maybe this courting thing was like bein' a cowboy . . . if you just practiced and tolerated the bumps and bruises, you might get the hang of it sooner or later.

Miss Eleanor walked up to join him and said, "We'd better get in and grab our seats, things tend to fill up quickly. The folks that attend are dedicated creatures of habit, and they'll knock you down if you're between them and their regular seat. Of course, they'll help you up, too, since they're all good Christians." She laughed again and Jared hoped she was once again teasing him.

They took a seat by the aisle in the third row and Jared tried to get comfortable in the hard wooden pew. He was acutely aware of the nearness of Miss Eleanor and realized that she smelled faintly of lavender. It was a pleasant smell but he feared it might cause him to sneeze, leading to an embarrassment he did not relish. He was thinking about this for some time before he became aware of the words Reverend Richardson was using in his sermon. He heard him say something about "walking the straight and narrow" and focusing his attention more closely, he groaned inwardly, realizing that the Reverend was talking about people making choices. "Here we go again," he thought to himself.

Sure enough, the Reverend was saying it was important to know where you were headed, and in order to do that, you needed to know where you'd been. He talked about the bible's being a source that could help you figure that out but Jared's mind wandered a bit as he pondered the knowledge that he wasn't sure of where he had been. He knew he had learned to be a cowboy and was confident in those abilities but because his memory was so hazy about his childhood and his family, he was less sure about who he was as a person once he stepped out of the saddle.

He was deep in thought when Miss Eleanor elbowed him none-too-gently in the side and said, "You can't stay here all day. They've got to get ready for the church social tonight. Come on, I'll introduce you to Reverend Richardson. And by the way, I guess you can call me Eleanor now because you stayed awake the entire time, although you looked like your mind was in some far away place."

Jared laughed and said, "Sermons are supposed to make you think, aren't they?"

As they approached Reverend Richardson, he was talking to some other members of the congregation. As he turned and spotted Eleanor, his face lit up like the sunrise over the mountain. "Miss Eleanor, it's always a pleasure to see you," he said with a slight bow. "Would you mind introducing your friend?"

Eleanor nodded and said, "It's a pleasure to see and hear you as well, Reverend. My friend here is Mr. Jared Delaney, formerly of Texas, who has recently come to Cimarron. As he is in the midst of making choices about whom he spends his time with, I'm sure your sermon this morning was especially helpful to him."

Once again, Jared felt a flash of irritation at the subject of allegiances being introduced in the conversation immediately. He covered his displeasure as best he could, saying, "Pleased to meet you, Reverend. Your words this mornin' got me to thinkin' about my own situation, of which I'm still not certain. I'm tryin' my best to get to know folks and decide where my path lies in your community."

The Reverend nodded thoughtfully and said, "I can appreciate that. We are generally judged by the company we keep and judging from the company you're keeping this morning, you must be pretty brave." The Reverend smiled as he added the last part. "Miss Eleanor is not shy about challenging us to think about how we live our lives. It's one of the characteristics that make her an excellent teacher. I might add, she doesn't spare herself in that respect. But here, we're getting a little too serious. Let me just say it's a pleasure to make your acquaintance. I hope we'll see more of you in here on Sundays. Watch out for that rascal, Father Antonio, by the way. The good Father is always looking for new recruits and he can be quite persuasive if you're not careful."

From the look in his eye, Jared could tell that the Reverend was joking with him, so he just smiled and said, "I'll try to watch my step."

As they walked away, Jared impulsively asked Eleanor if she would be interested in joining him for coffee. He held his breath as she gave it a moment's thought then said,

"Why, Jared, I would be delighted to accompany you. Have you had a chance to try out the Mares café?"

Jared let out the breath he was holding and said, "I'm still learnin' my way around and haven't had the chance yet. If you think it's the place for coffee after church, I'll follow your lead."

She opened her parasol and they strolled down the street toward the café. As they walked, he heard some children over by a store giggle as they passed by which caused him to blush a beet-red. Eleanor, on the other hand, seemed unfazed by their laughter. As they rounded the corner and stepped into the coolness of the cafe, he said to her, "I wish I could be a little more like you and not care what people think about me."

She gave him an odd look and said, "What makes you say that?"

"Well, those young'uns back there had a good laugh at us and you didn't hardly seem to notice. Me, I get all flustered and can't seem to concentrate," Jared explained with a rueful grin.

"Jared," Eleanor said, "I care what people think but only people whose opinions I value. Not that I don't value the opinion of those children back there because I do. On some subjects, I'm all ears when they speak." Jared listened attentively. He was used to the company of cowboys and had little experience conversing with an intelligent young woman of his age. Eleanor continued, "Grown-up relationships just doesn't happen to be one of those subjects so I take it with a grain of salt when they laugh." She smiled shyly. "Anyway, I know they mean no harm."

Jared nodded and said, "I see your point. I didn't think they were tryin' to be mean, they were just havin' a little fun at our expense."

"They were, indeed," Eleanor said with a smile. "There are others, though, that I take very seriously. Nathan Averill, the good Reverend Richardson, his friend Father Antonio, the Kilpatricks, to name a few. They're folks I listen to carefully and I respect all they have to say. If one of them criticizes me, I take it to heart and think long and hard about what they've said."

Jared shook his head with understanding and said, "That's how I felt about Mr. Goodnight and some of the other cowboys on the JA over in Texas. Sometimes what they said stung a bit but deep down, I knew they were doin' their best to help me make a hand. That means a lot to a fella."

Eleanor laughed and said, "I guess I

hadn't thought about becoming a better person as 'making a hand' but that's not a bad way to describe it. I'm trying to 'make a hand' as a schoolteacher and there are times my patience wears quite thin." In a serious tone, she went on, "There are others . . . Morgan O'Bannon and most of the folks down at the Colfax Tavern, for example . . . who make it clear they share different ideals than I do about right and wrong so I don't put any stock in what they might think or say about me. If I come to respect you, I'll care very deeply what you think of me."

Jared was taken aback by Eleanor's honesty and wasn't sure what to say. Then, as he thought about what she had declared, he said, "That seems fair. I just hope I can measure up."

They entered the cafe and approached a table where Jared politely pulled out a chair for Eleanor. As he took off his hat and was seating himself, a man walked quickly over to the table and said, "Senorita Eleanor, I demand to know who this man is and what his intentions are!"

Jared was shocked and was searching for something to say when Eleanor burst into laughter and said, "Senor Miguel, my deepest apologies. I don't want you to think for a moment my love for you has died but this young gentleman is new in town and I felt that I needed to take him under my wing so he wouldn't go astray."

The man laughed heartily in response, then he said, "I suppose I can set my jealousy aside if you are doing a good deed." Turning to Jared, he said, "Welcome, sir, I am Miguel Mares, owner, cook and waiter at this establishment. Please excuse our little running joke, but Miss Eleanor brightens up my days by coming here and pretending that a beauty like herself would ever be romantically interested in an old buzzard like me."

"Nonsense, Miguel, you know that you alone bear the key to my heart, although I'm sure you let your lovely wife, Anita, hold it for safe-keeping," Eleanor said with another laugh. "This, by the way, is Jared Delaney. He's taken a position with the Kilpatricks as a cowboy starting tomorrow morning."

"Enough of my foolishness, then, you'll need your strength. What may I serve you today?"

Jared and Eleanor tried to only order coffee but Miguel was so insistent that they wound up having an early lunch. They didn't have time for much conversation during the meal as they were busy putting away the vittles that Miguel provided, but when they were done and settled with another cup of coffee, Eleanor turned to Jared and said, "I've heard some things from different folks about you but I'd like to get to know you first hand. Would you mind telling me a bit about yourself and how you came to Cimarron?"

Jared thought about what he'd said to Nathan Averill and decided he'd be a little more circumspect about his personal life this time. He looked down at the table and said, "There really ain't a lot to tell. When I was a young boy in the Texas panhandle, my folks were killed in a raid by outlaws come down on a tear from the Indian Territory. I don't remember much about either one of them, which I regret."

Eleanor looked pained at hearing this information and said, "Oh, I'm so sorry. That must have been awful for you. How on earth did you survive?"

"Well," Jared said, "a family, the Gilbertsons, took me in. Lucy, that's Mrs. Gilbertson, taught me how to read and write which accounts for my interest in readin' books. I found out when I got older that I could save up my Bull Durham coupons and send away for books." Jared said proudly, "I've even read some of the classics." Eleanor nodded approvingly and he felt a warm surge of pride as he continued with his tale. "When I turned sixteen, I took a notion to see more of the West, so I left the Gilbertsons and went out lookin' for work. I caught on with a couple of different ranches and over a couple of years, went on some cattle drives before I went to work for Mr. Charles Goodnight. That's where I learned to be a top hand." As he made the last statement, Jared realized that it might sound like he was bragging and he didn't want to give Eleanor the wrong impression. He quickly said, "I don't mean to sound prideful."

Eleanor smiled. "It sounds to me as if you have every reason to feel proud of your accomplishments. I didn't take it as boasting."

Jared was relieved Eleanor hadn't been offended by his comments but wanted to make sure she understood what his experience had been like. He said, "There was only one way of doin' things on the JA . . . Mr. Goodnight's way. You worked hard and did it right or you went somewheres else pronto. He didn't put up with laziness or rowdy behavior but when you did your job, it made you feel proud knowin' he was pleased, though he didn't let on very often that he noticed. Somehow, though, you could just tell. One time in the three years I worked for him, he said, 'Good job.' I'd be hard pressed to think of a time in my life when I've been happier."

"I suppose it's like rain in the desert," Eleanor said. "It's rare, so when it comes, it's special."

"I hadn't thought about it quite like that," Jared replied, "but that's makes a lot of sense."

"It sounds as if you really liked your life at the ranch," Eleanor said. "Why did you leave?"

"It's kinda hard to say," Jared said pensively. "I did like what I was doin' and I liked the cowboys I was workin' with. After a time, though, I just got this urge to try somethin' different, so I left Mr. Goodnight on good terms and went lookin' for new ways to use my skills. I wound up in Lincoln County down south and went to work as a deputy for Sheriff Mills. It didn't take me long to figure out he was a whole lot more interested in politics than in enforcin' the law." Jared had a sour expression on his face as he talked about his experience with Sheriff Mills, like he'd bit into a lemon. "I stuck it out for nine months before I had my fill then I drifted up this way lookin' for my next adventure." Jared stopped to catch his breath and found Eleanor staring at him intently. He wondered if she had been looking at him that way the whole time he was talking. She seemed to measure her words before speaking to him.

"For someone who said he didn't have a lot to tell, you said quite a bit," she teased him. Then turning serious, she said, "If you didn't like Lincoln County, you're not going to like Cimarron much either. I know you've heard about Morgan O'Bannon, who is bad enough in his own right. What makes things worse is that he works with or for, depending on who you talk to, a bunch of scoundrels known as the Santa Fe Ring."

"I've heard some stories about those fellas," Jared said. "What's their game?"

"They're politicians and so-called businessmen in Northern New Mexico who are really thugs and thieves. They've got their fingers in just about every pie, at least the ones that show promise for making money. They don't care about anything but lining their own pockets. If you get in their way, they'll have you cut down!" Eleanor said heatedly. "That's where Morgan O'Bannon comes in. That's the situation and it's why just about everyone you've talked to since you got to town wonders what side you'll wind up on. Eventually, you'll have to choose."

Jared thought about what Eleanor was saying and shook his head. "I appreciate you sharin' your opinions with me but with all due respect, I'm gonna have to make up my own mind. I haven't had the chance to meet this Morgan O'Bannon face to face. I'd like to look him in the eye myself before I pass judgement."

Eleanor shook her head gently and said, "I understand that but I just hope you don't take too long in making up your mind. Some things are quite clear and it doesn't take long to figure them out."

Jared was growing uncomfortable with the direction the conversation had taken and looked for a way to change the topic. He said, "Well, that's way too much talk about politics. I've told you about me, how is it an educated young lady like yourself wound up out West?"

Eleanor smiled and said, "You've been so forthcoming about your past, the least I could do would be to respond in kind." She took a moment to gather her thoughts, then continued. "I was born in St. Louis. My father was a lawyer there and my mother was a schoolteacher, although she gave that up when I was born so she could spend her time with me. My parents were the two smartest people I've ever known and I remember even as a small child listening to them have long debates. At first, I thought they were fighting because they'd get pretty excited. After awhile, I figured out they both just felt strongly about the topics they were discussing. When I was six years old, they were talking about something . . . I don't even remember what . . . and I offered my opinion. A lot of grown folks would have either ignored me or told me to be quiet but my parents listened to what I said and really seemed to consider it. I'll never forget that moment and I try to offer the same respect to the young people I teach today."

Jared shook his head in amazement. "That's somethin'," he said. "It was never that way for me, nor for anybody else I knew, that's for sure. Do you reckon that's why you speak up so freely?" As soon as he said it, Jared thought that perhaps Eleanor might feel that he was implying she was rude. He stammered, "I didn't mean any disrespect. I mean . . . well, I don't even know what I mean." He laughed at himself and said, "I guess what I'm sayin' is you're real different from the ladies I've met before . . . but I think that's a good thing!"

Eleanor laughed at his discomfort and said, "I suppose I am different from some women in that I feel confident what I say is worth consideration. I believe that, given the opportunity, any women with even a modest amount of intelligence would have as much to offer in conversation as most men." She smiled and said, "I realize that's not an opinion many men and even some women share."

Jared nodded and said, "You're right about that, I reckon. You see things different from what most folks out West are used to. Things are changin' though, and I think we got to be open to new ideas."

"I appreciate your willingness to consider a different viewpoint." She smiled a little shyly and said, "I also appreciate your concern about not offending me, although I really am a lot tougher than you seem to think."

Jared sensed warmth in Eleanor's comments that made him uneasy. It also made him feel good. It occurred to him that he was in unfamiliar territory courting a young lady, and he needed to get back on solid ground. He figured if he said much more right then, he'd probably make a fool of himself so he decided to give the lead back to Eleanor. "I reckon we got off track of how you got yourself out West."

"Well, we had what I thought was a good

life in St. Louis," Eleanor continued, "but my father believed things had gotten too crowded. Somehow, he got it into his head we should move out West. That time, my parents really did have an argument! I don't know how my father persuaded my mother, but before long, we headed out. I was eleven years old and it seemed like a great adventure to me." As Eleanor told her story, Jared found himself thinking about the differences between them. Around the time she was having a great adventure, he was an orphan struggling just to survive.

"We went by train as far as we could . . . not very far in 1866 since the transcontinental railroad was still mostly just a notion . . . then joined up with a wagon train to go the rest of the way. My father had a vague plan of going to California but as we were going through the Texas panhandle, my mother got sick. We kept on going but it turned out she'd developed pneumonia. The wagon train came through Cimarron and my father decided she was too weak to go on, so we stopped here. She died a week later."

Eleanor stopped speaking. Jared looked at her face and noticed tears had welled up in her eyes. Jared realized guiltily he'd come to a hasty conclusion when he assumed they were so different. Unsure, he wanted to comfort her, so he said, "I know myself that children sometimes lose their parents. I figure not much in life hurts any worse unless it's a parent losin' a child. I'm sorry."

Eleanor smiled through her tears and said, "Thank you, Jared, for your words of comfort. I didn't mean to get emotional, but even after all these years, it still hurts. My father did a fine job as a father, but he wasn't my mother. I've missed her terribly but I have many wonderful memories from my first eleven years. I can't imagine what it's like for you not to be able to remember your parents."

Jared thought about Eleanor's words and said, "It's hard. Funny, I mostly remember their voices but I can't put faces to'em." He didn't say that the other vivid memory he had was of a cold, hard voice and the coldest blue eyes he had ever seen. Maybe when he got to know her better, he might tell her about this. Instead, he said, "What happened to your father and how did you wind up teaching school here in Cimarron?"

Eleanor paused for a moment. Then she said, "For a time after my mother died, my father seemed to lack the will and energy to go on. I don't know what would have happened to us but for the help of a man you've met, though he was a bit younger then . . . Nathan Averill." Jared had wondered what the connection between the sheriff and Eleanor was and realized he was about to find out. "Nathan was already sheriff back then," Eleanor said. "He heard about our troubles and came to the hotel where we were staying, offered his condolences and asked my father about his plans. He said he'd heard he was a lawyer and that Cimarron was in need of a good lawyer. He told my father that some crooked politicians and lawyers in Santa Fe . . . he referred to them as 'yellow-bellied snakes,' I believe . . . were pulling a fast one with folks' land grants so they could grab up all the quality land around here."

"I heard about that," Jared said. "I know there's families that have held land around here for generations, then some low-down sidewinders come along and steal it out from under'em . . . and the law takes their side!"

Eleanor said, "That's the Santa Fe Ring I was telling you about. A lawyer named Thomas Benton Catron is the ringleader. Nathan told my father they were particularly going after Spanish families who'd been living in this part of the country for centuries. Nathan figured those folks had a lot more claim to the land than a bunch of money-grubbers who were only interested in how much profit they could make." Jared could feel himself getting hot under the collar. Having had to deal with a tough set of circumstances himself, he was naturally sympathetic to the underdog.

"At first, my father wasn't interested," Eleanor continued. "Nathan understood he was in the throes of grief, losing his wife and facing life raising a child in unfamiliar country. Nathan also understood, though, that what my father needed to pull himself out of his pain was a just and challenging cause." Eleanor smiled, "Nathan kept coming around every few days to check in on us. He was kind, teasing with me but also putting a gentle hand on my shoulder, knowing I was going through my own sorrow."

Jared thought about Eleanor's description of the sheriff. He realized the qualities she described were the ones he'd perceived that led him to open up about his past. Something about the sheriff . . . compassion, wisdom . . . showed through his down-home, folksy mannerisms. "I had the sheriff pegged as a pretty good man but I may have underestimated him. It sounds like he was just what you and your pa needed . . . a true friend."

Eleanor nodded and said, "That's exactly it. He wasn't insistent, but he was persistent.

He'd drop bits of information to my father about the latest shenanigans of the Ring and shake his head about what they were going to try to get away with next. It wasn't long before my father got interested and within a few weeks, he told Nathan he was available to help him any way he could. That fox, Nathan, said he just happened to have a bunch of documents at his office . . . 'legal mumbo-jumbo' he called it . . . and he was hoping my father could figure them out. My father jumped right in and pretty soon came up with his own legal mumbo-jumbo that's managed to keep most of these land-grabbing efforts tied up in the courts. He didn't beat the Santa Fe Ring but he slowed them down so much that people have been able to hold on to their land and live their lives much as they had before all this foolishness started."

Jared shook his head in admiration. "I'm like Nathan. I can't follow all that lawyer talk. I sure admire a man who can, though, particularly when he uses it for the good of folks like your pa did. Looks like you come from pretty good stock as we cowboys say."

Eleanor smiled warmly and said, "Coming from a real cowboy, I take that as high praise."

Once again, Jared felt that odd combination of pleasure and discomfort he feared would result in his saying something foolish. Again, he made the wise decision to turn the conversation back over to Eleanor. "So, how'd you become a school teacher?"

Eleanor laughed. "I guess you might say I grew into it. I started going to the one-room schoolhouse presided over by Hattie O'Hanlon. Hattie came from Ireland with her husband but he died from pneumonia just like my mother so she just poured herself into teaching school. She could be mighty fearsome if a student wasn't paying attention or was being disruptive but she had such a twinkle in her eye most of the time. If you showed any interest in learning, she'd lavish attention on you. Because of my experience with my parents, I didn't know any better and would challenge her in class by asking questions and even occasionally disagreeing. A lot of schoolteachers would have squashed me like a bug but Hattie took me under her wing. It was just the thing a young girl who had lost her mother needed. By the time I turned twelve, I was her unofficial assistant. Once I turned sixteen, she made it official. When she died three years ago, I took over."

Eleanor paused at this point and Jared spoke up. "I worked with an Irishman at Mr. Goodnight's ranch. He was the cook and his wife helped him and cleaned up around the place. She had that same twinkle in her eye you speak of but if you crossed her, her tongue was sharp as a razor. She lit into this old cowboy once and I swear, if he'd of been a dog, he would've slunk off with his tail between his legs." Eleanor smiled at that. Jared continued, "The way you speak of your father, I take it he's no longer with you. What happened to him?"

Eleanor's eyes flashed and she said, "He was ambushed three years ago, shot right out of the saddle. He was riding to Taos to the circuit court there to file another motion to slow down those Santa Fe Ring crooks. When he didn't come home the next day, I got worried and told Nathan. He rode out and found him lying dead beside the trail with his saddlebags empty. The only thing he'd been carrying was the legal brief he was headed over to file. He even had some money on him for a meal and a hotel room that night and that wasn't touched. You draw your conclusions about who was responsible. I've already drawn mine."

Jared wasn't sure what to say but was

saved from having to say anything because Nathan Averill walked in at that moment. "Looks like you survived the Reverend's sermon this morning, Mr. Delaney. You made it through Miguel's lunch and I see Miss Eleanor hasn't yet chewed you up and spit you out. I guess you're tough enough."

Jared laughed along with Nathan and Eleanor, saying "This is prob'ly a good way to prepare myself for gettin' back to the cowboy life tomorrow. Speakin' of which, much as I hate to leave good company, I'd better pack up and be headin' out to the Kilpatrick's." For a moment, he thought he might have seen a hint of disappointment in Eleanor's eyes.

"It's been a pleasure getting to know you, Jared. Will we see you in church next Sunday?"

Jared laughed again. "Wild horses couldn't keep me away. If Nathan's right, this'll toughen me up so I'd better just make sure I'm here." Jared doffed his hat and reached out to shake Eleanor's hand. He was surprised at how strongly she squeezed back and didn't want to let go but he felt uncomfortable with the intensity of the moment. Forcing himself to release her hand, he said, "Thanks for tellin' me so much about yourself, seein' as how I'm a stranger to you."

Eleanor smiled and said, "You're a good listener, Jared, and anyway, after hearing some about your life, I knew we had a lot in common."

Jared nodded. "You're right about that. I'd never really talked with anyone else who'd lost their parents, even though I've known a few in my time. Makes me understand a little better some of the things I've always felt about it."

Then he turned to Nathan. "I appreciate all your help, sheriff. I expect I'll be seein' more of you as it looks like I'll be comin' into town after the work is done next week."

As Jared walked out of Miguel Mares' cafe, he felt a tug on his heartstrings and almost turned around to go back inside. He paused and thought to himself, "What would I say? I'd just be makin' a durned fool of myself." He felt himself drawn to the two people back in the cafe but at the same time, part of him resisted. Strangely, he felt a little resentful. He wanted to trust them but told himself he really didn't know them and had no reason to accept their word. He remembered how he'd trusted the Gilbertsons and then found out they'd taken advantage of him. It occurred to him that he had a hard time knowing who to trust,

which he figured had a lot to do with the
fact he wasn't sure he trusted himself.
Finally, he shook himself as if to wake up
and walked down the street toward the St.
James Hotel.

CHAPTER 6

After collecting his meager belongings from his room and checking out, Jared walked down to the livery stable to get his horse and saddle up. As he passed the swinging doors of the Colfax Tavern, Heck Roberts saw him and beckoned him to come in. Jared waved, shook his head ruefully and pointed in the direction of the livery stable. Heck seemed to understand and hollered out to him, "Come see us real soon."

As he rode leisurely up the trail to the Kilpatrick's ranch, Jared's mind wandered down a number of different paths. He thought about his conversation with Eleanor and in particular, the way she had clung to his hand when they had parted. He wondered what he was getting himself into and told himself a cowboy didn't need hobbles to tie him down. That led him to think about the way everyone seemed to want him to jump into a fight he knew nothing about and of which he wanted no part. Eleanor and the sheriff seemed determined to pull him into some crusade to stand up for people he didn't even know and while he was sympathetic, he was equally determined not to get involved. He didn't know if he even wanted to stay in Cimarron. The last thing he needed was to get tangled up with the local troubles.

Although Heck Roberts had been friendly and solicitous toward him, there was something about the man that seemed off. He wondered about this O'Bannon fellow everyone was talking about. He'd known ranchers and cattle rustlers during his time cowboying but he couldn't recall ever knowing a rancher that was a cattle rustler as well. Some of the shadier ranchers he'd known weren't above using their cinch rings to change the odd brand and collect a few strays that drifted their way. As a general rule, however, most ranchers he'd known refrained from the practice, either out of respect for their compadres or the desire not to get into a conflict. The cattle business was a hard enough way to make a living without inviting trouble by stealing from your neighbors. If O'Bannon was indeed as involved in cattle rustling as everyone seemed to think, he must be a pretty powerful fellow who didn't much care what his neighbors thought.

Jared was so deep in his thoughts that it took him a moment to notice his horse was getting a little waspy. Shaking out of his reverie and reminding himself a cowboy always pays attention to his pardner, he leaned down to check his cinch. Just as he did, he heard a loud noise from off to his right and up a little higher. His mind immediately registered it as a rifle shot. He saw the violent, powdered spewing of rock chips to his left as he let his motion carry him on over and out of the saddle, somersaulting and rolling behind a boulder that fortunately rested right beside the trail. He was dimly aware of his shirtsleeve tearing when, as he tumbled by, he painfully scraped his elbow on the rock he chose for sanctuary. He drew his pistol and kept his head down, listening for any noise that might give away the location of his attacker.

At first, he heard nothing but the pounding of his heart but then he heard hoof beats riding away to the north. He waited a few more minutes, agonizing over whether the silence was only a trick to lure him out from his hiding place. Finally, he could stand to stay put no longer so he decided to chance it. He got up ever so cautiously and peered out from behind his boulder. He saw his horse had bolted down the trail about fifty yards where she was waiting nervously.

After several frustrating minutes where she shied away from his approach, he got close enough to grab the reins and began talking to her, rubbing her muzzle soothingly. Once he got her calmed down, he decided it was time to mount up. As he put his boot in the stirrup, he felt a sharp pain in his leg and realized he was bruised and scraped up pretty much from head to toe. He wondered how that could have happened without his being aware of it.

Jared thought about trying to track whoever it was that had taken a shot at him but decided it would be smarter to head on up the trail to the Kilpatrick's ranch before it got dark. Riding off, he found himself starting at every little sound. Every bird's twitter, every rock rolling loose, became the anonymous shooter who'd tried to bushwhack him. He wondered who would want to shoot at him and why.

Riding up to the Kilpatrick's ranch house, Jared saw a figure on the porch with what appeared to be a rifle. He rode in slowly and when Ned recognized him, he lowered his Henry.

"Howdy, Ned," Jared called out, "Seems like everytime we see each other, you're pointin' that durned Henry at me. I'm hopin' we can put that behind us one of these days real soon." Jared was joshing, trying to lighten the moment but he could see the look on his new boss's face was grim. Jared asked, "Did somethin' happen while I was in town?"

Ned blew out his breath and said, "Yeah, I guess you could say so. We lost fifty head last night and Juan . . . you ain't met Juan Suazo yet, he's our other hand . . . he got shot in the leg. Lucky he got hit with a pistol but he's still gonna be laid up for awhile." Jared thought how fortunate he had been that the shooter who tried to ambush him had missed. He blessed his luck for having a loose cinch to check as Ned continued on. "I rode into town to get Doc Adams. Lucky he hadn't been into the whiskey too bad. He followed me back and patched up Juan."

"Where's Juan now?" Jared asked.

"Juan stays in a little cabin about a mile from here with his wife, Maria. We took him over there so she could tend to him. I'm glad he's alive but he ain't gonna be much help for quite awhile which means you and me's gonna have to work that much harder."

"I'll do what I can, Ned," Jared replied. "I ain't afraid to pitch in and work hard."

"I 'preciate that, Jared," Ned said with a sigh. "With all this rustlin' goin' on, we gotta keep the herd together pretty close to the ranch." Frowning, Ned continued, "It's a sorry state of affairs when a man has to keep his herd within eyesight so they don't get stole out from under him. I know Nathan's doin' his best but he can't be everywhere at once. Looks like you're gonna have to earn your keep and then some. We better set you up in the bunkhouse and get you fed."

As they walked toward the bunkhouse, Ned noticed Jared limping and asked what was wrong. Jared told Ned about being shot at on the way out to the ranch, which got him stirred up again. "Those no-good, bush-whackin' varmits!" Ned exclaimed. "I reckon it was one of them rustlers hangin' around to see if anyone was gonna follow 'em."

"Maybe he thought I was a one-man posse," Jared joked.

"I don't see nothin' funny about the situation," Ned snapped back. Jared remained silent, stung by the rancher's rebuke. When they got to the door of the bunkhouse, Ned stopped and said, "Sorry I snorted at you like that. It's just I'm not only worried about my herd, I'm worried about Lizbeth . . . you and Juan and Maria, too. These rascals won't stop until they have my steers and eventually, my land. They'd like to run me off, but if they have to kill me, I don't think they'd mind that. Either way, it keeps things a might dicey."

"No offense taken, Ned. I was just tryin' to lighten things up but I guess I was out of line. I'm willin' to do my part to keep the cattle together and keep an eye out for those bandits."

"I appreciate that," Ned said as they unloaded Jared's gear. "Let's go on back to the house and get some of Lizbeth's cookin' in you so you can get some sleep and be ready for the mornin'."

When they walked back to the house, Lizbeth welcomed Jared with a big smile, saying, "Jared, it's good to have you with us. I know Ned told you about the excitement we had last night and I appreciate you're still bein' here. I half-expected you'd get back on your horse and ride away when Ned gave you the news."

Jared smiled and said, "Not before I had some of your home cookin'! Ned promised me it's worth whatever dangers I have to face."

Lizbeth laughed and said, "Most cowboys would eat just about anything as long as it wasn't movin'. My food kind of just lays there on the plate but if that makes me a good cook, so be it. Have a seat there. I'll start bringing out the chuck."

After a supper that just kept coming, from steaks to potatoes and vegetables and finally, peach cobbler, polished off with several steaming cups of coffee, Jared bid the Kilpatricks good night and headed to the bunkhouse. It didn't take him long to hit his bunk and within minutes, he was asleep.

Sometime deep in the night, Jared awoke with a start. He figured he must've been dreaming again but for the life of him, all he could remember was a vague image of a man with his hat pulled down shading his face even though it was nighttime in the dream with only the light from the quarter moon. Funny, even with his hat pulled down and it being night, Jared could see in his mind the piercing, cold blue eyes which caused him to shiver even though the night was muggy and warm. He wondered if a noise had awakened him and walked out on the porch to see if anything or anybody was stirring. He saw nothing and went back inside.

It seemed he had just shut his eyes when

he was rudely awakened again, this time by the clanging of a spoon on a frying pan. He heard Ned holler, "Come on Jared, get movin', we got a lot to do today. Coffee's on and we got eggs, bacon, biscuits and gravy."

Jared stretched and slipped on his pants and boots. He felt a little quiver of anticipation in his belly about the day to come. It'd been over a year since he'd worked cattle and he was looking forward to doing something where there was a right and a wrong way to do things. You didn't worry about whose word to believe or which side to take, you just trusted your horse and did your job. It occurred to him he'd probably had better luck with horses than with people during his life. He'd generally found them to be trustworthy and dependable and on the occasions when he'd been kicked or bucked off, he could usually pinpoint what he'd done wrong and correct the mistake. He thought people were much more unpredictable and when things went badly, he was unsure of where and how he might've gone astray. As he thought about everyone trying to get him to take their part in the local conflict, he began to feel resentful and was a bit out of sorts as he walked toward the house.

When he walked in the door, Lizbeth was busy setting the table and just nodded and smiled at him as she continued her work. Ned looked up from where he sat with his coffee and said in a loud voice, "Well, Jared, I guess today you get to start provin' yourself."

As he was already in a bad humor, Jared flared up at this. "I worked on the JA for three years. If that ain't proof enough I'm a hand, I'll go right back out to the bunkhouse this minute and get my things."

Ned looked startled and tried to back up, saying, "Whoa, there pardner, I was just makin' conversation, I didn't mean to offend you. Are you always this snappy in the mornin'?"

Jared wasn't yet ready to back off and said, "I'm just gettin' tired of everyone thinkin' they can tell me what to do and pointin' me in whatever direction they think is best for me. I'll make up my own mind!"

Ned looked at Jared and replied evenly, "Jared, on this ranch, I'm your boss. I decide what work you do. If you don't like it, you're right, you'd be better off hittin' the trail." Ned nodded and attempted to take a conciliatory tone. "I appreciate you wantin' to be your own man. Things around here seem clear to me because I'm smack dab in the middle of'em. If I was an outsider like you, I might want to take a little time makin' up my mind. My problem is while you're makin' up your mind, people are dyin'. I need all the help I can get just to survive. I need to know you're with me cause if you ain't, you might be against me."

Jared stared back at Ned for a moment, still feeling a bit testy. He said, "I understand you're the boss and I got no problem with that. You're gonna find you won't even need to tell me what to do most of the time because I'll already be doin' it. As for the rest of it, you're right. . . . I need to see for myself what's goin' down before I make up my mind what part, if any, I want of it."

Ned said, "I need help real bad right now, so I guess I'll have to settle for that." Feeling the need to relieve the tense situation, Ned said, "While we're eatin', I'll tell you what we're doin' today." He gestured with his hand toward the table. "Here, take a seat."

Jared sat down and let out his breath, saying, "I'd purely like to hear about some real cowboy action after all these months driftin' around. Be nice to get back to somethin' I know. What've you got planned for the day, boss?" Jared tried to lighten up the situation as well and Ned seemed to relax a bit.

"Well," Ned replied, "I want to show you the spread while we get some work done. I figured we'd ride out and check some fence-line. Those low-down scoundrels may have clipped some wire."

Jared was surprised at the talk of fences. "I wasn't aware you were usin' bob wire, Ned," Jared said. "I'm used to open range. It's free-grazin' where I come from. I reckon you might have to show me how to patch it up if they been a'cuttin' it."

"I can do that," Ned replied. "Next, we're gonna gather part of the herd that's out a ways. We'll bring'em in closer where we can keep an eye on'em. I'll also take you by Juan's cabin so you can meet him and Maria. That'll keep us busy a good part of the day."

"Fine by me," Jared replied cheerfully, trying to make up for his previous surliness. "I'll pack away some of Lizbeth's fine breakfast, get my gear and I'll be ready to ride."

They ate the rest of the meal in silence and Jared excused himself to go saddle up. When he walked out, Lizbeth came out of the kitchen and said to Ned, "Want one more cup before you go?"

Ned shook his head and said, "No, thanks darlin'. I don't need any more coffee and I don't need any more worries. Just when I think I like that boy, he turns on me and acts like a bee got into his chaps. I can't figure him out."

Lizbeth moved over to where Ned was sitting at the table and rested her hand gently on his shoulder. "Ned, he's young and he had a hard life before he ever got here. I was in town yesterday getting supplies and Nathan told me about the boy's bein' an orphan. Losin' your parents that young can make it hard for a person to trust. He'll come around eventually but we're gonna have to be patient. I believe there's a good, strong man beneath that crusty outside layer."

Ned shook his head and laughed, "Lizbeth, I swear, you'd look for the tender side of a rattlesnake." Ned's expression turned serious. "This time, I hope you're right. We need a good hand and a good friend who'll stand with us when there's trouble . . . and we both know there's gonna be more trouble." With that, he gave her hand a squeeze, rose and walked out into the first light.

In spite of feeling a bit uneasy about Jared's

testiness at breakfast, Ned had to admit he was impressed by his skills as a cowboy. They surveyed the damage where the rustlers had cut the wire and stampeded the cattle through the fence. Jared laughed and said, "Reckon I'll get my first lesson in fence-mendin' right quick." Later, as they rounded up cattle to bring them closer to the ranch house, it became clear that Jared knew his way around a herd.

"Jared," Ned said, "if you thought I had any doubts about you bein' the real deal, get that out of your head right now. Looks like you know your stuff."

Jared felt a surge of pride as his boss gave him those words of praise. "Thanks, Ned. I've had some real good teachers and besides, I always seemed to just have the knack. I think some folks got it and some ain't. Maybe I was just blessed."

"I'd have to agree with that, pardner," Ned replied. "Say, we're pretty close to Juan and Maria's cabin, let's ride over so I can check on him and you can meet him. You might wanta be careful what you say about these troubles we're havin'. Besides bein' pretty hot about gettin' shot, Juan is of a mind that they shot him because he's Spanish. There's folks in O'Bannon's crew that don't take kindly to the Spanish families that've been here for a lot longer than they have and they're pretty quick to insult them. That's a sore topic for Juan."

Jared said, "I'll watch what I say." He paused, then asked, "You seem pretty convinced the rustlers were O'Bannon's men. Have you got any proof? Might there be other rascals around that'd try somethin' like that?"

Ned sighed and said, "Jared, I know you're not sure about all of this trouble but I know who did it and I'd just as soon not discuss it any further. We started the day with a bit of a scuff, I don't want to end it that way, too."

"Sorry, boss," Jared said, throwing up his hands in surrender, "I shouldn't have brought it up. I'll shut my trap."

They rode on in silence, enjoying the scenery of the high plains with the mountains off in the distance. As they topped a rise, Jared spotted the cabin and Ned said, "Race you to Juan's place."

Jared needed no further challenge and immediately spurred his horse to a gallop. He beat Ned by ten yards to the house and turned in his saddle as his boss rode up beside him. "Thought you'd never get here," he laughed.

Ned laughed, too, as he shook his head in

amazement. "You sure can ride! Reckon we ought to strike up some horse races with the other outfits around here. I could win back some of the money I been losin' on these cattle gettin' stolen."

Again, Jared felt that flush of pride and smiled at his boss and new friend. "You say the word and I'll take on all comers. We'll split the winnin's and go to Montana."

Ned laughed and said, "I reckon Lizbeth might have somethin' to say about that."

Jared laughed back and said, "Yeah, I suppose we couldn't leave Lizbeth's cookin' behind, could we."

As they walked up to the door of the cabin, a young Spanish woman opened it and came out. She looked terrified and said breathlessly, "You frightened me, riding up here like that. I thought you were the rustlers come back to kill us."

Ned looked crestfallen, thinking how it must have seemed to Juan and Maria with him chasing a stranger. He said, "My goodness, Maria, I'm so sorry! We got into high spirits and decided to have a race. We never even thought about how you might take it. Please accept my apologies."

Maria nodded as she caught her breath. "I accept your apology, Senor Ned. I'm sorry things have come to this sorry state that you can't have a little fun without scaring someone. Juan tried to get out of bed to get his rifle. I think he has some pain." She turned to look at Jared and said, "Is this the new hand you told us about?"

Ned nodded and said formally, "Maria Suazo, I'd like to introduce you to Jared Delaney, a fine cowhand out of Texas. We're mighty lucky to have him."

Jared doffed his hat and said, "Pleased to meet you, m'am. I'm sorry about the troubles you and your husband have run into. I hope he gets to feelin' better real soon."

Maria smiled and said, "My husband is a strong and brave man but don't tell him I said so. He'll think I'm feeling sorry for him and he'll stay in bed for much longer because he thinks I will treat him like a little baby. I have to be hard on him so he does not lay about for the rest of the spring."

Jared laughed. "Your secret's safe with me."

Ned laughed as well and said, "Let's go on in and see if we can help encourage Juan not to spend too much time dodgin' work."

They walked in and looked over in the corner by the window where Jared saw a young Spanish man trying to sit up. Maria rushed to his side and in contrast to her earlier words, said, "Juan, don't try to get up. Save your strength."

Looking up at Ned, Juan said, "Maria must think they shot me in the ear as well as the leg and that I can no longer hear. You see what sympathy I get in my own home." He looked Jared's way and said, "I'm glad to finally meet this cowboy we've been hearing about. Ned tells me you are going to make my life easier when I get back on my feet."

Jared nodded at Juan and said, "I bet you been cowboyin' long enough to know there ain't nothin' easy about it but I'll try to pull my share of the load. Like I told your wife, sorry to hear about your troubles. I hope you get to feelin' chipper real fast."

"I plan to be up very soon to go after those no-account gringos who ambushed me," Juan said with a fiery look.

Ned shook his head. "Juan, calm down, we don't want you to start bleedin' again. As for goin' after those varmits, temptin' as it is, we can't spare you from the ranch. Besides, that's Nathan Averill's job anyway. We spread ourselves too thin here, they'll just hit us again and we'll lose more cattle. I can't afford that."

Juan didn't look convinced. "If you say so, Senor Ned, but I just want one open shot at those cabrons." Turning his head back toward Jared, Juan said, "You've signed on to a big hornet's nest, Jared Delaney. It will get worse before it gets better in this war and those O'Bannons are some dangerous characters."

Jared thought about Ned's warning and tried to respond in an even manner. "Juan, I'll take care of my job and my compadres but I ain't lookin' to take sides in any war. I just want to be a workin' cowboy, draw my pay and let others worry about the politics."

Juan, looking puzzled, turned his head back toward Ned. "Have you not told him about the way things are, Senor Ned?"

Ned said, "Jared's been filled in about what's happenin' but he wants to take his time and get to know the lay of the land for himself." Juan shook his head and seemed about to say more when Ned raised his hand and said, "Enough. We didn't come over to get you in a lather, we just came to see how you were feelin'." He turned to Maria and asked, "Do we need to get Doc Adams back out here or is he doin' all right?"

Maria looked at Juan and then back at Ned. "He's healing but it's early to know for sure. Doc said if there is no infection, he should be able to be up and around in a week or so but he won't be ready for heavy work for much longer. I know this is not good news but it is what we were told. He did say Juan was very lucky the bullet didn't hit bone or nick an artery."

"That Doc, he's a good fellow," Juan said, "but I'm not sure he knows what he's talking about. I think he had been drinking some whiskey when he came to see about me. I'll be back on my horse very soon. Maybe then I will teach this Jared Delaney how to ride."

Jared wasn't sure how to take Juan's words until he saw the cowboy smiling. He decided to give back what he was getting. "I wouldn't be much of a cowboy if I took advantage of an invalid. I'll give you a year or so before I teach you how a real cowboy rides."

Juan laughed at that but then grimaced in pain. After a moment, he said, "I guess I'll know I'm ready to ride again when it doesn't hurt to laugh at such nonsense." He shook off the pain and said in a more serious tone, "Welcome. I look forward to riding with you."

Jared nodded, "Likewise, amigo. We'll show Ned some tricks when you're ready."

Ned laughed and said, "That's all I need! Outlaws stealin' my cattle and my hired hands gangin' up on me. Come on, Jared, let's get horseback so we can work a little of the sauce out of you." He turned to Maria and said, "Take care of him, Maria. Don't hesitate lettin' me know if you think he needs Doc again. I'll ride in and fetch him myself. Doc may take a nip of whiskey now and again but he knows his job. We've got to get this husband of yours up and about."

Maria nodded and took Ned's hand briefly. "Thank you, Senor Ned, for looking after my Juan. We both appreciate it even though he won't say it to you himself."

"No need, Maria, I understand," Ned said as he turned to go outside. "Do what she says," he said back over his shoulder to Juan, "or she may decide you're too much trouble and go find a quieter life." Juan shook his head and smiled, not looking the least bit worried.

CHAPTER 7

They worked until sundown gathering cattle and mending fence, then headed back to the ranch house where Lizbeth had prepared a huge meal for them. Jared was tired and hungry but feeling good about being back in the saddle doing work he knew and loved. There wasn't much conversation at supper but what did occur was pleasant and friendly. Jared retired soon after his evening cup of coffee and had no trouble falling into a dreamless sleep. The rest of the week continued in the same vein, with Jared following Ned's instructions and proving himself.

At the end of the day on Friday, Ned informed Jared they would only be working the morning on Saturday. "There's a church social and Lizbeth's dead set on bringin' her fried chicken to show those ladies who can really cook. I think she's bakin' apple cobbler, too." Ned grinned. "Our toughest chore tomorrow will be keepin' our paws off the food so the picnic basket makes it into town. Lizbeth'll skin us alive if she catches us gettin' into it."

When Jared heard about the social, his first thought was of Eleanor but he was embarrassed to say anything to Ned. Instead he said, "I didn't know you and Lizbeth were church-goin' folks?"

Ned shook his head and said, "Well, I'm not so much. It's hard gettin' into town, livin' out here like we do, but it means a lot to Lizbeth. She likes to hear what Reverend Richardson has to say every so often and she likes catchin' up on the latest gossip around town. It's not a lot to ask to keep her happy." Ned looked serious and Jared realized maybe the situation was taking its toll more than he'd realized. Ned continued, "Lizbeth tolerates a lot, livin' out here and puttin' up with the dangers, to boot. I don't tell her how much I appreciate it near often enough but the least I can do is give in to her wishes on things like this."

Jared was somewhat at a loss for words but managed to say, "She's a good woman, Ned. You're lucky to have her."

Ned brightened up and replied, "A fact which she reminds me of every chance she gets. Now let's get some grub in us."

After supper, Ned picked up his coffee cup and motioned to Jared to join him on the front porch. "Let's go set a spell and drink some of this fine coffee. No need to rush off to bed since we have a short day tomorrow . . . that is, unless you need your rest to get ready to face Miss Eleanor tomorrow," Ned said with a grin.

Jared blushed and said in an unconvincing manner, "Oh, is she gonna be there?"

Ned guffawed with laughter and said, "I'm sure she hadn't crossed your mind until I mentioned her."

Jared chuckled along with Ned. "Well, maybe I've thought about her once or twice. A hand can't be thinkin' about cows every minute of every day. I guess she just naturally came up in my thoughts."

Ned shook his head and said, "Come on, let's go watch the last of the sunset. When Lizbeth is done cleanin' up, I reckon she may get her fiddle and play us a tune."

Jared looked surprised. "I didn't know Lizbeth played the fiddle. That's somethin' . . . a fine cook and a fiddler, too!"

Ned said, "Her mother taught her to play and left her the fiddle when she passed on. She plays lively tunes and some sweet, sad melodies that'll break your heart. You didn't know her family came over from Ireland, did you? Before she married me, she was Elizabeth O'Neill."

"Why no, I didn't," Jared said. "With my name bein' Delaney, I always suspected my family came from there but with losin' my parents early, I never really knew. I look forward to hearin' what she can do on that fiddle."

They talked quietly as they watched the sun set over the mountains. Soon, Lizbeth came out and sure enough, she was carrying an old violin. As she pulled up a stool, Jared said eagerly, "Ned just told me you play. I wish I could play music but I don't reckon I've the knack."

"Maybe you just never had the chance," Lizbeth replied. "If you don't try somethin', you won't know if you got the knack or not. Maybe sometime I could show you a few things on the fiddle and you could give it a whirl."

This touched Jared deeply. He said, "Lizbeth, that'd be dandy. Thanks for bein' willin' to take the time. Now, why don't you play somethin'."

Lizbeth nodded and said, "I suppose I could. Ned likes the jigs and reels but I'm feelin' a little melancholy. I think I'll play this tune my mother taught me."

With that, Lizbeth began playing the saddest melody Jared had ever heard. As he listened, he had the feeling he'd heard it before. He was mortified to find tears welling up in his eyes and he was glad dusk had fallen so Ned couldn't see. When Lizbeth was done, Jared waited a moment before responding. When he composed himself, he said, "That was about the prettiest thing I ever heard, Lizbeth. I don't know how it could be but I swear I've heard it before."

Lizbeth said, "Thank you for your kind words. It's an Irish melody my mother taught me when I was a girl. It's got words, too. She used to sing it to me sometime. With your last name bein' Delaney, maybe your family knew some tunes from the old country."

Jared had the briefest flash of a memory, a vision of a woman who must've been his mother singing softly to him as he lay in his bed. Just as quickly as this flitted across his mind, it disappeared. He shook his head. "Maybe so, I just can't remember. That melody touches my heart somethin' fierce. Makes me want to do somethin', though I don't know what. I guess that sounds loco, don't it?"

Lizbeth smiled at him and said, "Maybe to someone who's not Irish but it makes sense to me." With a laugh, she said, "I think we're gettin' a bit 'too Irish' for Ned. I'll play somethin' livelier to perk us up." With that, she brought her fiddle up and sawed off a jaunty reel that set their feet a'tapping. She played on for another hour before Ned decided he'd be needing his strength in the morning to fight off the temptation of Lizbeth's food.

"Jared, you'd better head to the bunkhouse now or Lizbeth will keep you up all night with that fiddle. She says the Irish call it a ceili. Folks stay up until dawn singin', playin' the fiddle and other odd instruments and drinkin' their Irish moonshine."

Lizbeth laughed and said, "That would be poteen, or potato whiskey, Ned darlin', and yes, that's a tradition my family brought over from the old country. There's been more than one sunrise we sang into the kitchen back before I was an old married lady. Now you boys head on off so you can rest up for tomorrow. I want you alert if the widow Donaldson corners you and decides to tell you what's in her blueberry cobbler. After she's had a little nip on the sly, she may tell you the secret ingredients. I'm countin' on you to remember so I can best her at the next church social!" With that, she gathered up her fiddle and walked inside.

Ned and Jared lingered a few moments longer on the porch. Jared fidgeted a bit as he tried to think of a way to ask the question that was on his mind. Finally, he blurted it out in a rush. "Ned, I don't know how to say this without bein' blunt, so please don't take offense. Seems to me Lizbeth would be the best mama in the world and you ain't half bad yourself. Why don't you have a passle of young'uns runnin' around?"

Ned leaned his chair back against the wall and appeared to be deep in thought for a long moment before answering. Jared became so uncomfortable he was about to apologize for his impertinence when Ned responded. "I understand why you'd ask the question, no offense taken. The answer is that Lizbeth had her heart set on havin' children but every time she got in a family way, she wound up losin' the child. Finally, the doctor told us if that kept up, she might die. We talked about it and I told her that as much as I wanted children, I wanted more to have her with me for the rest of our natural lives." Jared nodded soberly and Ned continued. "She didn't say much but I know she went to visit an old Spanish lady livin' outside of town. Folks say she's some kind of medicine woman . . . a currendera. Now, Lizbeth drinks a smelly concoction every mornin' and we haven't had the problem since."

Jared spoke up. "I'm sorry, Ned, it must be hard."

Ned shrugged. "Sometimes she gets a faraway look in her eyes. It could come from bein' Irish but maybe it mean she's thinkin' about the babies she'll never hold. It's sad but with all the troubles goin' on, I'm almost glad we don't have one more human life to worry about and protect."

Jared felt a touch of bitterness. After a moment, he said, "Life's odd. I'd give anything to have my parents back and Lizbeth wants to be a mother, yet we're both denied our wishes. Don't seem fair."

Ned laughed ruefully and said, "I don't know where you came up with the notion life was fair but I reckon yours and Lizbeth's circumstances would get it out of your head." He stood up, stretched and said, "We could stay up all night discussin' the ways of the world or we could turn in and get rested up for tomorrow. Don't know about you but I know which one I'm choosin'." With that, Ned walked into the house and Jared headed out to the bunkhouse.

During the night, Jared didn't have any nightmares but he had a dream where he saw himself in a kitchen in a sod house out on a vast prairie. Somehow, he recognized himself even though he was a young child of maybe seven years. The woman in the kitchen with him had her back turned and all he could hear was her voice. When he awoke right after sunrise, he couldn't remember any of the words she'd said, only that her voice was gentle and soothing. He experienced such an intense feeling of sadness and longing that it was physically painful. He closed his eyes and rubbed his face to wipe away the memory, then pulled himself awake and out of his bunk. He heard noises from the ranch house, got dressed and walked over to get a cup of coffee. He knocked and Lizbeth called out from the kitchen for him to come on in. When he walked in, Lizbeth turned toward him and for just an instant, he had a soaring feeling he was looking at his mother. This feeling was quickly replaced by the bitterness he'd experienced the night before when he thought of how unfair it was that he was denied his parents and Lizbeth was denied her children. Lizbeth must have noticed the strange look on his face because she poured him a cup of coffee, carried it over to him and put her hand out to touch his cheek.

She said softly, "I know you carry a powerful hurt inside you but you ain't alone with that. It's hard holdin' on to those memories without gettin' eaten up by the bitterness. You got to live in the present and look to the future. If we're always lookin' back, we never see what might lie ahead."

Jared took the coffee from Lizbeth and smiled at her, though his eyes retained their sadness. "I reckon you're right," he said, "but sometimes it seems like the future ain't worth much if you don't have a family to share it with."

Lizbeth looked him in the eye and said, "Why Jared Delaney, who says you don't have a family? You can create your own family right here in Cimarron if you give the right people your love and loyalty and stand by'em no matter what."

Jared had a flash of that old feeling of not being good enough, like he'd let someone down. He avoided her eyes when he replied. "You say that like it's a simple thing. Givin' someone your love and loyalty no matter what takes a lot . . . maybe more than I got to give."

Lizbeth looked at him strangely and said, "When you look in the mirror, you must see somethin' different than I see. You got what it takes to be a fine man. I only hope one day you'll see it, too."

At that moment, Ned walked into the kitchen and bellowed, "Top of the mornin'." Seeing the looks on their faces, he realized he'd stumbled in on a serious conversation, which left him befuddled. When neither spoke, he said, "Sorry for walkin' in on your heart to heart. I was hopin' to get some breakfast to help me make it through the ride into town smellin' your wonderful cookin', Lizbeth."

Lizbeth looked into Jared's eyes for a moment longer then laughed. "Ned, I'll cook you up some breakfast if only to protect that 'wonderful cookin' ' from you. I'm gonna beat the widow Donaldson in the cobbler contest today even without knowin' her secret ingredient. I'll not have you sneakin' a piece on the ride into town!" With that, Lizbeth returned to the cookstove and began preparing breakfast.

The rest of the morning passed quickly as Ned and Jared took care of the horses and rode out to the nearest fence line on the north side of the ranch to check for any breaks. Ned suggested they ride over to Juan and Maria's cabin to check on them as well. They approached the cabin much more slowly than they had the last time they'd ridden up. Ned called out, "Buenos dias, amigos."

Maria walked out the front door. "I guess I was wrong," she said. "I thought cowboys never learned manners but here you are, riding up politely instead of like wild savages." The disapproval in her tone was belied by the twinkle in her eye. Jared was struck by the strength of this woman's personality and thought she must be a great partner for Juan. Prior to meeting Maria, he'd had the impression that Spanish wives were subservient to their men but that was certainly not the case with the Suazos. Yet it was clear to him in seeing Maria with her husband, tending to his wounds, that she loved him dearly. He wondered what that might be like and his thoughts involuntarily turned to Eleanor Coulter. Just as quickly, he dismissed the notion, thinking that couldn't happen with a drifting cowboy like himself.

Ned laughed and said, "We ain't fast learners when it comes to manners. If it makes you feel better, you got help in gettin' me trained. Lizbeth works at it night and day but she says it's an uphill struggle. She thinks there's a donkey in my family tree. Somethin' about me bein' stubborn

121

like a mule."

Maria laughed back and said, "Your wife is a wise woman, Senor Ned. Don't take it too badly, though, mules are known to be hard workers."

"Thanks . . . I think," Ned replied. He then turned serious. "How's Juan comin' along?"

"He's not doing badly," Maria answered. "I'm keeping the wound clean and changing the dressing every day so there's no sign of infection. He's walking a bit although it's still painful . . . not that he would ever let on that he feels pain, but a woman can tell. Would you like to come in to speak with him? He's resting but I can wake him up."

Ned shook his head and said, "No thanks, Maria, no need for that. We just came by to let you know we're headin' in for the church social. Do you need anything from town?"

Maria had a number of items she needed and after she'd shared them with Ned, he said, "Keep an eye peeled for trouble, Maria. If anything happens, stay quiet and let it happen. Not that I want to lose any more cattle but you've already had your share of trouble. It ain't worth your gettin' hurt or killed. If somethin' goes down, just watch close to see if you recognize anyone and look for which direction they ride."

Maria nodded soberly and said, "We'll do our best, Senor Ned. It wouldn't be easy for Juan to stay quiet but he knows he's wounded pretty bad and there's nothing he could do. I just hope nothing happens."

"That makes two of us, Maria," Ned responded. "I may be lookin' for trouble that ain't comin' . . . today at least. Still, we gotta be ready." With that, he turned his horse and Jared turned to follow.

As they rode back to prepare to head into town, Ned said, "I didn't want to say anything about this in front of Lizbeth cause I don't want to worry her but I'd appreciate you helpin' me keep a sharp lookout on the ride into town. I don't think those rascals will try somethin' but you never know. I don't want us to get bushwhacked."

Thinking back on his recent experience of being shot at, Jared agreed. "I ain't lookin' to get bushwhacked either, Ned, particularly not before I've had a chance to compare Lizbeth's and the widow Donaldson's cobblers!"

Ned laughed at that and as they rode back up to the ranch house, He said, "You're a good man, Jared Delaney."

Jared smiled in response but in the back of his mind, he felt a nagging sense of doubt.

CHAPTER 8

Jared was on guard. All his senses alert as he scanned the horizon for signs of danger. In the end, the ride into town proved uneventful. Ned rode in the buckboard with Lizbeth and Jared rode along beside them leading Ned's horse. Lizbeth did most of the talking and it was obvious she was excited about seeing the women in town to catch up on the gossip and swap recipes. After going on for some time, however, she suddenly asked Jared, "Do you plan to spend time with Miss Coulter today?"

Caught off guard, Jared stammered, "Uh, I hadn't really given it much thought."

Lizbeth laughed at him and said, "You know it's a sin to tell a lie, don't you, Jared?"

Jared blushed. "I reckon you caught me on that, Lizbeth," he said. "Maybe I have given just a little bit of thought to Miss Coulter but I swear, I can't figure her out."

"What can't you figure," Lizbeth asked.

"Well, for one thing, I was wonderin' if she had a steady beau that I don't know about," Jared said. "I don't want to stumble into the middle of somethin' and get crosswise with some local fella."

Lizbeth smiled and said, "You don't have to worry about that, Jared, she's not attached."

Jared nodded but still looked worried. "I guess that gets me to my next question, then. Why don't she have a regular fella? She's sure nuff pretty and plenty smart, to boot."

Lizbeth looked thoughtful. "That's a fair question," she said. "I don't know as I have the answer but I got an opinion. You want to hear it?"

Jared didn't want to betray his eagerness to hear more about Eleanor. He responded in what he thought was a casual manner. "Well, we got a few minutes before we get there. I reckon there's no harm in hearin' what you got to say."

Lizbeth laughed at him again and said, "There you go, lyin' again." When he started to protest, she just waved her hand at him and continued on. "For one thing, Jared, it ain't like Eleanor is an old maid. She's about the same age as you. I don't hear anybody askin' why you're not hitched up."

Jared started to argue but what Lizbeth said made sense to him so he just shrugged his shoulders. "You got me there, I reckon. What else?"

"There's a couple other things to consider," Lizbeth said. "For one thing, most of the eligible bachelors are smelly old cowboys . . . no offense to either of you," she said with a grin. "They got no ambition or direction and to tell you the truth, they just wouldn't make a very good catch." Again Jared tried to think of a rebuttal. Again, he came up empty, so once again, he just shrugged and Lizbeth continued. "You answered your own question a minute ago if you were payin' attention." When Jared looked puzzled, she said, "Think about it. She's a pretty girl, no doubt but she's also smart and outspoken. A man's gotta stand pretty tall to measure up to Eleanor Coulter. He'd have to be able to match wits with her and appreciate her intelligence and spunk. Not all men are looking for those qualities in a wife."

Jared considered what Lizbeth had said. "That makes a lot of sense, I guess. She can be a might intimidatin' when you first meet her, downright prickly at times. If a fella weren't accustomed to it, he might be tempted to turn tail and run."

Lizbeth leaned a bit in Jared's direction, looked him in the eye and asked, "So . . . what are you plannin' to do?" Unfortunately . . . or maybe fortunately, there wasn't time for Jared to answer because just then, they pulled up to the town square. It was a grassy patch with a whitewashed wooden gazebo in the middle, and Jared looked over to see Eleanor Coulter talking with a group of women. He felt a surge of excitement, which he tried to ignore, telling himself that she'd only been hospitable to him because he was new in town. As they parked the buckboard and tied up the horses, Eleanor broke away from the group and hurried over.

"Good afternoon, Ned and Lizbeth. I'm pleased you could come!" Turning to Jared, she smiled excitedly and said, "As for you, Jared Delaney, since you're something of a tenderfoot when it comes to these events, you'd better stick with me so you don't get yourself into trouble."

Jared felt an odd mixture of happiness and relief. It was obvious, even to him, that Eleanor had been waiting for him and was pleased to see him. He tipped his hat to her and said, "It's good to know I'll be safe in your company."

Behind him, Ned snorted with laughter

and muttered under his breath, "Safe as you'd be with a pack of wolves on your heels, I reckon!" Lizbeth gave him an elbow in the side to shush him, laughing as she did so. Eleanor and Jared chose to ignore them.

Jared leaned over to Eleanor and said, "Come with me, I want to show you somethin'."

Curious, she followed him to where he'd tied his horse and watched as he opened his saddlebag. He turned to her and proudly displayed two ragged and well-worn books.

"Why Jared," she said in amazement, "those are by William Shakespeare."

"Yep," he said proudly. "*Julius Caesar* and *A Midsummer Night's Dream*. I got some more at the bunkhouse, I just brought these two to show you."

Eleanor said, "I remember you told me you could read but I must confess, I just assumed you read those dime novels. I never imagined you read the classics."

Jared smiled shyly and said, "Well, truth be told, I like the dime novels, too, but I really like the stories Mr. Shakespeare tells." He grinned and said, "I got to admit it took me awhile to get used to the way he talks. They sure had a different way of speakin' back in those days."

Eleanor smiled and said, "You're right. Some folks let that keep them from enjoying the stories. I'm impressed you didn't let that stop you." Jared could tell how pleased Eleanor was that he was well-read and it occurred to him that his stock as a suitor may have risen in her eyes. He felt like he was walking on a cloud as Eleanor led him away to where the food was laid out on a long table.

Along the way, she introduced him to townspeople and some of the ranchers from the outlying area who'd come to spend time with their neighbors. Jared also noticed quite a few families from the Spanish community. When he mentioned this to Eleanor, she said, "Reverend Richardson and Father Antonio encourage their congregations to mingle. They believe it promotes harmony in the town. Traditionally, they've remained separate but as Father Antonio says, we're all God's children. With all the troubles these days, we need to find ways to work together."

Jared nodded and said, "Makes sense to me. It ain't the color of a man's skin, it's what kind of hand he makes. I've known some mighty fine vaqueros in my time and was always proud to work along side of'em."

Walking through the crowd, Jared was

again struck by the contrast in people's reactions towards him. Some averted their eyes and moved out of his path, as if he might taint them in some way. Other people greeted him in a friendly fashion and some even called him by name . . . strange. Apparently, folks had heard of him already and knew he was working for the Kilpatricks. This surprised him but Eleanor assured him this was how the town operated. Rumor and gossip efficiently spread the news and spiced it up a bit to make it more interesting. One man asked him if it was true he and Sheriff Mills had tracked down and hung seven outlaws during his time as deputy down south. He had to laugh at that one and told the man as far as he knew, Sheriff Mills hadn't tracked down anything tougher than a saddle horse that took off one day while his owner was in the mercantile. The man laughed but seemed disappointed just the same.

The afternoon continued in this way for the next several hours with Jared getting acquainted with the townspeople and correcting misinformation about his past. He met the widow Donaldson but to his chagrin, she didn't say a word about the ingredients of her cobbler. He was glad he was able to tell Lizbeth honestly that he found her cobbler to be preferable to the widow's. He figured if that hadn't been the case, he'd pay for it all the next week with injured looks and smaller portions at meal times.

Nathan Averill showed up about mid-afternoon and approached them, smiling and tipping his hat to Eleanor. "Howdy, Eleanor and Jared. I thought I'd better mosey down this way and see if I needed to protect the town from any marauding picnickers who might have gotten out of hand and attacked someone with fried chicken drumsticks."

Jared laughed and said, "It was touch and go durin' the cobbler contest when the widow Donaldson found out she was comin' in second place behind Lizbeth. Reverend Richardson was able to distract her with some 'important church business' and that saved the day."

Nathan chuckled at that and Eleanor shook her head with mild disapproval. "Aren't you two the funniest things. You can have your laugh but these church events are important to the town. In these times, anything that brings folks together is worthwhile."

Both men put up their hands and Nathan said, "Eleanor, I take it all back! You're right, I was wrong. I'll never make fun again!"

Eleanor shook her head again but smiled and said, "Until the next time something strikes your funny bone. I know you, Nathan. You like to lighten things up to get people's minds off their troubles. I have a feeling your friend here is the same way."

Jared backed up a step in mock fear and said, "Nathan, I'm afraid Eleanor believes I've fallen in with bad company . . . that company bein' you. I hope you're ashamed of yourself, bein' sheriff and all."

"Yes, indeed I am," replied Nathan, looking not the least bit ashamed of himself. "Well, I need to get back to my office to do some blasted paperwork. The circuit court at Taos is perpetually sendin' over a passle of documents they deem important. I read'em but often fail to see what they have to do with the good folks of Cimarron." Jared and Eleanor chuckled together as Nathan went on. "Beats havin' an honest job, though. I'll stop back by in a little while to see how you two are gettin' along." With that, Nathan walked off in the direction of his office. Jared watched him and noticed that as he passed the Colfax Tavern, he stopped for a moment and seemed to be studying the activities through the swinging doors. He shook his head, looking a bit perplexed, and continued on down the street.

The rest of the afternoon was a happy blur to Jared. Eleanor seemed to get more comfortable around him, which allowed him to see the warmer, softer side of her personality. He recalled his description of her as "prickly" in his conversation with Lizbeth and decided he might revise his estimation of her after spending more time with her. He talked with so many people, he couldn't remember all the names but found everyone to be pleasant and eager to get to know him. The one uncomfortable moment came when Father Antonio looked around at the throng of people, then at Jared and remarked that he was pleased to see Jared had made a good choice of compadres. Jared let it pass, but a few minutes later, he mentioned it to Eleanor. "I wish attendin' a church picnic didn't give folks the impression I'm in one camp or another. Can't you people just enjoy yourselves and not get so agitated about choosin' up sides?"

Eleanor shook her head and said, "I know you're trying to be cautious but many of us have lived here most of our lives. We understand how things are. Some people are routinely pushed around by Morgan

O'Bannon's men for the simple 'crime' of being Spanish. They have no doubt there are two factions here . . . they see it and feel it every day." Jared could see Eleanor's passion rise as she defended her fellow townspeople but then she just as quickly calmed herself. "You're right about one thing. We can't let this interfere with our lives so that we can't enjoy the simple pleasure of a church social." With that, she reached down, took his hand and said, "Let's not talk about it. Have some more cobbler. You can choose sides between Lizbeth and the widow Donaldson.

Jared threw back his head and laughed, saying, "I know which side I'm takin' in that dust-up, I guarantee you!"

They wandered over to the table where the desserts were and although he looked longingly at the widow Donaldson's blueberry cobbler, Jared was very careful to only take a serving from Lizbeth's apple cobbler. The hours passed and dusk began to fall. Ned came over to Jared and said, "Lizbeth and I are ready to head on back to the ranch. You comin'?"

Jared looked at Eleanor and said, "I believe I'll take a room at the St. James so I can be available for church in the mornin' if that's acceptable to you, Miss Coulter."

Eleanor looked pleased and said, "I think that's a grand idea, Mr. Delaney. You appear to have the potential for becoming a civilized gentleman but I believe it's going to take a few more sessions with Reverend Richardson at church to polish those rough edges."

Jared laughed and said, "Well, then, I guess that's settled. I'll help Ned and Lizbeth load up their dishes and then maybe we might discuss supper."

Eleanor replied, "I don't know how you can even think about food after all you've eaten this afternoon. Shall we find a quiet place to enjoy a cup of coffee to finish off the day?"

Jared tipped his hat, saying, "Good idea. I'll be right back," and walked off with Ned.

Ned gave Jared an amused look. "Well, you survived the church social. Eleanor is a fine young lady but she keeps a fella on his toes."

Jared laughed and said, "She does, at that. I'm still tryin' to figure it out . . . she'll say somethin' that gets my dander up, then she laughs and I realize she's havin' me on. Then she gets all excited and makes a speech. Next thing I know, she'll be sorta sweet and I get flustered all over again. I ain't complainin' though, it's just I'm not used to courtin'. I reckon I do have some of those rough edges she mentioned."

It was Ned's turn to laugh as he said, "Lizbeth could spend hours tellin' you about my rough edges! For all Lizbeth's talk about 'smelly old cowboys,' I believe it's what keeps'em interested. If we were smooth and polished, it wouldn't be a challenge and they'd lose interest pretty darn quick."

Jared looked puzzled. "I never thought about it that way. This romance business is complicated! It's sure simpler bein' a cowboy. Things are pretty much black and white. You know what to do and you sure know when you didn't do it right."

Ned smiled and said, "Well, don't forget that. I don't want you stayin' for church tomorrow and forgettin' about comin' back to work. We'll need to get after it first thing Monday mornin' cause Juan won't be able to help out for another couple of weeks. The last thing I need is for you to be lollygaggin' around town while I'm out there workin' and lookin' over my shoulder!"

Jared frowned and said, "I forgot about you lookin' over your shoulder. You sure you and Lizbeth are all right to ride back this evenin' without me?"

Ned nodded and said, "We'll be fine.

Lizbeth can handle the buckboard and I'll ride along behind her keepin' a sharp eye out. There's no need for you to go. If they wanta ambush us, they can shoot all three of us as easy as they can two."

Jared still looked uncertain. "I don't mind changin' my plans if you want me to."

"Don't worry none," Ned replied. "I'll have my Henry in my hands which'll give'em pause. It'll be gettin' dark, too, so they'll have a harder time pullin' off an ambush. We got a rustler's moon tonight so the aimin' is trickier."

Jared nodded. "I hadn't thought about the rustler's moon in awhile. When I was at the JA, Mr. Goodnight's reputation was such that cattle rustlers didn't want nothin' to do with him, so it wasn't a time we took special care."

Ned said, "You got that right. There's no good time to steal cattle from Charlie Goodnight, not even durin' the rustler's moon. Wish the same was true here in Cimarron." He shook his head ruefully. "Well, it's late and the ranch ain't gettin' any closer. I reckon we oughta head on up the trail. Will we see you while there's still light tomorrow?"

Jared laughed again and said, "After church and a good meal, I'll have had all the civilized livin' I can tolerate. My 'unpolished charms' might've worn thin with Eleanor by then, too. I'll head on back by mid-afternoon. Any chores you need doin', save'em for me and I'll take care of'em so I can work up an appetite for Lizbeth's supper."

"I swear, I believe you got a hollow leg, as much as you eat. Don't worry, I'll do my part to help you work up that appetite." Ned and Jared went back to where the women were waiting and they said their goodbyes. Lizbeth gave Jared a sisterly peck on the cheek, which embarrassed but pleased him. As the couple rode away, Jared and Eleanor walked back to the picnic area. Jared said, "I need to get my horse bedded down at the livery and stop at the St. James to get a room. After that, I'll be ready for some supper."

Eleanor nodded. "I'll collect my dishes and take them back to my room behind the school, then meet you at the St. James. Anything more than coffee doesn't sound appetizing though," she said with a smile.

They went their separate ways, then met up again at the St. James. Jared ate steak with potatoes and Eleanor, true to her word, only had coffee. They talked for several hours although later, Jared couldn't remember exactly what they discussed. He had vague recollections of her describing humorous characteristics of various townspeople. He knew they talked about their hopes and dreams for the future. Whatever they discussed, it left a funny feeling in his stomach, like he'd swallowed butterflies . . . strange, but pleasant! They avoided discussing the troubles with Morgan O'Bannon and the Santa Fe Ring, sensing that their friendship needed to grow stronger before visiting the topic again.

When they finally reached a lull in the conversation, Eleanor said, "I've had a lovely time, Jared, but if I don't get some sleep, I'll be the one nodding off during Reverend Richardson's sermon. I'd never hear the end of it from the children at school."

Jared laughed. "I understand. The school marm has a reputation to protect." He stood up and with an exaggerated bow, said, "May I walk you home, Miss Coulter?"

Eleanor laughed at Jared's highjinks but shook her head. "Thank you, kind sir, but you're right, I have my reputation. I don't want anyone thinking I'm anything less than a lady so it would be best to say our goodbyes here. My room is only two blocks away and I've always made it safely before, I don't know why this night should be any different. Thanks for your offer, though."

Jared felt a flash of embarrassment and quickly said, "I'd never do somethin' to cause folks to think less of you, Eleanor. I hope you didn't think I was bein' forward!"

Eleanor laughed. "I knew you were being polite. When I said that underneath that rough cowboy exterior, you're a gentleman at heart, I wasn't joking. Should I call by in the morning and have them go upstairs to bang on some pots and pans or can I count on you to meet me at the church?"

Jared chuckled and said, "It wouldn't be a pretty sight if someone banged on pots and pans outside my door. Cowboys get a might jumpy and come a'boltin' out of bed to the sound of loud noises. I'll meet you in front of the church, I promise." With that, they said good night and Jared watched from the door as Eleanor made her way to her room behind the school, vigilant until he saw the glow of a candle showing through her window.

CHAPTER 9

Jared awoke, cold and nervous, with a vague recollection of dreaming about the rustler's moon. He couldn't recall anything specific but it left him with a cold, nervous feeling in the pit of his stomach. His dreams were like the early part of his life, foggy and closed off to him, as if his mind was a room with the door shut and the shades drawn. He didn't know what was in the room but it felt dangerous and deadly. If he knew what was there, he could confront it and deal with it but not knowing left him feeling helpless. That was a feeling he hated with all his being.

He dressed and went downstairs where he had two cups of coffee to help clear the cobwebs. Then he walked over to the church and was gratified to see that he'd gotten there before Eleanor. Several members of the congregation made small talk about the church social of the previous day. It gave him a pleasant feeling, like he was becoming a part of the community but at the same time, it made him uneasy. He really hoped to stay as far away from the local troubles as possible, yet he found himself being inexorably drawn into the fray.

Whatever uncomfortable feelings he was experiencing vanished when Eleanor joined him in front of the church. She seemed to be in a cheerful mood as she greeted him and they walked in and found seats. The Reverend Richardson made some comments about the church social and some announcements of upcoming events before he launched into his sermon for the day.

As best Jared could tell, the sermon was about being concerned for your fellow man, particularly the ones who had less than you did. Unlike the previous sermon he'd heard, there was nothing in this one that made Jared uncomfortable. As a cowboy, he was used to sharing whatever he had with his pards and expecting the same in return. When the service was over, he and Eleanor paid their respects then went over to Miguel Mares' cafe for lunch. Miguel came to seat them immediately and made a fuss over Eleanor, winking at Jared as he did so. He brought them large servings of the Spanish food common to Northern New Mexico, which Jared ate con mucho gusto. As they were polishing off their meal with apple pie and coffee, Jared said to Eleanor, "I'm curious about your friend, the sheriff."

Eleanor looked at him. "What is it you want to know?"

"I'm not rightly sure," Jared said hesitantly. "You seem to think a lot of him and so does Ned. He's cut from a different cloth than old Ham Mills down in Lincoln, that's for certain." Jared paused as he tried to collect his thoughts. "It's just, I don't know, with all the troubles goin' on around here, I'm tryin' to figure out who I can trust." Jared looked perplexed. "Maybe I'm bein' foolish."

Eleanor said, "I don't think it's foolish at all. If you're asking my opinion, here it is. I trust Nathan with my life and I believe you can, too."

Jared considered what Eleanor was saying. He looked down and said, "Sometimes I don't trust myself, Eleanor. Makes it tough to know who else to trust."

Eleanor reached out and touched him lightly on the arm. The touch, light as it was, coupled with the look on her face, conveyed an affection that surprised, pleased and scared him all at the same time. "I can't take away your pain, Jared," she said softly, "and I can't tell you what to do. I can tell you there's good people in the world. Accepting their friendship can go a long way towards healing you."

Jared considered Eleanor's words as well as her touch. He smiled shyly at her and said, "That's somethin' worth thinkin' about." He found himself thinking that her friendship, in particular, might have a powerful healing effect on him but wasn't sure how to put that in words without sounding like a rube. They sat quietly for another moment but Jared was uncomfortable with the silence and felt a need to break it. Not knowing what else to say, he asked, "Where'd old Nathan come from? I mean, has he always lived here in Cimarron or did he come here from some other place?"

Eleanor considered his question. "I was just a little girl when I met Nathan. When you're a child, you don't think too much about things like that. Nathan was just *there* . . . seemed to me he always had been." She smiled a little at her recollection, then added, "I do know that before he came here, he lived in the sandhills of Nebraska. I couldn't tell you what he did although he's bound to have had experience as a lawman before coming here."

"What makes you say that?" Jared asked.

"Because he's so good at it," Eleanor said. "He knows what's right and wrong, he knows the law, he's steadfast . . . and when there's trouble, he gets there quick and handles it." Eleanor seemed to think back on previous experiences. "I've seen Nathan handle situations so smoothly people didn't even realize they were being 'handled.' He never bullies anyone or pushes them around, he just solves the problem."

"That's quite a skill," Jared responded. "He's such a likeable fella, you might underestimate him if you weren't careful. From what Ned's told me, I reckon that'd be a big mistake."

"He's tough, all right," Eleanor said. "More than one troublemaker has made that mistake. Generally, they've wound up behind bars."

Curious, Jared asked her to tell him more about Nathan's exploits. She shared several stories which led to more tales about Cimarron and the Colfax area. Jared was caught up in the conversation but suddenly he gave a thought to the time. Although he was enjoying himself immensely, he felt a sense of restlessness that he attributed to his need to get back out to the ranch. Eleanor seemed to sense his uneasiness and said, "Jared, I know you're feeling the tug of your responsibilities to Ned and Lizbeth. If you need to take your leave, I'll understand."

Feeling a sense of relief, he said, "If you don't mind, I sure nuff need to be gettin' back. We've got a passle of chores to do to get ready for tomorrow mornin'. With Juan laid up still, there's all the work two cowboys can do and then some."

Eleanor really seemed to understand this, making Jared feel more at ease about their budding relationship. He was always going to be a cowboy and it was important to him that she understand and accept the nature of his work.

"Must I wait until the next church social to see you, Mr. Delaney?" Eleanor asked casually.

Jared replied nonchalantly, "I don't think it'll be that long before I head back to town. That bed at the St. James is a lot more comfortable than the one in Ned's bunkhouse so that's a mighty big attraction . . . the steaks there taste mighty good, too."

Eleanor's face fell and she said, "Why, I was hoping perhaps I was a part of the attraction drawing you back to civilization." When she saw Jared's mischievous grin, she realized he'd been teasing her and said, "Why Jared Delaney, I had no idea you had a sense of humor. I guess I'll need to be more alert."

They both laughed as they rose from the table and Jared paid for their meals. Thanking Miguel for the excellent fare, they made their way outside in the direction of the St. James so Jared could settle his account and get his horse from the stable. Passing the Colfax Tavern, Jared sensed Eleanor tensing up but neither said anything and no one inside the tavern seemed to take note of their passing. Little did he know that, much as in his early years, events were developing beyond his awareness which would have a profound effect on his life.

CHAPTER 10

The office behind the bar area of the Colfax Tavern was much more lavishly furnished than the patrons knew, since none of them was ever allowed inside the inner sanctum where Morgan O'Bannon conducted business when he was in town. As Jared and Eleanor passed by, Morgan was seated in a hand-tooled leather chair behind the mahogany desk with his custom made boots up. He was going over the previous night's receipts with Heck Roberts when they both glanced out the window and noticed Jared and Eleanor walking past.

"That young cowboy has gotten pretty cozy with the townspeople, especially that annoying school teacher," Morgan commented. "Too bad. I could use a fella with his skills. After all, I do have a ranch to run along with my other interests."

O'Bannon chuckled and seeing this, Heck Roberts laughed along. "You certainly do have rather diverse business interests, Mr. O'Bannon, if I do say so myself," Roberts preened. "I agree about the cowboy. I was hoping we might persuade him to enjoy the pleasures of the tavern and get him interested in working for us. Nathan Averill made a play for him right after he hit town, too."

Morgan looked up. "Really?"

"I guess he thought he'd be able to use his talents, too. Far as I can tell, he brushed that aside pretty quickly. I hear he's gone to work for Ned Kilpatrick. Ned's short-handed since that no-good Spanish scoundrel, Suazo, had his little accident." Roberts laughed at his little touch of irony.

"You know, Heck, we might find a way to use that young man's talents yet. There's somethin' familiar about him, I just can't put my finger on it." O'Bannon looked pensive. "Keep on being friendly but not too pushy. Offer him a free drink and if you get the chance, expose him to Christy's charms. She might be able to bewitch him and lure him into our camp." O'Bannon continued to look like he had a thought hanging around in the back of his mind but couldn't quite retrieve it. He said, "I can't say why but I have a feeling this'll get interesting as things develop."

CHAPTER 11

Over the next few weeks, Jared was as happy as he'd ever been in his life. He worked hard helping Ned out, impressing him with his skill as a cowboy and his willingness to tackle hard chores. As Juan Suazo began getting back on his feet, he spent time watching Jared work and they developed a friendship based on mutual admiration and continual good-natured teasing. Juan told Jared that as soon as he was healthy, he would take pity on him and teach him how to be a vaquero . . . a real cowboy. Jared responded by saying he doubted Juan would ever get that healthy. Sometimes, Juan and Maria would stop by the ranch house for dinner and on several occasions, Lizbeth was persuaded to bring out her fiddle.

One evening, to everyone's' surprise, Lizbeth handed Jared the fiddle and he played a ragged but recognizable lullaby. It turned out he and Lizbeth had been getting together for fiddle lessons a couple of times a week when they were able to break away from their chores. Lizbeth claimed he had a good feel for the difficult instrument and everyone was impressed with his new skill, giving him a round of applause when he was done.

When the applause died down, Ned looked at him and said, "You know, Jared, I'm not sure I like the fact you been fiddlin' around with my wife." Jared blushed beet-red and tried to think of a way to reassure Ned they hadn't done anything wrong. In his discomfort, he failed to notice everyone else grinning until Ned broke into laughter and he realized Ned was making a joke at his expense. Lizbeth sent Ned a withering look which shut him up for a time. Jared handed the fiddle back to Lizbeth and she played some more fiddle tunes for them. In addition to her Irish repertoire, Maria had taught her the melodies of some old Spanish tunes which Lizbeth had been able to pick out on her fiddle. They enjoyed the music while a cricket choir chirped in the background until Ned announced he was getting a bit long in the tooth and wasn't able to stay up as late as the youngsters. After some good-natured teasing in which everyone agreed with him that he was indeed over the hill, they turned in and the next day, began again.

A feeling of camaraderie and shared purpose brought them together. Jared had experienced something similar working the JA but the addition of the women at the Kilpatrick ranch made it feel more like family. When contrasted to his experience growing up with John and Lucy Gilbertson, he realized he felt more accepted by the Kilpatricks than he'd ever felt as a child. It was a good feeling but it made him uncomfortable, as if somehow he didn't deserve it or someone would snatch it away when he least expected it. He didn't understand this feeling and avoided thinking about it, yet it lingered under the surface, interfering with his being able to fully appreciate his newfound family.

The other thing preventing Jared from relaxing and settling in with his new friends was the constant threat of danger hanging over them as they waited and wondered when the next attack would occur. One cold, clear morning as they were rounding up strays in the high country, Jared said, "Ned, we ride around like spooky mule deer waitin' for a mountain lion to pounce. Do you really think those rustlers, whoever they are, are comin' back any time soon?"

Ned sat up in the saddle, looked around and then looked straight at Jared. "They're comin' back. It ain't a question of 'if,' it's a question of when. And who they are is Morgan O'Bannon and his bunch, make no mistake about it."

"You're pretty sure about that," Jared replied. "Tell me about this O'Bannon fella. Has he always been ornery?"

Ned laughed briefly, then turned serious again. "Morgan O'Bannon is the oldest of Sean O'Bannon's three boys. They didn't come to town too often, which was fine with folks since they always started trouble when they did come. Big Sean enjoyed throwin' his weight around. He seemed to particularly have it in for the Spanish folks that had lived in Cimarron for generations."

"Huh," Jared grunted. "Why was that?"

"He resented that they'd been here longer than he had. He wanted to make it clear to'em it didn't make any difference to him cause he was the top dog."

"Old man sounds like a bully if you ask me," Jared responded.

"I reckon old Sean came from a long line of bullies," Ned said, "and he sure passed the trait along to his sons. I was in school with the youngest, Jake, and we had some scuffles. My proudest moment was the day

I bloodied Jake's nose when he was pickin' on my best friend."

Jared laughed. "I didn't know you was a hero, Ned."

Ned grinned back. "He'd have beat me to a bloody pulp if we'd finished the fight. Lucky for me, Nathan, who'd recently become sheriff, happened by. He stopped it before it got goin' good. If he hadn't shown up, I don't think Miss Hattie could've stopped Jake."

"Is that the lady who took Eleanor under her wing?" Jared asked.

"The very same," Ned replied. "She was a piece of work. The fact she had trouble handlin' Jake shows what a handful he was."

"He must've been," Jared said. "From what Eleanor's told me, Miss Hattie could breathe fire."

"That's a fact, but Jake, he never showed respect to no one. That ain't changed to this day, far as I can see. As I recollect, that was when Jake stopped comin' to school. It was also the beginnin' of the bad blood between the O'Bannons and Nathan Averill."

"You're tellin' me some sort of feud developed between Nathan and these folks because of a schoolyard scuffle?" Jared asked in amazement.

"I reckon that's where it started," Ned

154

said, "though it was bound to happen sooner or later. The O'Bannons were bullies and Nathan wasn't the sort to step aside and let it go. He took his duties seriously, Nathan did. I reckon that put him on a collision course with the O'Bannons."

"Nathan's quite a fella," Jared commented. "I'd like to know more about him, too."

"That'll have to wait," Ned said, "I'm tellin' about the O'Bannons right now. I expect I'd get confused if I took a turn to tell you about Nathan."

Jared laughed at Ned, who continued. "Anyway, Jake was the youngest, Pete was the middle boy and Morgan was the oldest. They was all pretty wild and the Colfax Tavern was the place to be on a Saturday night if you were lookin' for fun or trouble."

"Reckon things ain't changed all that much when it comes to the Tavern," Jared said.

"That's a fact. This was before Heck Roberts' time, by the way. Morgan brought him in when he came back from the war, but I'm gettin' ahead of myself." Ned took a swig of water from his canteen before continuing. "What I heard was, one night Morgan was whoopin' it up at the tavern, drinkin' and pushin' other cowboys around, clearly lookin' for trouble. He was different back then than he is now."

"How's that?" Jared asked.

"He was loud and pushy, always ready to get in a fistfight. Quite a hand with the ladies. Sometimes, though, he could be friendly, helpin' folks out with chores and things just cause he was in the mood."

"That sure don't sound like the fella I hear about," Jared said.

"Nowadays, he's quiet and polite, dressed up like a gentleman rancher . . . yet you get the feelin' he's like a rattlesnake, ready to strike. There don't seem to be a hint of human kindness in him now." Ned laughed. "I'm gettin' off my story again. Anyhow, the way I heard it, Morgan took offense at some young cowboy hangin' around a tavern lady he was interested in. He slapped the girl and when the cowboy stood up to defend her honor, Morgan whacked him across the head with a whiskey bottle. The cowboy went down like stone."

"Come on, Ned," Jared said, "that stuff happens all the time. What's the big deal?"

"Morgan didn't stop there," Ned said. "He pulled out his pistol, plannin' to shoot him where he lay. Just then, Nathan Averill came in the tavern and told him to put his pistol away or die where he stood."

"Sounds like Nathan has a habit of showin' up at the right time when it comes to the O'Bannons," Jared said.

"There's some truth to that," Ned said with chagrin, "though I wish it was true more often these days. Anyways, Morgan turned around real slow and smiled at Nathan. He holstered his pistol and walked toward the bar." Ned leaned forward in his saddle, getting in the spirit of his story. "Just as he got there, he turned and went for his gun but Nathan was expectin' somethin' like that and had followed him to the bar. As Morgan drew, Nathan pistol-whipped him across the left ear, knockin' him flat. Morgan was up quick as a snake but Nathan knocked him down again. He aimed his pistol at Morgan's head and said if he tried it again, he'd put a bullet between his eyes." Ned paused for effect, letting Jared imagine the tension between the two men. "Morgan lay there lookin' back at him, then smiled the coldest smile you ever seen. He told Nathan he was done, pushed his pistol across the floor and asked if it was all right to get up. Nathan told him to do it slow and easy which Morgan did. Nathan told him to head on back out to the ranch so he didn't get in any more trouble . . . then he said somethin' I know he's had reason to reconsider over the years."

"What's that?" Jared asked.

"He told Morgan he hoped he'd learned a lesson he wouldn't forget. Morgan turned at the door and said very calmly, 'Sheriff, I'll never forget this . . . you can count on it.' Nathan and Morgan have remained bitter enemies, though they haven't had an open conflict since then. Their paths don't cross much but when they do, it's like you're standin' in an arroyo and the flash flood is comin'. They're always polite and Nathan acts almost friendly, joshin' Morgan about some thing or another, but you can cut the tension with a knife. Nathan's one of my best friends and I'd do just about anything to help him but I swear I wouldn't want to be within five miles when the storm finally hits and the flash flood comes."

Jared looked skeptical. "I'll have to take your word since I've never laid eyes on O'Bannon but Nathan strikes me as a mild-mannered old cuss. It's hard to think of him as some kind of flash flood. And why would the O'Bannons hold a grudge for so long over youthful highjinks."

Ned said, "Make no mistake. The O'Bannons are proud and mean enough to bear a grudge just for what I've told you about but there's more to the story."

Jared chuckled. "Ned, somehow I figured there had to be." Just then, a cow broke from the gather and took off over the rough terrain. Jared spurred his horse and brought her back into the herd effortlessly, then trotted back over to where Ned waited.

Ned said, "Go ahead, laugh, but don't ever make the mistake of underestimatin' old Nathan. He's friendly and polite with everyone and I know he's gettin' along in years. When the situation calls for it, though, he's as tough as anyone you ever seen. Some folks say Nathan's the only man Morgan is afraid of, though I promise you, no one has the salt to say it out loud."

"All right," Jared said with a little laugh, "I'll trust your word on Nathan, at least until I hear the full story on him. Now, I want to hear the rest of *this* story. You keep wanderin' all around it without gettin' to the point."

Ned chuckled. "Yeah, I get goin' in one direction, then take a little jog in another. First thing you know, I got myself off track. I've a tendency to ramble if I ain't careful."

"You know, I believe your wife has mentioned that fact," Jared said with a laugh.

Ned looked flustered for a moment, then he shrugged. "Well, here's the most important part of the story though there's a piece that'll never be told cause only Morgan knows it. What I know is mostly hearsay but I believe it's true as far as it goes."

Jared directed most of his attention to Ned's words but part of his mind focused on the surroundings, reading the sights and sounds. The cattle didn't seem skittish and birds were chirping, signs that suggested no threats were nearby. Ned continued with his tale.

"When the War Between the States broke out, it seemed pretty far away, though we did wind up gettin' into it a bit down by Glorietta Pass. After about a year, though, Morgan O'Bannon just up and went east to enlist in the Union Army. We couldn't figure out what he was up to but we knew he was up to somethin'. The O'Bannons never cared a lick about any cause that wasn't their own." Ned gave a disgusted look and spat on the ground. "Then we heard Morgan was appointed quartermaster for General Sherman, which struck us as odd."

"That does seem odd," Jared said. "He seems like the kind of fella that would be an officer leadin' soldiers into the thick of battle."

Ned nodded in agreement. "That's what we thought, too. A few months later, it began to make sense. Wagons showed up at the O'Bannon place with loads of supplies that didn't seem like what you'd expect at a ranch . . . bolts of cloth for uniforms, tools and the like. Seems old Sean was sellin' things back to both armies at an inflated cost and turnin' quite a dandy profit. We heard of shipments of gold bullion that wound up out at the O'Bannon place, too, but no one ever laid eyes on'em . . . at least no one who would admit to it."

Jared shook his head in disbelief. "You're tellin' me Morgan O'Bannon was smugglin' from the Union army? How'd he get away with such a thing?"

Ned replied, "Smugglers was pretty common durin' the war but the O'Bannons made the rest of'em look like pikers. I don't know how he pulled it off but I do know that besides bein' mean and fearless, Morgan is one smart fella. Whatever he was doin', he made it work so well he even got promoted a couple of times. There's no tellin' how rich they'd have gotten but for one thing they didn't account for."

"What was that?" Jared wondered.

"There was a war goin' on," Ned replied. "Morgan's unit was at the Battle of Kennesaw Mountain in the middle of '64. Their side lost that day and a passle of Union soldiers were captured, includin' Morgan. They took'em to that new Andersonville prison the Confederates had recently opened."

"So Morgan just spent the rest of the war coolin' his heels in a Confederate prison?" Jared asked.

Ned got a very serious look on his face. "You must not know much about the War. Given a choice between goin' to Andersonville and goin' to Hell, the smart choice'd be to go on down to Hell. Out of somethin' like twenty thousand prisoners that were kept there, twelve thousand died . . . starvation, diseases and worst of all, torture. Morgan survived but there's no tellin' what he went through. Whatever happened, he never said nothin' to folks around here."

"How'd he get out and what happened then?" Jared asked eagerly.

"Slow down, now, you don't wanta rush a good story." Ned pulled out his bandana and wiped his brow before he went on. "After the war, they went into Andersonville and found survivors lookin' like skeletons, so starved they couldn't walk. They took'em to Union hospitals and began nursin'em back to health."

"Morgan was one of'em?" Jared asked.

"That he was," Ned replied. "Not long after, army officials began to investigate irregularities between the supplies they had on hand and what their records showed. They tracked the problems in Sherman's division to Morgan. It's likely he'd have been court-martialed and hung but he vanished out of the hospital."

"What do you mean, vanished?" Jared asked. "People don't just vanish."

"No one knows how he did it, though I've heard rumors Heck Roberts was involved. For a spell, no one knew where he was. Rumor has it he went to the Indian Territories and led a band of marauders throughout northern Texas. They'd raid outlyin' farms, stealin' the livestock and killin' folks as they went."

Jared felt a cold wave of dread go down his spine. "Morgan was robbin' folks in north Texas right after the war? That's when my family was wiped out. You don't suppose he had anything to do with it, do you?"

Ned looked thoughtful and said, "I don't know how to tell, Jared. Even if it's true Morgan was runnin' roughshod back then, he wasn't the only one. There was some tough hombres ridin' the Indian Territory at that time. Prob'ly any number of 'em could've been responsible for your folks' tragedy. Do you have any recollection of what the varmits looked like?"

In his mind, Jared saw the cold blue eyes and heard the voice, soft and hard at the same time. Shaking it off, he said, "I have flashes of memories but they don't make sense. It's like when lightnin' strikes in the dark . . . you get a fast look around but you can't quite tell what you're lookin' at. If I got a good look at the killers, I don't recall it. It's like bein' behind a door that every so often opens just a tad. When I try to look through the crack, the door slams shut."

Ned nodded. "I know what you mean, I hate that feelin'. You almost remember somethin', like it's ticklin' the back of your brain but you can't quite scratch it to bring it out. Maybe someday you'll recollect. I'd surely want to know what happened, if only so I could close that chapter of my life and move on."

Jared looked rueful and said, "I don't know as how that chapter'll ever get closed."

"Well, where there's life, there's hope, I always say," Ned replied. "Now, let me finish this yarn so we can get back to movin' these old cows along." Ned stood up in his stirrups to stretch his legs, then went on with his story. "Like I said, nobody knew where Morgan was but he must have been

164

keepin' in touch with his family. One day . . . '68 or '69, I can't recall . . . old Sean's heart give out and he just up and died. A week later, Morgan came ridin' in on a big bay stallion. Took over runnin' the ranch smooth as silk, like he and his daddy'd been plannin' it all along. What folks noticed though, was that he was different."

Jared looked puzzled. "Different how?"

"Before he left," Ned answered, "he'd been wild and unpredictable. When he returned, he was hard and dangerous. In his younger days, he'd lose his temper and get into a fight every now and then. This new Morgan was quieter but in a scary way, like a snake, watchin' with flat eyes, ready to strike." Once again, Jared noted the unsettling comparison to a venomous serpent. "Whatever happened in Andersonville and durin' those wild days in the Indian Territories, it changed him forever but not for better."

It occurred to Jared that the changes Morgan had undergone may have dramatically changed the lives of others as well but he didn't comment on that. "What happened after that?"

"Morgan took up leadership of the family, no questions asked. His brothers never made a peep, they just fell in line. They're still hotheads, no different than back in the school yard days. I'll tell you, though, I'd rather face ten hotheads like Pete and Jake than one Morgan." Ned took off his hat and scratched his head. "Give the devil his due, he's got that ranch operatin' at a profit. It's common knowledge he rustles cattle, but no one's caught him at it." He smiled a bitter smile. "No one 'cept Nathan has tried all that hard, though. It ain't exactly healthy."

Jared looked skeptical. "Ned, if it's common knowledge, there's likely proof. If there's no proof, how's everyone so certain? Just cause a fella went away to war and came back changed don't make him an outlaw."

"Folks around these parts've been toleratin' abuse from the O'Bannons for years. It ain't hard for us to believe the worst about'em. Like I said, Morgan's smart. When he steals cattle, he don't take'em right to the ranch."

"What does he do with'em?" Jared asked curiously.

"The canyons south and west of town go on for miles. He'll hide'em up there, change the brands and bring'em in a few at a time so it's harder to catch him at it."

"Has Nathan tried to track him?"

Ned shook his head wearily. "Nathan's done his best to gather evidence against Morgan but bein' as he's often without a deputy, he ain't had much luck. Those canyons go on forever. It's been hard to get the goods on him. Nathan's found signs where it appeared someone had gathered cattle and branded'em but by the time he got there, they were long gone."

"Why don't he go out to the ranch and check the brands? Seems like he could tell if somethin' looked funny."

"That's where that no-good lawyer, Tom Catron, from over in Santa Fe, comes in," Ned said. "Morgan won't let Nathan on his ranch without a search warrant. So far, Catron's been able to block him from getting one."

Jared frowned. "If Nathan can't get the goods on O'Bannon, maybe he ain't the one doin' the deed."

"Maybe you need to meet Morgan yourself and make your own judgement," Ned replied testily.

Jared nodded. "You may be right, Ned, I don't mean to doubt your word. People've been after me to join up with'em and I don't even know all the riders in the race. First day I hit town, that Roberts fella at the Colfax Tavern was tellin' me what I should and shouldn't do when all I wanted was a beer." Jared paused as he thought back on his first encounter with Roberts.

"You mentioned Morgan brought Heck back with him from the war. What's the story there? I noticed he don't talk like folks around these parts."

Ned replied. "Heck Roberts is a Yankee, through and through, most likely from up around New York, though no one knows for sure. Word is that Heck was Morgan's assistant quartermaster and was in on the shenanigans. When they cracked down on the smugglin', he made his getaway and wasn't captured when Morgan was. Folks think he had a hand in Morgan's escape from the hospital. They also say he rode with him in the Indian Territories."

"He don't seem like one for ridin' and shootin'," Jared said. "Strikes me as more the type for talkin' and shuckin'."

Ned laughed. "He ain't one for gettin' his hands dirty. They say he mostly scouted out banks and farms that'd be easy pickin's for Morgan's gang. There's times when things've gotten outa hand at the tavern though, and they say Heck's pretty handy with a shotgun. He's not a fella you want to mess with, I'll tell you! He may be a Yankee but he's got a mean streak."

Jared nodded and said, "I had a feelin' when I met him. He was friendly enough but I got the notion he was sizin' me up to see how he might use me. Can't say as I much liked it."

Ned looked up at the sky. "Would you look at this. While we been talkin' the sun's been gettin' higher. Let's get these cattle down to the south pasture. We'll be close enough to head in for some food." Ned and Jared began moving the cattle, never realizing they were being observed from the grove of trees on the hill overlooking the field where they'd been talking.

On the other side of the hill below the grove of trees, Jake and Pete O'Bannon returned to their horses and quietly mounted up. They walked the horses about a half a mile before speaking. "Don't seem like they're showin' the same pattern every day," Jake said in a puzzled tone. "They move the herd up to the high country, then move 'em back down before I expect 'em to. Damned if I can make sense of it."

"That's the point," Pete replied smugly. "They're tryin' to do things such that we can't predict so we won't know where and when to hit 'em again. It's pretty plain to anyone who ain't an eejit."

Jake gave his older brother a look of irritation and said, "I know, Pete, I's just sayin' what you was sayin' but in a different way. Ain't no call to be makin' fun of me."

"Take it easy," Pete said with a smirk, "I'm just funnin' you." Pete's expression changed and he looked thoughtful. "I notice Kilpatrick and that Delaney fella seem to be gettin' on pretty well. When they get to talkin', they ain't payin' real close attention to what's goin' on around'em. When the time is right, we can take advantage of that."

"Yeah," Jake said disdainfully, "They get to gossipin' like old church biddies. Hells bells, we could snatch the herd right out from under'em."

"Snatchin' the herd ain't what we're gonna do, eejit," Pete said, "We got other plans for them boys. Let's get back to the ranch and tell Morgan what we saw." The brothers spurred their horses into a lope and headed west.

CHAPTER 12

Several days later, Eleanor was having Sunday lunch with Reverend Richardson and Father Antonio at the Mares café. They were having a lively discussion when the door suddenly burst open and Pete and Jake O'Bannon swaggered in, accompanied by two other cowboys. All four were disheveled and smelled of whiskey. Without taking off his hat, Jake surveyed the room. His eyes fell upon Tomas Mares, Miguel's oldest son, who was standing behind the counter.

"Hey, pepper-belly," Jake yelled, "Get us a table. Come on, get a move on! We ain't got all day. Some of us ain't like you lazy beaners. We put in a full day's work."

Tomas looked at the cowboys, then glanced over his shoulder toward the kitchen where his father was cooking. It was only noon on Sunday, but it was obvious the cowboys had been drinking and were spoiling for a fight. Tomas decided to ignore their insults and smooth over the situation. He took a deep breath, came around the counter and said, "Good afternoon, senors, come over to this table here and we'll serve you a fine meal."

As he turned to lead the cowboys to their table, Jake stuck his boot out and tripped Tomas, sending him stumbling. He almost fell but was caught himself on a chair.

"Look, Pete," Jake laughed, "He's not just a lazy Meskin, he's a clumsy one, too. The boy can't even walk straight."

Tomas regained his balance and his eyes flashed. He gathered himself to lunge towards Jake. Eleanor had been watching the encounter from where she sat and as Tomas came up, she rushed over to where the men were, putting herself between Tomas and Jake O'Bannon. She looked Jake in the eye and said, "This is a civilized café for civilized people, Mr. O'Bannon. If you can't behave in a civilized manner, you need to go elsewhere."

Jake blinked, momentarily thrown off balance himself at being confronted by a woman. He looked around at the people in the café and realizing they were watching intently, he recovered. "Look here, boys, pepper-belly needs the school marm to protect him."

Tomas edged forward and said, "You would not talk so big if it was just you and me out in the street, eh, cabron." Tomas was not as tall as Jake but he was stocky and strong. He looked like he could hold his own in a fistfight. He also had the look of one who'd been pushed as far as he was willing to be pushed.

Pete laughed at Jake, egging him on. "Hey, little brother, he just called you a name. You ain't gonna take that, are you?"

Jake looked at Pete, then back at Tomas. His eyes narrowed ominously. He said, "I don't know what you called me cause you don't speak English that good but I heard what you said about me and you out in the street. Why don't you get your lazy Meskin tail out from between your legs and follow me outside if you want a piece of that pie."

Eleanor was terrified the confrontation was going to escalate and wasn't sure what to do. Reverend Richardson and Father Antonio were good men but they weren't fighters. The rest of the customers probably wouldn't mind seeing Jake and Pete get their comeuppance, but they weren't likely to lift a finger to help. In fact, most of them were doing their best to become invisible. She was afraid if Miguel came out of the kitchen without knowing what was going on, the cowboys might pull their guns and get the drop on him before he could get his shotgun. She was trying to come up with a plan and not having much luck when the front door opened and Nathan Averill walked in. He sized up the situation and putting his hand down next to his Colt pistol, walked over to within six feet of where the cowboys stood. Eleanor noticed he'd managed to position himself so that if there was gunplay, he'd be shooting toward the counter away from the customers.

"Howdy, boys," Nathan said in a friendly tone. "Looks like your Saturday night party's gone on a little too long, don't it? Might be a good idea for you fellas to head on back to the ranch. Get some rest so you'll be ready for a hard day's work tomorrow."

The words hung in the air for several agonizing seconds. The sheriff's body language belied his pleasant tone. He was clearly ready. Eleanor held her breath. Pete glanced to one side at Jake, then the other at the two cowboys. He nodded to the cowboys to spread out but Nathan immediately saw what they were up to. In the same calm voice, he said, "I wouldn't move if I was you boys. I'm a might skittish in my old age. You never know how I might react.

It'd be a shame if I had to shoot you and spoil all these nice people's lunch, now wouldn't it?"

The cowboys stopped in their tracks, looking uncertainly at Pete for direction. For a couple of seconds, everyone stood motionless waiting for someone to make their move. The silence was broken by the click of a shotgun hammer being drawn back. Behind the counter, Miguel Mares pointed his weapon at the cowboys and said, "The sheriff is right. I don't want to upset my customers by spilling your blood all over their Sunday meal. Leave pronto and you might live to see another day."

Pete and Jake looked at each other, then at the two men who had the drop on them. None of the patrons moved a muscle or drew a breath as they waited and prepared to dive for cover if necessary. Finally, Pete shrugged and said, "Jake, I ain't all that hungry right now. Let's head on back to the tavern and wet our whistles some more. It don't smell all that good in here anyhow with all them frijole eaters hangin' around."

Pete walked very deliberately toward the door. The other cowboys followed, looking relieved. Jake turned to Tomas and said, "You're lucky you had that girl and the old man lookin' out for you, pepper-belly.

Otherwise, you'd be dead and this town'd be better off with one less Meskin." He turned and stared at Nathan, saying, "You got the drop on us this time, old man. One of these days, it'll just be me and you. Then we'll see how tough you really are."

Nathan returned Jake's stare for a moment, then with a ghost of a smile, said, "You never know, Jake, someday you may have to find out. For now, though, you'd better follow your pards on out of here before you get in any deeper." Jake looked around and seemed to realize for the first time that his compadres had left and he was alone. He stared at Nathan for another couple of seconds, then without another word, walked out of the café.

For a long moment, no one breathed or moved after Jake walked out of the café. Then Nathan and Miguel stepped quickly over to where Tomas and Eleanor were standing and Miguel said urgently, "Tomas, are you all right?"

With his eyes still flashing, Tomas responded, "Si, papa, I am all right but I would feel better if you had let me go out in the street with that pendejo!"

Nathan reached out and put his hand on Tomas' shoulder, saying, "You're a brave young man, Tomas, but the O'Bannons don't believe in fair fights. Pete or one of those other lowdown sidewinders would've shot you in the back while you were havin' it on with Jake."

Tomas didn't say anything, he just continued to stare angrily out the front door as if Jake could feel the heat from his eyes. Miguel nodded and said, "Senor Nathan is right my son, the O'Bannon family has no honor. They hate our people." Turning to Nathan, Miguel said, "Just the same, I feel the way my son does. I'm sick and tired of their insults. I want to have it out with them once and for all."

Eleanor, who'd been standing by, joined in at that point. "It's despicable how they act. It makes my blood boil, Miguel! But I meant what I said to Jake about this being a place for civilized folks. We can't resolve everything with a gunfight, no matter how badly the O'Bannons behave."

Turning to Eleanor, Miguel answered, "You are a shining light of my life, Senorita, but I must disagree with you. Sometimes a man has to make a stand. The O'Bannons only understand one thing . . . violence. Sooner or later, it will come down to that, mark my words."

Nathan patted Tomas on the shoulder, then turned to Miguel and Eleanor. "You may be right, amigo, but if it comes to that, it's my job as sheriff to handle it. That's what they pay me for. I don't want the good citizens of Cimarron takin' the law into their own hands."

Miguel nodded but seemed unconvinced. "I respect you, Senor Nathan, but the law only offers so much protection. Those scoundrels walk into my café, threaten my son and scare my customers, then they walk away. You stopped it but they are still free men. You know as well as I that they will do the same thing again when the mood strikes them."

Nathan shook his head. "I know it's frustratin', Miguel, but they didn't break any laws, otherwise I'd have run'em in to jail. They came right up to the line but they didn't cross it. All I could do was make'em move along. Their time'll come, though. When it does, I promise you I'll do everything in my legal power to put'em away for a long time."

"I know you'll do your best, Senor Nathan, I don't doubt that," Miguel said, "but they insult the honor of my family and my people. At times like this, I forget there are good people here who treat each other with respect and make it worthwhile to live in Cimarron."

"But you're right about that, amigo," Nathan replied. "There are a lot more decent folks around than bad apples like the O'Bannons, it's just they don't make as big a ruckus. Speakin' of which." Nathan turned to address the customers. "You folks can get on back to your dinin' now, the excitement's over."

Turning back to Miguel, he said, "I do think it's over for now. I'll keep an eye out in case those boys swing back by here after they've had a few more cups of courage at the Colfax Tavern." He nodded to Tomas and Miguel, tipped his hat to Eleanor and walked out the door.

Miguel motioned for Tomas to follow him back to the kitchen. Eleanor returned to her table where Reverend Richardson and Father Antonio waited anxiously.

As she sat down, Reverend Richardson said, "Eleanor, we're so sorry. We wanted to help but we didn't know what to do."

Eleanor reached out and patted the reverend on the arm. "You and Father Antonio are men of God, not gunfighters. I wouldn't expect you to know what to do in an altercation like that. Please don't worry about it."

Father Antonio said, "But I can't help but worry about it, Senorita. If Sheriff Averill hadn't come along, things could well have turned bloody." Father Antonio was clearly agitated. "I don't understand why those cowboys hate our people so much. It seems we're guilty of the crimes of having brown skin and being here on the land first."

"Most of us don't feel that way!" Eleanor said emphatically to Father Antonio. "I hate the fact that a few ignorant people cause such pain and animosity. They divide the community when we're really all in this life together. I just hate it!"

"Si, I know you do, senorita," Father Antonio answered gently. "These insults grow tiresome, though. I am afraid they take their toll on all of us. If it weren't for the efforts of my good friend here to bring our congregations together, I might give up hope."

Reverend Richardson nodded in acknowledgement of the gratitude expressed by Father Antonio. He looked thoughtful for a moment. "You know, Eleanor, I was thinking about what you said about the division that could result from such venom. You don't suppose that might be part of the motivation behind this, do you? I've known Morgan O'Bannon long enough to believe he's capable of using such tactics in his efforts to take over Cimarron and the rest of

Colfax County. I wouldn't put it past him to use this sort of hateful behavior to drive a wedge between the whites and Spanish. Perhaps he subscribes to the theory that dividing people makes them easier to conquer."

Eleanor blinked. "You know, Reverend, I'd never thought of that. I attributed it to ignorance and being mean-spirited. As you say, Mr. O'Bannon is both smart and devious enough to come up with that sort of strategy. Maybe we should mention the notion to Nathan and see what he thinks."

In the backroom of the Colfax Tavern, Morgan listened to Pete recount what had taken place at the Mares Café. Morgan chuckled, then said to Jake, "What would you have done to that Mexican kid if Averill hadn't shown up when he did?"

Jake shrugged and grinned. "I don't know. I might've taken him out in the street and skinned him. I didn't expect him to rear up at me like he did, him bein' a young kid and all. That fancy school marm almost got herself slapped into next week, shootin' off her mouth that way." He turned to Pete and said, "Why didn't you let us go ahead and make our play? We could have taken'em, I bet."

"You'd bet that, wouldn't you, you eejit!" Pete said derisively. "You'd just ignore the fact the Meskin cook had a twelve gauge pointed at our backs and that lawman had the drop on us. You'd of got us into a helluva mess is what you'd a done. That's why I made the call, not you. Don't you worry, folks are gonna pay before it's over."

Morgan nodded. "Pete's right, little brother, in the end, it'll work out our way. Those still alive will be sorry for thinking they could stand up to us." Anyone hearing the venom in Morgan's voice wouldn't have doubted his word for a second. "Here's what you both need to remember. I want you stirring up trouble but I don't want you killing anyone out in the open. Jake, I particularly don't want you skinning Mexicans in the street. I don't give a hoot in hell whether those people live or die but I mean to take over this part of the country. That's what is most important, not some ignorant Mexican kid. Keep yourself in check and don't go off half-cocked or else you might destroy everything I'm trying to accomplish with one stupid act. Do you get my drift, little brother?"

Jake looked away from the intensity of his oldest brother's gaze and answered in a surly manner, "I got you, Morgan. I's just havin' a little fun is all. I'll keep my temper under control . . . but those damn people make me see red sometimes."

"I don't care what color you see, Jake, just so you follow my instructions to the letter. Stir up trouble between the Mexicans and the other town folks so they're suspicious and slow to come to each other's assistance. Once we've taken over, we'll sort out who needs a little more education in how to be a proper citizen . . . I'll put you in charge of that personally." A sadistic grin spread over Jake's face.

Morgan got up from behind the desk and put his arms around his brothers' shoulders. "In the meantime, we need to cause friction between the school marm and that young cowboy. If we can get them squabbling and create tension between Delaney and Ned Kilpatrick as well, we'll have strung out our most dangerous adversaries . . . other than Sheriff Averill, that is. I'll have to come up with something special for him." Sparks seemed to fly from Morgan's eyes when he spoke the sheriff's name.

Jake snorted, "He's an old man, Morgan. If he hadn't snuck in and got the drop on us this mornin', we'd of taken him in a heartbeat."

Morgan looked at his brother with amusement. "Once again, this is why you don't plan the strategy, Jake. You don't know how to evaluate your enemies objectively and you underestimate them as a result. Nathan Averill is getting on in years but he'd still be a handful in a fight. If we play our cards right, we'll just get him fighting who we want him to fight and it won't be us. Try to be patient. This will play out in good time, you'll see. In the meantime, stay away from the sheriff."

CHAPTER 13

After church, Jared begged off lunch because he needed to go by the mercantile to get some items for Lizbeth. He got into a long conversation with George Russell, the owner, and when he finally finished the task, he found himself with a powerful thirst. He was to meet up with Eleanor around two for a short visit before heading out to the Kilpatricks' but he had a little time to kill. He hadn't been to the Colfax Tavern in quite a spell. The idea of a beer sounded good to him. "One beer," he thought as he sauntered down the board sidewalk. "How could it hurt?"

When Heck Roberts saw Jared walk in, he was surprised but he remembered Morgan's directive and smoothly shifted into his "hail fellow well met" façade, motioning Jared over to the end of the bar. "Afternoon, cowboy," he said heartily, "How's about a beer on the house?"

"I don't mind payin', Mr. Roberts," Jared answered uncertainly," but I sure would like a beer. It's a mighty dry afternoon. I'd like to wet my whistle."

"Call me Heck, boy. It certainly is a dry afternoon," said Heck affably. "I believe a top hand like yourself deserves at least one beer on Mr. O'Bannon. Cowboys should be treated with respect although that's not always the way it goes around these parts."

Curious, Jared asked, "What do you mean? I sure been treated square by everyone I run into. Did somethin' happen?"

"Well," Heck said conspiratorially, "You mightn't have heard yet, it only happened an hour or so ago. Pete and Jake O'Bannon and a couple of their pards were treated rudely over at that Mares café. They came in for lunch and one of the boys, the older one I think, told them they didn't serve 'their kind,' whatever that means."

"That don't make sense," Jared said. "Why would he do that?"

"These Meskin folks around here don't seem to like cowboys. I think they're jealous of their skills or some such nonsense." Roberts shook his head disapprovingly at the temerity of the 'Meskins.' "The boy got threatening, even calling Jake out into the street. Lucky for him, Jake was in a pretty

186

good mood and just shrugged the whole thing off. That old codger of a sheriff showed up in the middle of it and wouldn't you know, he took the side of the Meskins. I don't know what the world is coming to when the law takes the side of the brown-skinned folks against those with white skin without even knowing the facts."

Jared thought the whole story sounded a bit off and he suspected that Roberts was tilting it in the direction of the O'Bannons. He didn't know Miguel Mares well but in his encounters with the man and his family, he'd never been treated with anything less than respect. He said, "Heck, that just don't sound right to me. I was of the impression Miguel Mares treats folks pretty much the way they treat him. As long as you're respectful, he'll return the favor. As for Mexican folks bein' jealous of us cowboys and our skills," Jared scoffed, "I reckon I need to remind you we learned pert near all we know from the vaqueros in the first place. I can't hardly see how they'd be jealous but they might feel they've been squeezed out."

Heck said, "You're fairly new around here and you've mostly heard from folks like Sheriff Averill and that school teacher lady. I just hope you keep in mind there's always another side to every story. Maybe things aren't exactly the way they first appear."

Jared grew weary of yet another conversation about taking sides. He downed his beer and said, "That's all mighty interestin' but I've got to meet up with that school teacher lady you mentioned, then head on back out to the ranch to get ready for a hard week. I appreciate the beer." With a tip of his hat to Roberts, Jared walked out squinting into the sun and headed toward schoolhouse where he knew Eleanor would be working on some lesson plans for the upcoming school week. As he approached the school, Eleanor walked out of the classroom looking agitated. He walked up to her and said, "I just had the strangest conversation with Heck Roberts. He said the O'Bannon brothers went into Miguel's café and got treated rude. He said Nathan took Miguel's side in the deal. Don't that beat all?"

Much to Jared's amazement, Eleanor exploded. "I can't believe you're taking the O'Bannons' part in this matter," she said shrilly. "I was there. That's not what happened at all!"

"Whoa there," Jared said defensively. "I'm not takin' anyone's part, I'm just tellin' you what I heard. You got no call to go jumpin' down my throat."

"Why were you even in the Colfax Tavern?" Eleanor demanded. "Those people are low-class! That Roberts fellow mistreats the poor women that work there."

Jared was feeling resentful about the turn in this conversation. He said, "In the first place, I only went in there to have a beer and kill a little time. In the second place, where do you get off thinkin' you can tell me where I can and can't be? You're my ladyfriend, not my mother!"

Eleanor glared at Jared and tried to collect herself. "I know I'm not your mother. I'm really not sure what that has to do with our conversation right now. And as for my being your ladyfriend, I'm not sure we've established that yet, nor am I sure I want to, given how you're treating me."

Jared sputtered, "How I'm treatin' you! What about how you're treatin' me? All I did was tell you about a conversation I had with a fella. Next thing I know, I landed in a patch of cactus. I don't know why you're so all-fired prickly!" Jared felt like he'd done something wrong but for the life of him, he didn't know what. "I got work to do out at the ranch," Jared said huffily. "I believe I'll just head on out that way 'til you calm down a bit."

He turned on his heel and walked toward

the livery stable to his waiting horse. He didn't look back so he missed seeing Eleanor begin to cry as she watched him walk away. If he had looked back, it might have softened his heart. He might have turned around, gone back and asked her what was wrong. He might have taken her in his arms and comforted her. He might have let her know he was on *her* side. He might have apologized for his angry words. She might have done the same. They might have discussed what had really happened at the café. But he didn't look back.

When Jared got to the Kilpatrick's, he took care of his horse, then took his saddle with him and went straight to the bunkhouse, intending to do some patchwork on the leather. As he worked with needle and thread, he stewed about the argument with Eleanor and succeeded in convincing himself he'd been the injured party. He thought it was probably a good thing he would be out at the ranch all week so she would have time to consider her actions and see the error of her ways. He anticipated that once she'd reflected on her behavior, she'd most likely want to apologize to him. He was contemplating whether or not to accept her apology right away or make her suffer a bit longer when he heard the sound of a spoon banging on a pot announcing supper. At the table, Ned seemed preoccupied, so Lizbeth attempted to engage Jared in a conversation but he was in no mood for talk. After receiving terse answers to her questions about how his time in town had gone, Lizbeth looked at both men and said, "Looks like I got turned around and wound up in an old bear's den. You two are a couple of grumps." After both men grunted in response, Lizbeth gave up and they ate in silence. Jared declined her offer of cobbler, a sure sign something was wrong, and excused himself to the bunkhouse.

The next morning, Jared was up on time and over for breakfast but his feelings were still smarting from his argument with Eleanor. Lizbeth could tell he was upset and after serving him, asked, "Did something happen while you were in town?"

Jared wasn't sure what to say because he knew Lizbeth and Eleanor were friends. He figured if he told her what happened, she might take Eleanor's side and then he'd find himself crosswise with another friend. He decided the less he said the better. "Eleanor and I had a little spat . . . it'll blow over. I don't really want to talk about it." He thanked her for breakfast, grabbed his hat and walked outside where Ned waited impatiently.

"I didn't think you'd ever get done in there," Ned said irritably. "What were you and Lizbeth gabbin' about anyway?"

Jared looked at Ned incredulously and said, "We weren't gabbin' about anything, I was finishin' my breakfast. What are you in such a goldanged hurry about anyway? You got a bee in your bonnet?"

"No, mister smarty-pants, I don't," Ned replied with annoyance. "I just want to get a good days work under my belt and I expect the same from my hands. We can't get finished if we don't get started."

Jared stared sullenly at Ned for a moment, then without a word, mounted up and spurred his horse. Ned had to spur his horse as well in order to catch up which he finally did after a couple of hundred yards. "Whoa, there, cowboy," he said a bit breathlessly, "You don't know where we're goin' yet."

Jared slowed to a trot and said, "I thought you wanted to get started. I figured you'd catch up and tell me what to do sooner or later."

"You're in a mighty fine mood this mornin'," Ned observed. "What's eatin' you?"

Jared considered telling Ned about the argument with Eleanor, figuring he might see things his way. If they hadn't just been cross with one another, he might've done so but he was still feeling irritable so he just said, "Nothin', I didn't sleep well last night. I ain't in the mood to talk but I'm ready to work if you are."

"Fair enough," Ned replied, "Follow me. We're headin' over to the high pasture this mornin'. I want to get those cows down lower and closer to the ranch. I got a feelin' somethin's up. I don't like havin' my herd spread out too far. We'll gather'em up and move'em down. I expect if we hit it hard, we can get it done by this afternoon. Let's get a move on." Ned broke into a long trot and Jared followed.

They arrived at the high pasture about a half hour later and began working the cattle. Once again, Ned was struck by what a good hand Jared was. He always seemed to know where to go and what to do without any direction from Ned. Even though he was in a sour mood, it didn't seem to affect his cowboy skills. Ned thought to himself. "When his disposition improves, I'll let him know he's doin'a good job. Looks like he could use a little buckin' up." They worked for a time with Ned holding the gather while

Jared rounded up the strays. Close to noon, they were nearly done and stopped to talk about what to do next, not realizing that once again, they were being watched and stalked.

CHAPTER 14

Jake turned to his brother. "I don't know, Pete, you think we can do this the way Morgan wants it done? If we can't, it may be too risky."

Pete's smile was cruel. "Ain't no time like the present, little brother. You're the sharpshooter, get to work."

Jake lay on his stomach with his rifle resting on a rock, pointing in the general direction of Jared and Ned down in the valley below. He chuckled at his brother's comment, then sighted in on the riders. Ned was in front with Jared a few yards behind and off to the side as they herded the cattle across the open field. As Jake took aim, Jared reached down to grab his canteen. Jake took advantage of the opportunity, squeezing off a shot that clipped one of the reins Jared was holding loosely in his left hand. Jared's horse reared, catching him by surprise and he was thrown from the saddle, landing unceremoniously on his back. As he lay there dazed Ned reacted, grabbing his rifle from its scabbard as he leapt from his horse. A quick look around showed no natural cover, so he did the best thing he could under the circumstances and ran behind one of the cows. The cow, sensing the unrest, danced around. Another shot rang out and the cow dropped like a stone. Ned went down with the cow, continuing to use it for cover as he shouted to Jared, "Catch your horse and hightail it to the ranch. They may be pullin' somethin' there, too. Go take care of Lizbeth, now!"

Jared tried to clear the cobwebs from his head and respond to the crisis but he felt paralyzed with a strangely familiar fear. It was like something had ahold of him and he couldn't shake free to get up and follow his boss's directions. His body was trembling and he felt like he was going to be sick. He felt hot and cold at the same time. In the distance, he heard the urgency in Ned's voice but it took a couple of beats for the words to register. With an effort that felt like he was moving a huge boulder off his body, he forced himself up to a sitting position. He shouted back, "I can't leave you here with those bushwhackers. I'll get my rifle and try to flush'em out."

From behind his perilous position, Ned screamed back at Jared. "Do what I say! You're useless here, go do somethin' that needs doin'!"

Up on the hill, Pete and Jake heard the voices carry and grinned at each other. Pete said, "Pump a few more rounds into them cows, then let's get outta here. I think we got lucky with this ambush, little brother."

Jake fired several more shots into the valley, killing three more cows, then the two brothers backed away from the edge of the cliff and went to where their horses were tethered. They mounted up and quickly rode away.

As Jake was shooting the cattle, Jared sprinted to his horse and was trying to get it under control so he could grab his rifle from the scabbard. As he managed to pull it free, he realized the shooting had stopped and he heard the sound of hoofbeats fading into the distance. He kept his horse between himself and where the rifle fire had come from until he was fairly certain that the danger had passed, then made his way to where Ned was slowly getting up and collecting himself.

As Jared approached, Ned looked at him coldly and said, "I gave you an order, boy. I told you to go to the ranch and look after

Lizbeth. Why are you standin' here gawkin' at me?"

Jared felt a mixture of humiliation and anger wash over him. "Ned, I didn't want to leave you here in danger. Can't you see that?"

"What I saw," Ned replied through clenched teeth, "was a cowboy who couldn't handle his horse and was no help in a fight. You couldn't even do what I asked when I told you to go check on Lizbeth. What good are you?"

Jared staggered back as if he had been hit by a blow from Ned's fist. In the back of his mind, he heard a voice once again saying to him, "You're not man enough." His anger rose up like a flash flood. "If I'm not good enough to work for you, maybe we should part ways. Far as I can see, you got a third-rate outfit here anyways. You can't keep cowboys workin' and you blame all your troubles on that O'Bannon fella. Maybe the problem is you."

It was Ned's turn to look stunned. He shook his head and said very softly, "Mister, if that's how you feel, I want you off my land just as fast as you can ride. Go by the bunkhouse and gather your stuff but don't waste a minute speakin' to my wife or to Juan and Maria. You're not man enough to carry their saddle blankets."

For a moment, Jared's mind searched for a way to take back the angry words he'd spoken. He knew in his heart they weren't true and he thought if he just owned up to his mistake, maybe he could repair the damage. Then his pride got the better of him and he said, "If that's the way you want it, Kilpatrick, that's the way it'll be. You owe me for my time. I'll expect you to leave me my money at the desk of the St. James the next time you're in town."

Jared mounted up and rode away towards the ranch house. Ned found his horse over in a grove of trees and quickly mounted up. He thought about trying to get the scattered cattle back together and move them to the south pasture but decided it would be better to get back to the ranch house as quickly as possible to make sure Lizbeth was all right. At that point, he didn't trust Jared Delaney to look out for his wife.

When Ned arrived at the ranch house, Lizbeth was standing on the porch with a dish towel in her hands. As he dismounted, she approached him in confusion. "What in the world is goin' on, Ned? Jared came stormin' in, went straight to the bunkhouse, grabbed his gear and rode off without a word. When I asked him what was wrong, he wouldn't answer me."

Ned told her about the ambush and about Jared's shoddy performance. When he told her what the two had said to each other, Lizbeth shook her head. "Ned, don't you think you're being too hard on the boy? He was tryin' to help you and did the best he could in a bad situation."

Ned threw up his hands in exasperation and said, "Why're you takin' his part? Men were shootin' at us and I needed a hand who could keep a clear head and follow orders. He froze. I can't have that in my hired hands. I thought he was made of stronger stuff but I see I was wrong. What's more, when I told him the way it was, he turned it around and blamed me. He wasn't even man enough to admit he was wrong."

"I know, Ned," Lizbeth sighed, "but don't you ever remember a time in your life when your pride wouldn't let you admit you'd made a mistake?"

"Course I can, Lizbeth," Ned replied, "but this wasn't about which way to lead cattle, it was life and death. We can't afford those kind of mistakes. I think we're better off without him around here." All at once, it was like the air went out of Ned. He said dejectedly, "I don't know what I'm gonna do about all the work pilin' up, though. Juan ain't ready to ride a full day yet and he don't have the strength to do the fence mendin' and such, neither."

Lizbeth put a hand on her husband's arm. "I know things are rough. You know I've mended a fence or two myself and I can fill a hole. Say the word and I'll get to work. I can go light on the cookin' and chores and go where you need the most help."

Ned smiled a sad smile at his wife and said, "Darlin', that means more to me than you'll ever know but I don't think it's come to that yet. I'll go into town in a day or so and check with Nathan to see if any cowboys have drifted through. There's always someone lookin' for work. I doubt they'll have the skills Jared has, though." Ned shook his head. "He may not've been much in a fight but he knew what's what when it came to cowboyin'. He was a hand, I'll give him that." Ned took off his hat and gazed out to the north before turning back to his wife. "Funny, that's what I was thinkin' about right before the shootin' started. I was gonna tell him, too. Looks like now I won't get the chance." With that, Ned turned and went to put his horse up before coming back to eat his meal with Lizbeth.

■ ■ ■ ■

Jared fumed as he rode into Cimarron. The more he thought about it, the more he believed Ned had been unreasonable and disrespectful. It'd been bad luck, not bad horsemanship, that found him reaching for his canteen as the shot spooked his horse. When he refused to follow Ned's orders, it'd been out of loyalty to a man he'd thought of as a friend.

"I guess that's over," Jared thought to himself. "Well, he wasn't much of a friend to turn on me like that." The thought crossed his mind that he wasn't much of a friend either if he could lash back at Ned like he had but he put it out of his mind. He started thinking about his prospects now that he was unemployed and wondered if any of the other ranches might be hiring. He thought briefly of moving on to Arizona to look for work but then he thought about Eleanor. They were on the outs temporarily, but he figured things would be better once she apologized.

He wondered what she would say when he told her how unreasonable Ned had been. He knew she'd been friends with the Kilpatricks a lot longer than she had been with him but he figured when she heard what happened, she couldn't help but see his point. As he considered the multiple consequences of his dustup with Ned, he felt a sharp stab of regret, particularly about Lizbeth. She'd been nothing but kind to him, sometimes acting like a big sister, other times like he thought a mother might act. He hadn't just lost a job, he felt like once again, he'd lost a family. An overwhelming sense of sadness washed over him briefly but he dredged up his anger about what Ned had said. The two feelings collided and struggled with each other in his heart, then the sadness receded into the background, replaced by bitterness. Being told he wasn't man enough for a task was the ultimate insult. It struck him to the core although he couldn't explain, even to himself, why it mattered as much as it did. As he rode along, he began to have an idea about what he might do next and he thought to himself, "We'll see who's man enough, Ned Kilpatrick."

CHAPTER 15

In the backroom of the Colfax Tavern, Morgan O'Bannon and Heck Roberts listened intently while Jake and Pete recounted what had happened at the Kilpatrick ranch. "You shoulda seen'em, Morg," Jake laughed. "They was fussin' like a couple of old biddies, goin' back and forth. We couldn't make out all they was sayin' but they were both pretty hot."

Morgan smiled a thin smile that didn't extend to his eyes. "That's what we want, to drive a wedge between Kilpatrick and Delaney. We'll play that cowboy like a concertina. He'll never even know he's being manipulated." O'Bannon's smile widened as he thought about Jared's total lack of awareness of his intricate machinations. "When we make our move, I want the kid in our camp. Tom Catron and I have had our eyes on Kilpatrick's ranch for quite awhile. I don't want some no-account drifter to be the wild card that upsets my hand."

Pete shuffled his feet nervously and said, "Morgan, I still ain't clear on why we gotta share our profits with Mr. Catron over in Santa Fe. Seems like we're doin' all the work."

Morgan gave Pete a withering look. "I would have expected that question from Jake. I'm surprised to hear it from you, Pete." Pete looked down at his feet while Jake started to protest. Morgan continued, over-riding Jake's sputtering. "As I've tried to make clear to both of you, Catron handles the legal business in the capital. He understands how land grant laws operate. Because of him, once we take over Kilpatrick's ranch, it'll be ours . . . lock, stock and barrel. It'll be legal and there'll be nothing Kilpatrick or anyone else can do about it. Believe me, he'll earn his share." Morgan turned away for a moment, looking out the window with a hard glint in his eye. "I plan to take that land and settle some old scores with Averill at the same time. Let's see if we can get Delaney where we can keep an eye on him and put him to some use."

He turned to Roberts and said, "Heck, be on the lookout for a chance to enlist the kid's services. Like I told you before, Christy could be some help if she gets the opportunity. When the time is right, I want to meet this young man and see if I can persuade him to cast his lot with us."

Turning to his brothers, Morgan said, "You boys did a nice job. Pa would be proud of you if he was here to see what you've done. Head on back to the ranch now and make sure things are running smoothly." With just a hint of irony, he said, "We do have a cattle operation to run. I have a hunch that may be the best way to convince Delaney to throw in with us. I think he just wants to be a cowboy and doesn't have the grit for the harder dealings." With a wave of his hand, he signaled the meeting over and went to his desk.

CHAPTER 16

Jared rode into town and got a room at the St. James Hotel. After he stowed his gear, he checked the grandfather clock in the lobby and saw it was a little after one in the afternoon. He knew Eleanor was busy with school until three so he decided to kill a little time. He debated about stopping in to see Nathan but he knew the old man was good friends with the Kilpatricks. He could just imagine what he'd say when he heard about their dust-up.

"I don't need that old sidewinder tellin' me it was all my fault things went south the way they did," Jared thought. Considering his options, he decided to wander over to the Colfax Tavern and see what was going on. He recalled Ned's warnings about Heck Roberts but he remembered Roberts had always been civil towards him. Right now, he needed someone who would be friendly and see his point of view. Besides, a beer would taste mighty good, washing some of the trail dust and bitterness out of his mouth. With the decision made, he walked down the street in the direction of the tavern.

"Well, look what the cat's drug in," Heck Roberts announced to the room as he watched Jared come through the swinging doors of the tavern. "It's that fine cowboy from Texas, Jared Delaney." The fact there were only two other customers in the establishment at the time didn't seem to phase Roberts. "What brings you to town in the middle of an afternoon in the middle of the week, Delaney? I'd expect you to be chasing Ned Kilpatrick's cows all over creation about now."

"I ain't gonna be chasin' Kilpatrick's cows anywhere from now on," Jared spat out. "We had words. I told him I was through with him and his third-rate outfit. He wants to blame everyone else for his troubles, including me. I won't stand for it! Now, how's about a nice cool beer to take the edge off?"

Containing his surprise at how quickly Morgan's plan had come to fruition, Roberts set about to take advantage of the opportunity. "Why, of course, young man, one beer coming up and a smooth shot of whiskey on the side to make it go down better." Roberts quickly served Jared before he could protest and told him the whiskey was on the house. "Compliments of Mr. O'Bannon," he told Jared.

"Not that I mind a free shot of whiskey," Jared said, "but why would Mr. O'Bannon want to buy me a drink? We've never met and he's not even here."

Roberts laughed and said, "I can see you're a clever young fella. I'm not going to slide anything by you. The truth is, Mr. O'Bannon left me specific instructions that if you came in, I was to buy you a glass of whiskey on his behalf."

"That's mighty neighborly of him but it still don't answer my question about why he'd want to do it in the first place," Jared replied. "Why would Morgan O'Bannon give two hoots in hell about me?"

"The honest to goodness truth, Jared," Roberts said with a smile, "is Mr. O'Bannon has heard of your reputation. He's set his sights on enticing you to come work for him at his ranch. With all due respect to Ned Kilpatrick, the O'Bannon spread is three times the size and a first-rate outfit to work for, all in all. He'd like to meet you personally and have the chance to tell you about his ranch. He hopes you might consider a change in employment." As he said this,

Heck thought to himself, "Although I'll bet even he wouldn't have predicted it would happen this fast!"

Jared felt flattered a big-time rancher like O'Bannon was interested in hiring him. Accompanying that good feeling was one of bitterness at Ned Kilpatrick for condemning his performance earlier in the day. He took a draw on his beer and a sip of his whiskey to rinse the bitter taste out of his mouth. Setting aside his misgivings about O'Bannon, he told Roberts, "Tell Mr. O'Bannon I'd be happy to meet him and talk about employment opportunities. It just so happens I'm available now and was plannin' on lookin' for work anyway." He took another big gulp of beer, then swallowed his whiskey and set his glass down with a satisfying thump.

One beer and a shot of whiskey led to several others. Jared soon found himself unloading all his frustrations about Ned Kilpatrick on the sympathetic ear of Heck Roberts. As his tongue loosened and his thoughts got muddled, he decided Roberts was a pretty smart fella after all since he seemed to agree with everything Jared was saying. He felt vindicated that Ned was being unreasonable and was just beginning to launch into another tirade about what a rascal he was when he suddenly remembered he'd intended to meet Eleanor after school. He asked Roberts the time and he pointed toward the end of the bar. The grandfather clock showed three forty-five.

"Damnation," Jared exclaimed, "I'm late to meet my ladyfriend!"

Roberts laughed. "It's better to never keep the ladies waiting if you can help it. When you're done, come back for a nightcap. Mr. O'Bannon usually shows up sometime after the supper hour and passes time with the clientele. He'll be interested to hear about the change in your employment situation. I'll bet he'll want to talk with you right away about the opportunity this presents.

"Sounds like a mighty fine idea, Heck, old buddy," Jared slurred. "I'll be back after I have a talk with my ladyfriend and get some supper in me." As he said the words, Jared felt a strange feeling, almost as if a shadow had passed overhead, momentarily blocking out the sun. He chose to ignore the feeling.

Jared staggered a bit as he walked toward the school and realized he'd had too much to drink. He thought about stopping by Miguel Mares' cafe for a cup of coffee to clear his head before he faced Eleanor. He rejected the notion because he was already later than he wanted to be and didn't want to have to track Eleanor all over town if she'd already left the school. He felt guilty about running late, especially since his tardiness was a result of spending time in a place Eleanor disapproved of. The guilt was followed quickly by resentment. "Why am I actin' like a scolded schoolboy?" he thought. "I'm not the one who's done somethin' wrong."

He walked along unsteadily, trying to maintain his equilibrium. He gathered his thoughts so he could explain clearly to her the disrespectful manner in which Ned had treated him and justify his decision to leave the ranch that had been his home for the past months. He was so preoccupied with these thoughts as he walked up to the schoolhouse that he almost fell inside the door when Eleanor opened it to come out just as he was reaching forward to grab the handle. He lurched against her and she had to steady him so he didn't fall.

"Jared," Eleanor exclaimed, "What are you doing here?"

Jared, his head still woozy from the alcohol, got flustered and became angry with Eleanor. "I thought you'd be happy to see me," he said with an edge of bitterness. "Sounds like you're accusin' me of somethin' instead. For your information, I'm here right now because that lowdown skunk, Ned Kilpatrick, don't know when he's got a good thing. We had words and I left his outfit!"

It was Eleanor's turn to be flustered. She said, "What are you talking about? Ned has been one of your best friends. Why are you calling him names?"

If Jared had been thinking more clearly, he'd have had the good sense to back up and start over with Eleanor, explaining what had happened and giving her a chance to digest the information. Unfortunately, his judgment was clouded by the whiskey. He was still smarting from the conflict with Ned, so he instead went on the attack with Eleanor. "I might've known you'd take up for Ned. I can't believe you folks, pretend-in' to be my friends then turnin' against me."

Eleanor grew more confused as the conversation went on. "I don't know what you're talking about." She sensed something different about him, then she smelled the alcohol on his breath. "Jared," she said, "I'm trying to understand why you're in town in the middle of the week and why you smell like a distillery. I don't know what you mean about people turning against you. If you'd explain to me what's going on, maybe I could catch up with you."

"Catch up with me and bushwhack me is more likely!" Jared exclaimed. "Ever since I came to town, you and Nathan Averill and Ned have been on me about you bein' the ones in the right, tellin' me what a scoundrel Morgan O'Bannon is. When there's trouble, Ned's the one who turns on me. O'Bannon's people are the ones who listen to my account. What am I supposed to think?" Without waiting for a reply, Jared rushed on. "I want to know right now if you're with me or not, even though I'm through with Ned Kilpatrick?"

Eleanor drew herself up. "Jared, I don't know what's gotten into you besides a bunch of whiskey. I don't even know how to answer your question. I'm sorry you and Ned had words. I'd certainly like to hear what happened but I don't appreciate your coming in here and demanding that I agree with you about something when I don't even know the details. It's not fair of you to put me on the spot in this way and I don't appreciate it."

Jared felt himself losing his temper but was powerless to control what he said. "I'll tell you what's not fair, Eleanor. It's people who pretend to be your friends and then turn on you when things get hard. That's happened to me all my life. I should've known better but you're all pretty slick. I guess I fell for your lies."

Eleanor recoiled from his accusation. Then with some fire of her own, she responded. "That's harsh and uncalled for. I won't stand to be talked to in that manner. I thought you were a gentleman and a decent person but I can see I misjudged you on both counts. This conversation is over, as is our friendship." She brushed past him and walked off down the street without looking back.

It was Jared's turn to be stunned. He tried to comprehend what had just happened but his mind wasn't processing the information. He realized the whiskey had muddled his thinking, making him say things he didn't mean. "Damn me for a fool, drinking in the middle of the day," he thought angrily.

He wanted to run after Eleanor and say something to change her mind but he didn't know what to say. Besides, his pride was getting in the way again. He felt the struggle inside between the Jared who wanted to believe Eleanor and the others really cared and the Jared who didn't trust anyone to get close enough to hurt him. He laughed bitterly as he realized all the talk of taking sides that had dogged him since he first hit town had finally come down to this moment. He could follow his heart and run after Eleanor or use his head and not leave himself open to getting that heart stomped upon. In the end, his head, with all the pain and mistrust it carried, won out. He made his choice. He walked away through the afternoon shadows in the direction of the Colfax Tavern.

CHAPTER 17

Jared awoke in a cold sweat, disoriented and confused about where he was. He fought down the panicky feeling as he remembered he was in the bunkhouse at the O'Bannon ranch and had a long day ahead of him moving part of the herd up to a higher pasture. The day would be made easier by the fact he'd be riding with five good cowboys who knew their jobs and worked together with a minimum of friction.

In the three weeks since he'd come to work for Morgan O'Bannon, he'd found most of the hands to be likeable and easy to work with. After the negative things he'd heard about O'Bannon from Eleanor, Ned Kilpatrick and Nathan Averill, he'd been apprehensive about accepting the job when Morgan offered it to him but the pay had been almost double what Kilpatrick had paid him and the conditions were far superior. He'd been pleasantly surprised to find an outfit that was well run and a group of cowboys who got along just fine with the exception of an occasional fistfight over a girl at the Colfax Tavern. These disagreements were always confined to the bar, though. The cowboss, Bob Evans, didn't tolerate fighting on the job. Any cowboy who let his temper get in the way of his work was given his wages and shown the gate.

When Jared met Bob, he was pleased that the cowboss had heard about his reputation as a top hand and was willing to give him leadership responsibilities right away. Jared was worried some of the other hands might resent this but they'd also heard about his work on the JA and were willing to grant him an extra measure of respect from the git-go as a result of that.

The only exceptions were Morgan's brothers, Pete and Jake. The other cowboys had been curious about what it had been like to work for "Old Charlie," as they called him, but Pete and Jake had made snide comments about Jared's having worked for "that old has-been." Jared didn't want to get into a scuffle with the boss's brothers, but he felt compelled to tell them they must've gotten bad information somewhere because Mr. Goodnight was more cowboy than anyone on this ranch, himself included. They could see he was getting worked up and tried to play it off as if they were just joshin' him but Jared could sense animosity. Any time he was around the brothers, one or both would make some sly dig, always with the pretense of joking around. Not wanting trouble, Jared did his best to stay out of the brothers' paths as much as possible which wasn't difficult as they weren't involved in the day to day operation of the ranch most of the time.

In fact, he wasn't sure what they did. They would leave every few days with a small group of cowboys and come back two or three days later looking worn out. Then, they'd spend several days hanging out at the Colfax Tavern, drinking and spending time with the working girls. Jared was curious about this but didn't want to create a ruckus in his new situation. He didn't ask any questions, attributing it to the privilege of being the boss's brothers.

In contrast, Morgan had been extremely polite and respectful, commenting on his skills as a hand and generally making him feel welcome. At their first meeting at the Colfax Tavern after his ill-fated encounter with Eleanor, he'd been struck by his eerily familiar icy blue eyes. Even as Morgan offered him a job and touted his reputation as a cowboy, there was something about him that inspired a feeling of dread, but he chalked it up to the negative things he'd heard from Nathan, Eleanor and Ned. Even after working at the ranch for three weeks, however, he was still uncomfortable around O'Bannon. It was like the man was sizing him up in some way beyond that of evaluating his worth as an employee.

Unlike Pete and Jake, Morgan was often present at the ranch overseeing the daily routine. He'd meet with Bob Evans a couple of times a week to discuss the management of the cattle and he also had a foreman in charge of a crew that worked in the two buildings off to the west of the main ranch house. Jared wasn't sure what was in the buildings but he knew they were more like storehouses although they were the size of a barn. In a friendly way, Bob made it clear to Jared the cowboys were to keep their distance from the buildings, as they had nothing to do with their work with cattle. This also made Jared curious but he knew Morgan was a wealthy man and assumed he might be involved in selling other goods in addition to his cattle. He thought briefly of what Ned had told him of the family's alleged smuggling during the War Between the States. He wondered if there might be some truth to it after all but decided it was not something that concerned him.

In Bob Evans, Jared hoped he might've found a new friend. Bob was a few years older than Jared but had spent his life working cattle and as far as Jared could see, he was a first rate cowboy. He was clearly in charge of the hands but seemed to lead with a mixture of experience and good humor that inspired respect rather than fear. He told Jared he'd grown up on his family's ranch above the Canadian River in the Texas panhandle near a little town called Dumas, named after some Frenchman who passed through the area. He was the fifth of six brothers. It was clear to him he was never going to have a big role in running the family ranch so he set out to make his own way. He worked several big outfits in Texas and New Mexico and made quite a few trips up the trails with herds. He'd been with the O'Bannon outfit for two years, he told Jared, and by and large, found it to his liking. When he told Jared this, it seemed there was something slightly off about the manner in which Evans spoke, like something didn't set too well with him. In keeping with his approach of not asking too many questions, however, Jared let it pass. He figured if he got to know Bob better, he could ask him about it.

After a good-sized breakfast and several cups of cowboy coffee, Jared saddled up along with the other hands and rode out in the direction of the cattle they'd be rounding up and moving. As he loped along, Bob rode up beside him and said, "Mornin', Jared. You ready for a full day?" Without waiting for an answer, he said, "When we get these cows moved, we'd better go check the fence on that south pasture. I think some of them Meskins done run their goats through it and we're gonna have to patch it up. Those folks don't seem to have the sense God gave a goose!"

Growing up in Texas and spending time in New Mexico, Jared had encountered this attitude before but he'd never really been a big believer in it. He thought briefly of his former friends, Juan and Maria Suazo. He said, "There's folks that don't have good sense and folks that do but I never really thought they was divided along the lines of Spanish and white. I've met some pretty smart Spanish folks and some pretty dumb gringos, when I think about it."

Bob looked sideways at Jared and said, "Don't tell me you're one of them frijole and tortilla lovin' fellas. That kinda thinkin' don't set well with the O'Bannons. The way they see it, these Meskins've had it too good around these parts for too long. Now it's time for us gringos to have our day. As your friend, I feel obliged to tell you if you're gonna make it in this outfit, you might wanta watch what you say about that."

Jared wondered what kind of friend Bob would turn out to be after all. He knew that as much as he admired Bob's cowboy skills, his respect for the man had dropped a notch because of his narrow-minded attitude. "I'm hopin' if I do a good job as a hand, there won't be much problem about what kinda people I like to spend my free time with, if you know what I mean."

Bob looked a bit disconcerted and told Jared, "I didn't mean no offense, Jared, I just wanted to let you know what's expected here at the O'Bannon's spread. Most places, bein' a good hand would take the cake but I reckon there's a little more to it here. Sometimes that means we gotta toe the line and do things we ain't exactly happy about just cause it's part of the job."

Jared felt a sinking feeling in his stomach as the issue of being pressured to toe someone else's line came up yet again. He said, "You know, Bob, I came to Cimarron lookin' to work as a cowboy, which seemed simple enough to me. From the day I arrived, people been tellin' me I've got to take their side in somethin' I don't know about or understand." Jared knew his exasperation was showing but decided he needed to be as clear as he could be with Evans. "That's what drove me away from Ned Kilpatrick. Now, just when I think I've got me a good job, you tell me I've gotta think the same way as everybody else who works here or I can't make it. What if I decide just to do my job and keep my thoughts to myself?"

Bob shook his head stubbornly. "I might work that way other places, but around these parts, you gotta figure out which way the wind blows and decide if you're gonna go with it or against it. Believe me, it's a mighty strong wind. The smart thing is to go with it. That's all I got to say about it." Jared noticed that Evans couldn't look him square in the eye as he spoke. It occurred to him that maybe the man's character couldn't keep pace with his cowboy skills. Evans spoke up to the rest of the hands, saying, "Let's get these cattle movin' and go tend to that fence." With that said, Bob spurred his horse and moved on out front of the group of cowboys, leaving Jared to speculate on his last words and wonder which direction he would ultimately decide to go.

CHAPTER 18

In Miguel Mares' café on a Saturday, the sheriff sat with a visibly upset Eleanor Coulter. She said, "Nathan, You should have seen him that day. He was like a stranger, completely different from the man I thought I knew. He'd been drinking, which he shouldn't have, but there was something more, a bitterness I hadn't seen before. Ned and Lizbeth were nothing but good to him. I just don't understand how he could turn on them that way."

Nathan took a deep breath before responding. "Eleanor, I'm not defendin' the young man but I suspect there's more goin' on than meets the eye. Somethin', or more likely, somebody got between Jared and Ned. My guess would be their name is O'Bannon. You don't think it was an accident they offered Jared a job at almost twice what Ned was payin' him, do you?"

"No," Eleanor replied, "but he didn't have

to take it, did he?"

"No, he didn't," Nathan said wearily. "I'm not sayin' the boy doesn't have a lot to learn or that he shouldn't account for his mistakes. I'm just sayin' he hasn't really understood or accepted the situation he stumbled into here in Cimarron. I'm not willin' to write him off as a lost cause yet, no matter what kind of dumb decisions he's made. I wish you'd at least think about talkin' to him if you get the chance."

Eleanor gave a frustrated sigh. "That's part of the problem, Nathan, I haven't had the chance. He spends most of his time on O'Bannon's ranch and the rest of his free time at that hell-hole of a tavern, doing God knows what."

Nathan could see Eleanor was hurt by Jared's apparent defection to the seedy nightlife of Cimarron. Having inside information of his own, he knew a certain lady of the evening was occupying quite a bit of his time and attention. "There ain' no easy answers, I'm just asking you not to give up on Jared. There's some grit in that boy down deep. Sooner or later, it'll come to the surface."

With the briefest glimpse of a smile, Eleanor said, "I hope you're right, Nathan."

Nathan said, "I hope I am, too. Meantime,

I'll do some checkin' around. My gut tells me those rascal O'Bannons are up to somethin'. I doubt it's anything good."

A few hours and a few drinks later that same Saturday, Jared sat in a room upstairs with Christy, complaining once again about the way he'd been treated by Ned Kilpatrick.

"I don't get it, Christy, I thought he was my friend," Jared said. "He's lucky I felt that way, too. If another man had said those things to me, I'd of given him a whuppin' or worse, right on the spot."

Christy nodded in an understanding way. "I know you would, Jared, honey. He's lucky you didn't lose your temper any more than you did. But come on, let's forget about that and have some fun. You got a good job now. The O'Bannons'll treat you right."

Jared smiled and said, "You're right, I need to forget about what happened and get on with my life." His head felt fuzzy and his thoughts were confused, much as they'd been most Saturdays since he went to work for the O'Bannon outfit. "You know, Christy, even though they treat me good at the ranch, they're still tryin' to tell me what and how to think . . . and I ain't talkin' about my job. That I could understand. There's somethin' out there that ain't right but I can't put my finger on it."

Christy reached for the whiskey bottle by the bed. "Jared, honey, you think way too much. Let's have another drink and quit worryin' about all this nonsense."

Jared stretched out on the bed. "Hon, don't you ever think about things and try to make sense out of 'em? With everyone tuggin' at you all the time, it gets kinda confusin' but I think a person's got to try to figure out the right thing to do. Don't you?"

Christy gave a bitter laugh and replied, "Jared, you big, dumb cowboy, look at me. Look around! Where do you think you are? Do I look like I spend a lot of time thinkin' about right and wrong? I'm just tryin' to get by and maybe squeeze a little pleasure out of this mean old life. Right and wrong ain't got a lot to do with it."

Jared sat up on the bed and took Christy's hand. "I ain't so dumb I don't know what you do to get by but there's more to you than all that. You're smart and funny. You can be awful nice when nobody's lookin'. I hate when you talk down about yourself!"

Christy got a funny look on her face. "I know you want me to be somethin' more than I am but sometimes things're just what they seem. I like you just fine but it ain't gonna stop me from makin' my livin' . . . if you can call it livin' . . . doin' what I know how to do." She looked away from Jared and said, "If you were smart, you'd get away from me, Morgan O'Bannon and this whole town. You'd clear out for some other place that wasn't so tricky." The sudden intensity in her voice surprised Jared. "You got no idea what you've stumbled into. It's ugly and gettin' uglier."

"Christy," Jared smiled, "When I'm with you, I can't even think about ugly. Let's have that drink."

Christy shook her head and thought to herself, "Don't say I didn't warn you, cowboy."

Sunday morning, Jared awoke with a serious headache and a foggy memory of yet another nightmare of the man with the ice blue eyes. With his head pounding, he decided to ponder the significance of this later in the day after some coffee and a good breakfast. As he sat up on the edge of the bed and started to put on his boots, Christy rolled over and smiled at him. With a glance, she took in his dark hair, blue eyes and lithe frame. She said, "Where you goin' so early, Mr. Delaney? Take off them boots and lie back down, I'll make sure you don't regret the decision."

Jared was tempted but his head was hurting too badly and he thought he should get back out to the ranch pretty quick after he had some food. "That's the best offer I've had today but I need to get on back to work pretty soon. I got to talk to Bob about movin' the herd down to a lower pasture. We may have a big cat workin' in that high section. We need to get them calves away so we can hunt that rascal down."

Christy pouted and said, "You work way too hard, Jared. By the way, this was only the first offer you got today but you're right, it'll be the best." Her frown deepened. "Guess that means I gotta get back to work with the payin' customers."

Jared saw the pained look on her face. He put his hand on her arm. "Christy, hon, I'm makin' good money and savin' up part of my pay each month. Pretty soon, I could get you a place of your own. Then you wouldn't have to spend your time bein' nice and friendly to smelly old cowboys like me."

Instead of perking up like Jared had expected, Christy seemed more despondent. "I know you mean well but I am what I am. Ain't nothin' you can do to change that so I wish you wouldn't try. There's things that keep me tied here that you ain't got no kinda notion about."

Jared shook his head in puzzlement. "Maybe you're right, but if you don't tell me, I sure won't know what's goin' on or why. Does Heck Roberts have some kind of hold on you?" Since he'd spent more time at the Colfax Tavern, he'd noticed that while Heck was friendly with the customers, he was curt with the girls, sometimes making jokes about their 'getting a beating' if they didn't do what he wanted fast enough. He'd noticed girls with bruises, always on their arms and never on their faces. He didn't know if Heck had done it or maybe some drunked up cowboy who got a little rough.

Christy turned away from Jared and said, "I don't want to talk about it. Go on back to your cows and leave me be."

Jared tried to cheer Christy up but his efforts went nowhere. He finally gave up, telling her he'd see her next Saturday night when he came in to town. He tried to give her a kiss but she pushed him away, which hurt his feelings. He told her he was sorry although he wasn't sure what for and walked downstairs to head over to the cafe. Heck was already behind the bar and nodded to Jared. "Morning, cowboy, is Miss Christy taking good care of you?" he asked with a laugh.

Jared bristled at the notion that she was

"taking care of him," like he was just one of her customers. Stiffly, he replied, "Christy's and my business ain't none of yours. If I want you to know what we're up to, I'll tell you. If I don't tell you, that means you don't need to know."

Heck's jaw tightened and his eyes squinted. For a split second, Jared thought he was going to come at him. Then, gaining control, he gave Jared a smile. "You're right, cowboy, it's not my business. I can see you have feelings for her and I'm sure she does for you. What you've got together is different from what she does the rest of the week."

As Heck spoke, he appeared to have a twinkle in his eye. Jared couldn't tell if he was having fun at his expense or if he was serious. He waited to see if Heck had anything more to say. When he didn't, he said, "That's right. Sorry I'm a little touchy, I've got one heckuva headache," he said ruefully. "I'm in serious need of coffee and some food. I'll see you later, Heck, I'm goin' to the café."

Heck grinned at him and said, "I understand, Jared, you go on and take care of yourself. We don't want any of Mr. O'Bannon's cowboys dying from a hangover, now do we?" If Jared had had eyes in the back of his head as he walked out the swinging doors, he would have been chilled by the look the bartender gave him.

After Jared left, Heck went upstairs and opened the door to Christy's room without knocking. She was still on the bed and when she heard the door open, she rolled over to see Heck striding over to her with his hand raised. She cowered on the bed, covering her head and neck but he stopped without hitting her.

"It would be a real shame," he said in a low and menacing voice, "if a working girl forgot what she was getting paid extra to do and got off the trail with a certain cowboy. In fact, it could get very painful for the girl. Get my drift?"

Christy nodded without speaking. After looking at her long and hard, Heck turned and stalked out of the room. As he closed the door, one tear rolled down Christy's cheek. She didn't even bother to brush it away.

CHAPTER 19

Jared ate a big breakfast but it didn't make him feel much better. He tried to be friendly to Miguel Mares but the owner would have none of it, answering him curtly and walking back into the kitchen from which he never reappeared. This stung but Jared knew how close Miguel was to Eleanor. He felt a pang of loneliness when he thought about her. Although he'd seen her from a distance around town, she'd made no effort to talk to him and his pride wouldn't let him approach her. From time to time, he considered that perhaps pride was overrated.

Riding out to the O'Bannon place, he thought about what had happened and found himself getting confused all over again. He felt justified in his anger towards Ned Kilpatrick and hurt that Eleanor hadn't immediately agreed with him in the matter. Couldn't she just see the truth and do what was right? He considered this thought and had to laugh at himself. There were many in Cimarron who'd asked him the same question. His answer had always been that he needed to understand the lay of the land before he made a decision. Thinking that Eleanor should be held to a tougher standard than he held himself to seemed ridiculous.

Clearly, he'd been too hasty in how he reacted towards her. He wished he could talk this over with her but realized he had no idea how to initiate such a conversation. He feared too much water had passed under that bridge and she had moved on, forgetting about him completely. His initial reaction to this thought was his old familiar feeling of bitterness that she would treat him in such a fashion but he stopped himself. He realized he had not behaved in an honorable manner towards her. If he was going to assign blame, he needed to take a share for himself.

Missing Eleanor was almost a physical pain in the pit of his stomach. He'd never had a steady gal . . . being a cowboy had precluded that sort of activity. Thinking about their time together, he realized how quickly he'd grown comfortable with the experience. He recalled tender moments they'd shared, savoring the warmth he remembered in her eyes. He also remembered times she'd gotten 'prickly,' challenging him about different notions. At first, this had made him uncomfortable, but soon, he came to enjoy the challenge. It forced him to think about what he believed and why. It was different having women for friends. If another cowboy challenged him the way Eleanor had, he might've wound up in a fistfight and yet with her, it often resulted in his seeing something from a new and unfamiliar point of view. It dawned on him he felt that way about Lizbeth as well, though he had no romantic feelings for her. She comforted him and made him feel better in a way none of his cowboy pards could ever do. He thought Ned Kilpatrick was one lucky fella, even with all his troubles at the ranch.

As he rode on, a thought crossed his mind . . . there were no women on the O'Bannon ranch. He never heard the O'Bannon sons speak of their mother, although they frequently talked about their father. The only female companionship they seemed to seek was that of the working girls at the Colfax Tavern and that was only to satisfy their lust. He compared this to the men in Cimarron whom he respected . . .

Nathan, Ned, Juan Suazo, Miguel Mares, even Reverend Richardson and Father Antonio. Those men treated women with respect, while the O'Bannons treated them as something less than human, only necessary to meet their physical needs and then to be cast aside. He tried to reach across the foggy recesses of his mind to where his mother and father hid and determine the nature of their relationship. Was it one of convenience like the O'Bannons or did his parents have the kind of friendship that Ned and Lizbeth had and that he and Eleanor had been cultivating before he so thoughtlessly threw it away?

Preoccupied with these thoughts, Jared was surprised when he looked up as he approached the ranch and saw Bob, Pete and Jake with a few other cowboys branding some cattle in one of the pens. He couldn't imagine why they'd be doing something like that, particularly on a Sunday morning, the only day the hands took the whole day off. He rode up to the pen. "Mighty strange for you boys to be workin' on a Sunday mornin', ain't it, Bob? Where'd these cows come from, anyway?"

Bob edged away from the others and guided Jared toward the bunkhouse. "Oh, them are just some strays Jake and Pete rounded up and brought in. We thought since they's just runnin' around loose, we might as well take'em in and find'em a good home." He laughed as he spoke but he seemed mighty nervous.

Jared looked sideways at Bob. "I'll say again, Bob, it's strange what's goin' on. Generally, we check the brand on strays and return'em to their rightful owners, don't we . . . or have I missed somethin'?"

Again, Bob seemed skittish as he tried to brush off Jared's comments. "Course we checked for a brand, Jared, you don't think we're cattle rustlers, now do you?" He laughed nervously again. "Come on, I got a job I need you to do. These boys can handle things here."

Jared allowed himself to be led away but he continued to have the feeling something was a bit off. His initial impression of Bob Evans as a good hand and potential compadre had been replaced by that of a man who was bitter, sneaky and not to be trusted. Cautiously, he said, "What'd you have in mind for me to do, Bob?"

Bob took off his hat and wiped his brow. "When Pete and Jake was comin' in this mornin', they saw fresh tracks. If you head on out to the high section out west there, you might have some luck findin' the big cat that's been givin' us so much trouble. You're a better shot than me, that's why I waited for you. I'd be obliged if you'd head on out that way and see if you can put an end to that rascal and his thievin' ways."

Jared nodded and said, "I came back a little early from town with that thought in mind. I'd be willin' to go take a look." Looking back over his shoulder at the pen, he said pointedly, "I'd agree with you, it's bothersome when somethin' . . . or someone . . . with thievin' ways gets after your cattle. I'll do my best to put an end to it."

Jared turned and rode out to the west to look for the mountain lion. Bob watched him intently until he disappeared over the rise, then rode back to the pen where he had a brief conversation with Jake and Pete O'Bannon. He told the cowboys to finish the job they were doing and he, Jake and Pete rode off in the direction of town.

As Jared rode out, he continued to feel that something was amiss at the O'Bannon ranch. He thought back over his time there, remembering other incidents that had seemed a bit off to him. There were occasions when the count seemed off. He'd noticed some strange looking O'Bannon brands, like the cowboy wielding the iron had been drunk. He thought about the veiled warnings Christy had given him during their pillow talk and the stories Ned had told him. The more he pondered these discrepancies, the more bothered he got but then he thought about the task at hand. This mountain lion would require his full attention and he realized he'd better pay attention. He told himself he'd ask some pointed questions once he was through with the hunt. "Maybe I'll just have a talk with Mr. Morgan O'Bannon himself," Jared thought.

He followed the cat's signs up the draw. Dismounting and tying his horse to a tree, he pulled his Henry rifle out of the scabbard. He hated not being horseback, but he was more afraid that if the cat came upon him suddenly, it would spook his horse. He'd be in a world of trouble if that happened.

Silently, he made his way down the draw, following the tracks, and was soon rewarded for his efforts. Luckily, there'd been rain a few days before and the ground revealed the information that the lion had passed that way recently. Like a ghost, he came around a short bend, looked up to his right and saw the cat crouched on a big rock not twenty feet away, looking in the opposite direction. He raised his rifle and as he did, the cat heard him. In a motion so fast it seemed a blur, it turned, gathered itself to attack and gave a nerve-shattering scream. Jared sighted and fired just as the lion uncoiled to spring at him. In that split second, he looked into the cat's eyes. The chilling thought flashed through his mind that the cat's eyes looked just like those of the man in his dream. His shot caught the lion in mid-leap. He crumpled in a heap not five feet from Jared, who levered another bullet into the chamber and stayed poised to shoot again if necessary.

He felt a trickle of sweat glide down the side of his face as he watched the animal for the slightest twitch. After what he figured was a safe passage of time, Jared concluded the cat was done for. He'd been holding his breath and now he let out a tremendous sigh, getting out his knife to skin the animal. A sense of pride washed over him as he realized he'd held his nerve in a life-threatening situation. With a mixture of bitterness and regret, he wished Ned Kilpatrick could see him in this moment in time. That thought passed quickly, however, as he went about disposing of the carcass.

CHAPTER 20

In the back room of the Colfax Tavern, Morgan O'Bannon held a war council with Heck Roberts, Bob Evans, Pete and Jake. Bob said, "Mr. O'Bannon, Delaney's been askin' questions. I think he's startin' to suspect we got more goin' on than just runnin' a ranch. You'd told me to keep an eye on him so I thought I'd better let you know. He came back early today and found us changin' brands on the cattle Pete and Jake brought in last night. I gave him the runaround so I don't think he knows anything for certain but he's sure nosin' around more than he oughta be."

"Thanks for the information, Bob," O'Bannon said curtly, "I appreciate it. You go on upstairs now, find yourself some female companionship. Tell'em I said to be real nice to you." Evans was nonplussed at being dismissed so brusquely but the idea of spending some free time with a working girl appealed to him. He took his leave quickly.

After Evans closed the door, Morgan turned to the others. "I want a full report. That young cowboy is catching on faster than we anticipated. We may need to move ahead quicker than we'd planned."

Heck nervously cleared his throat. "I'm afraid you're right, Morgan, we may need to act fast. I'm not sure we can count on Christy to keep pumping him for information. Not only is he getting a bit suspicious, I think she may be falling for him, too. I'm worried she may get cold feet and tell him what's going on. I'd have never thought she'd act this way but women are hard to figure."

Morgan shook his head and flashed his trademark cruel smile. "Who would have predicted our soiled dove would care at all for a cowboy, much less develop a conscience. I'm disappointed in the little lady but I believe you can handle her, Heck."

He turned to Pete and Jake. "After last night, we need to hold off on any more raids until we get this game set up. If we play this right, we can take Nathan Averill down, get rid of this pesky cowboy and take control of all the land around these parts that's worth having."

Jake shook his head in exasperation and said, "Morgan, wouldn't it be easier if you just let me go on down to the sheriff's office right now and call that old coot out in the street? Nothin' I'd like better than to shoot him down like a dog while all these lilly-livered town folk watch their hero die."

Morgan held Jake with a cold stare until he started to fidget. "Oh, he'll die all right, and the town folk will get the message but it won't happen your way. I want it to have the appearance of being cold-blooded murder but you're not who I had in mind as the culprit." Again, the cruel smile. "And anyway, Jake, you may not realize it but you're not good enough to take that old coot." Before Jake could respond, Morgan declared the meeting over.

CHAPTER 21

Ned finished off the last of his coffee and wearily pushed back from the kitchen table. "Lizbeth," he said with a frown, "I hate to ask you this after you worked so hard fixin' me such a fine breakfast but I need your help today. We're so short-handed with just me and Juan that we haven't had time to check the fence line in that section south of the ridge. I think O'Bannon's boys go out and cut down the fence ahead of time so when they make a night raid, they have their escape route already open."

"You figure they're gettin' ready to hit us again?" Lizbeth asked.

"I don't know," Ned said. "I may be worryin' for nothin' but I'd rather know for sure than stew about it all day until I find the time to ride over that way. I'm just tryin' to be ready in case there's trouble."

"I already told you I'd do anything you needed me to do, Ned," Lizbeth replied. "I know it's been tough on you and Juan since Jared left."

At the mention of Jared's name, Ned's face clouded and he shook his head. "The more I think about what happened, the more confused I get. I don't think I was wrong in criticizin' the boy although as you so helpfully pointed out," he said with a rueful grin, "I'd prob'ly have done a better job of it if I hadn't lost my temper."

Lizbeth raised an eyebrow at him. He continued, trying to explain his actions. "Things happened so fast, like a wildfire spreadin'. I was scared to death somethin' was gonna happen to you. I wish we'd both cooled down but Jared took off for town and next thing I know, he's workin' for O'Bannon. Somehow, it didn't seem like there was any turnin' back after that."

"I'm a bit puzzled myself," Lizbeth said, "about Jared goin' to work so fast for that scoundrel. I heard they offered him almost twice what he was gettin' here. He's good but no cowboy's that good. It think Morgan's playin' some sort of game and plans to use Jared as a pawn."

Ned nodded and said, "You know, I hadn't really thought about that. You're right about Morgan and his games. Jake and Pete are just plain mean but Morgan always has a plan that involves him makin' more money and grabbin' more land. I can't figure how he'd be usin' Jared."

Lizbeth took him by the hand. "Come sit back down for a minute. I've got an idea. I want to see what you think about it."

Ned grabbed another cup of coffee and allowed himself to be led back to the table in the kitchen. He took a seat. "All right, I'm listenin'."

"We all know Morgan and his outfit've been rustlin' cattle for years even if no one has caught'em red-handed and lived to tell about it, right?"

Ned nodded ruefully and said, "We do know that, don't we."

"Who stands in the way of the O'Bannons runnin' roughshod over all of Colfax County?" Lizbeth asked.

Ned thought for a second. "Well, it's clear enough Nathan is the one, that's for sure. He's the only one Morgan has any fear of, if you could call it that, or maybe grudgin' respect. He's about all that stands in the way of'em grabbin' every bit of land in the county. Some of us ranchers might be willin' to try to make a stand but without Nathan, most wouldn't have the nerve or see the point. They'd likely just clear out and go somewhere else where they might start over or at least hope to live a while longer."

"That's right, and if they do, their land goes up for public auction. Who's gonna bid against Morgan O'Bannon? Nathan is the key to the whole scheme," Lizbeth said. "If he's out of the way, there's nobody could stop Morgan and his crew from takin' over."

Ned looked puzzled and asked, "But how does Jared fit in?"

Lizbeth looked thoughtful. "This is where it gets a little tricky in my mind but I have a notion about it. It was clear from the time Jared came to town that Nathan thought highly of him . . . he asked him to be his deputy right on the spot, if you recall. I've talked with him some when I've been to town for supplies and I know he still has hopes the boy will straighten out. I have a feelin' Morgan intends to use that connection in some way to bring Nathan down. I don't think Jared, even as confused as he is, would join in somethin' like that willingly but he might get caught up in some trickery that Morgan plots."

Ned nodded thoughtfully. "Morgan's connected with Catron and those Santa Fe Ring boys but if he or his brothers shot down the sheriff in cold blood, there'd be an investigation. Nathan's got a few friends in Santa Fe, too. If anything happened to him, some of them would look at it pretty close. Morgan just might be plannin' to play Jared against Nathan in some underhanded scheme." Ned got a look of consternation as he pondered what his wife had suggested. "What do we do about all this?"

Lizbeth shook her head. "I ain't sure yet. I'm tempted to say somethin' to Nathan about it, just so's he could give it some thought, too. We might be missin' some details or not comin' at it from the right direction. Next time I'm in town, I might pay Nathan a visit. See what he thinks."

Ned rose from the table and said, "I think that's best. Right now, I gotta get horseback and get some work done. I'm guessin' Juan is already out waitin' for me. Don't forget about checkin' that fence. The more we talk about Morgan and his shenanigans, the more nervous I get." He paused, looking at his wife with concern. "You be careful out there, Lizbeth. If the fence is down, don't hang around there, just come get me and let me know the score. We'll be in the north section up on the plateau most of the day."

After Ned walked out, Lizbeth continued to think about Nathan and Jared. She thought Nathan might buy her idea about the game Morgan was playing but she wasn't sure what their next move should be. Jared had cut himself off completely from all of them and she didn't know how he would take it if he were approached about this. She didn't even know who would be best to approach him. She figured he would bristle if Ned came around and her fear was that Ned would again lose his temper. She didn't think Eleanor's pride would let her seek out Jared and she couldn't really blame her. She'd heard the rumors of Jared's carryin' on with that hussy, Christy, and she knew it hurt Eleanor more than she would let on. That left Nathan and her as the only likely choices to seek Jared out. She knew Jared was fond of her and had looked up to her as some mixture of mother and sister. She might be the one to have the discussion with him.

She cleaned up the breakfast dishes and continued to think about the best way to proceed. When she was done straightening up, she saddled her mare and rode out to the south section to check the fence. She was relieved to find it intact. She spurred her horse in the direction of where Ned and Juan were to let them know that, at least for now, things seemed to be all right. As she rode, she had the unpleasant feeling they wouldn't remain that way for long.

■ ■ ■ ■

Upstairs at the Colfax Tavern, Heck Roberts entered Christy's room without knocking. She looked up as she was pulling on her stockings and said sassily, "Well, just come right on in, no need to knock."

Heck shook his head dismissively. "We don't have time for that Christy, we've got to get going on this plan. You've got a part to play."

"Why, whatever are you talkin' about?" Christy said in a faux-Southern accent, "I'm sure I don't know what plan you mean."

Heck casually walked over to the bed and backhanded her hard across the face. She tried to hit him back but he caught her wrist and held it easily, bending it down until she cried out for him to stop. He smiled at her. "Are you done? Like I said, we don't have time for fooling around, we've got to get moving with Mr. O'Bannon's plan. It's happening tonight. If you know what's good for you, you'll do your part like I tell you."

Christy gave him a sullen look but nodded silently. As Heck began to explain to her what he expected of her that night, she got a worried look on her face but she knew better than to object or resist.

CHAPTER 22

Jared rode back to the O'Bannon ranch with the bloody hide of the mountain lion draped across the back of his horse who acted as spooky as Jared felt. As he spoke softly to the horse to calm him down, he thought of what he wanted to say to Morgan O'Bannon. He thought it best not to accuse him directly of any wrong-doing but he wanted him to know he wasn't dealing with a fool or a blind man. He decided if he didn't get a satisfactory explanation, he would draw his wages and move on. Maybe his time in Colfax County was winding down. He wondered if it hadn't been a mistake to come here in the first place.

You sure made a mess of things, he thought to himself, reflecting on the rifts he'd caused with Eleanor and the Kilpatricks. *There was good folks who cared about you and you run'em off.* He realized that by trying to stay out of the conflict and not take a stand, he'd wound up alone. It stuck in his craw but he resolved that before he took his leave, he'd sure enough stand up to O'Bannon if for no other reason than to salve his own conscience for the mistakes he'd made. *They can say what they will when I'm gone,* he thought, *but at least I'll know I tried to do the right thing by everyone.*

When Jared rode up to the ranch, he noticed Morgan's big bay stallion tied up at the hitching post by the main house. He had a knot in his stomach at the thought of confronting the powerful rancher but he figured the only way to untie the knot was to get it done. He walked up on the long porch and knocked on the door.

"Come in," Morgan called from inside. As Jared walked through the door, he heard the unmistakable sound of a shell being jacked into the chamber of a shotgun and reflexively went for his gun. "Whoa, cowboy!" Morgan called out from the other side of the great room, "No need for gunplay."

It was darker than it had been outside. It took Jared's eyes a moment to adjust to the difference. When he could see clearly, he saw Morgan on the other side of the room with a shotgun pointed at the floor.

"What's goin' on here, Mr. O'Bannon?"

he demanded in a voice that sounded more spooked than he would have liked.

"I'm glad you're here, Jared, we've got trouble on our hands," Morgan said. "I got word rustlers are going to try to make off with some of our cattle from out on the north section. I need you to head out there to keep an eye on the herd. I'll send some other hands out that way as soon as they get in but I need you there now."

Jared was nonplussed and his confusion showed in his voice. "What are you talking about Mr. O'Bannon? You're tellin' me rustlers are comin' after *your* herd?"

Morgan gave a sardonic laugh and said, "Yes, I know the rumors all over Colfax County. They say I'm the rustler but I assure you, that's not the case. They don't hit us as often as they do the smaller ranches because we've got more hands to watch over things but I guess they're getting pretty brazen." Morgan's voice became more urgent. "There's no time to debate with you about this. If you're still working for me, get out there with the herd now. What's your answer?"

Still puzzled, Jared said uncertainly, "Well, there was somethin' I wanted to discuss with you but I reckon it can wait. I sure do need to talk with you soon, though."

"Fine," said O'Bannon, "we'll talk all you want once we get this threat taken care of. Now get on your horse and ride." Morgan laid the shotgun across his left shoulder and strode out of the room, leaving Jared standing there alone.

Jared's head was spinning. Not knowing how else to respond, he turned and went back out to where he'd left his horse. He still had his Henry and adequate ammo so he decided he would follow directions and head out for the north section where O'Bannon had said the rustlers might strike. He left the big cat's hide out in the barn, mounted up and rode off.

Darkness fell and things got busy at the Colfax Tavern. Christy stood at the end of the bar nervously eyeing Heck Roberts. She rebuffed the advances of several cowboys with sharp-tongued comments about their personal hygiene and they went back to tell their friends that she was in a rattlesnake mood tonight. After that, they left her alone with her drink and her thoughts. Heck let her have one glass of whiskey. When she asked for a refill, he refused, saying she would need her wits about her before the night was over. He fixed her with a stare and leaned over to whisper, "You're not getting cold feet on me, are you Christy?"

She returned his stare for a second then sighed. "There's no point goin' against you or Morgan. I don't like it one bit but a girl's got to go along to get along. You'll have your way, don't worry."

Heck laughed and said, "I knew you'd come around. I told Morgan we didn't have to worry about you. I'm glad you're proving me right. If I was wrong, things'd get pretty messy for me but I promise, I'd make sure they got even messier for you."

Christy stared back at him for a moment then looked away. Heck laughed again then moved on down the bar to tend to some new customers. Christy looked up at the clock over the bar and saw that the time was 7:45. She tried not to watch the seconds tick away.

CHAPTER 23

Nathan Averill was putting the final touches on a letter he was writing to the magistrate in Santa Fe when the door flung open and Christy Quick from the Colfax Tavern rushed into his office. Startled, he regained his composure and said, "May I help you, Miss Quick?"

"You got to go right away, sheriff, that young cowboy, Delaney, is rustlin' cattle from the O'Bannon ranch. Heck just got word and sent me to tell you. Looks like he's been behind it all along."

"Whoa, there, slow down, miss," Nathan said, "That boy's confused but he ain't a cattle thief. I think someone's got their facts mixed up."

"I'm just tellin' you what Heck told me," Christy said, "One of the hands came barrelin' into the tavern, said he'd seen someone suspicious headin' toward the north pasture. They talked it over and figured it was Delaney. Heck said you prob'ly wouldn't believe it but I'm supposed to tell you to do your duty. That's what I'm doin'. I got nothin' more to say."

The story didn't set well with Nathan. Seeing how agitated the woman appeared, he said, "Maybe we should talk a little more about this, Miss Quick. I don't think you're tellin' me everything there is to know about this deal."

Christy shook her head nervously. "Sheriff, I'm just tellin' you what I was told, that's all. I need to get back to the tavern before I get myself in trouble."

Nathan looked closely at Christy and noticed a bruise below her right eye. "Please sit down, Miss Quick, I'll do my duty that Heck's so concerned about in a minute. Right now, I'm concerned about who's been slappin' you around."

Christy looked away and said, "It's nothin', I just ran into a door."

"A door that tends bar at the Colfax Tavern, I'd wager," Nathan said gently. "Come on now, sit down so we can talk. There's more goin' on than you're lettin' on. I don't want anybody getting hurt that doesn't need to, includin' you? I can't help you if you don't tell me the truth."

Something about the sheriff's tone of

voice seemed to reach Christy. She came over to the chair by his desk where she sat down resignedly. "Sheriff," she said, "I thought I could do this but I can't." She looked down and tears fell down on the front of her dress as she cried quietly.

Nathan let her cry for a moment, then reached out and gently patted her on the shoulder. "Miss Quick, I know a lot more than you think I do. We both know Heck Roberts is a bully and Morgan O'Bannon is a very bad man. They've been hurtin' folks around these parts way too long. It's time someone took a stand. I'll do everything in my power to help keep you safe if you'll be honest with me."

Christy looked up at the sheriff. He saw tears in her eyes but also a hint of a spark. "Sheriff, you can't keep me safe but I'm past carin' . . . and now I'm mad. Maybe you really can stop those varmits so I'll tell you the truth. Once I do, my life here is over and there's nothin' you can do about that. I'm tired of gettin' pushed around and I'm ready to make them that's done it pay." She paused for a moment, then said, "You're right, too, folks don't deserve to be hurt no more. I thought I didn't care but I guess I was wrong."

Nathan nodded reassuringly and said,

"You'd better tell your story before you think too much. I got a feelin' things are about to come to a boil around here."

To his surprise, Christy laughed out loud. "The pot's boilin' over for sure, Sheriff. Some folks are gonna get burned. You're right, Morgan is behind the cattle rustlin', has been for years. Heck's in it up to his ears, too. They set up Jared to take you for a cattle rustler and they sent me to set you up by tellin' you Jared was the rustler. They figured you'd go shootin' at each other and both wind up dead. Jake and Pete'll be there to make sure just in case you don't finish the job. It's an ambush."

Nathan leaned forward with a sense of urgency. "If you hadn't come clean, Miss Quick, innocent folks could've gotten hurt. They still might but at least I'm headin' into this with my eyes open. I can handle Jake and Pete but I got to figure out how to do it without spookin' Jared." Nathan sat back in his chair for a moment. "Thanks for what you've done. It can't be easy."

Christy gave a bitter smile and said, "Easy ain't somethin' I'm used to, Sheriff. I'll pretend I did what I was told, then find a way out of town fast as I can. Heck's made it plain he'll take me down if he goes so my life here is done."

261

"Are you sure you have to leave, Miss Quick?" Nathan said. "If I play this right, I'm gonna bring those rascals down like a house of cards. You might be able to stick around."

Christy shook her head. "Sheriff, you might just pull it off but I can't take that chance. Heck won't just black my eye, he'll kill me and before killin' me, he'll make me suffer. He acts all nice when he's tendin' bar but he's mean as the devil. He especially likes to hurt women."

"If you're dead set on this, Miss Quick, you're gonna need some help." Nathan got up and went to a cabinet behind his desk. He opened a door and then a small drawer inside the cabinet. "I've been savin' this for a rainy day. Looks like you need it more than I do."

Nathan held out a small leather pouch. Christy hesitated, then took it. She opened the pouch and saw quite a few gold coins inside. "Sheriff, I know I take money for favors but this is a lot of money. I don't see as how I can take your life savin's from you."

"Miss Quick, I'm a small-town sheriff, got no wife or kids. I don't even have a notion as to what I was savin' that money for anyhow. What you've done may save lives and start some powerful changes for the better around here. I'd say you've earned that money along with my gratitude and respect," Nathan replied.

Christy looked down as teardrops once again fell on the front of her dress. "I don't know that anything'll change around here. It'll likely turn out bad for me no matter what else happens." She raised her head up and looked the sheriff in the eye. "I'll take your money and your gratitude and especially your respect. It ain't somethin' I've had much of but I sorta like the feel of it." It dawned on her that the longer she stayed, the more suspicious Heck would be. "I better get back. Please be careful."

She walked out the way she came in, in a rush. Nathan sat for a moment thinking about what had transpired, then got up and went to his gun cabinet where he got out a carbine and a shotgun. He figured he'd put the shotgun in the scabbard on his saddle and carry the carbine.

Jared reached the herd as dusk began closing in. He saw no signs of anyone in the vicinity but the cattle seemed spooked. As the thought crossed his mind, he chuckled nervously, thinking perhaps it wasn't the cattle that were spooked but rather himself. He didn't know what to expect so he decided to ride around the area looking and listening for telltale signs of trouble.

He tried to ignore the nagging confusion he felt from his brief conversation with Morgan and focus on the job at hand but his mind kept coming back to it. He'd anticipated a discussion in which he would hold the upper hand, setting Morgan back on his heels with questions regarding the suspicious series of events taking place on the ranch. Instead, he found himself caught off guard by Morgan's allegations that others were the cattle rustlers. Reflecting on the conversation, he thought again that things didn't add up. He wondered what game O'Bannon was playing with this misdirection and decided he needed more pieces to the puzzle in order to figure it out. Of one thing, he was certain . . . Morgan was using him as a pawn. If he wasn't careful, he'd wind up as dead as the mountain lion he'd shot earlier in the day. In his mind, he saw the cold, cruel eyes of the big cat as it sprung at him and he couldn't help thinking that Morgan's eyes looked the same. With that unsettling thought, Jared turned his full attention to scouting the area for signs of trouble. It was dark by then with only a little light available from the quarter moon. Jared felt a little shiver rise up his spine. It occurred to him that the ridge overlooking the pasture left him a sitting duck if someone had an ambush planned.

Jake and Pete saw Jared ride up at dusk but waited until he rode around to the other side of the herd before they communicated through whispers. "We got one in the pen," Jake said quietly. "Now we just gotta wait for the other one to get here."

Pete whispered, "It'll be tricky to hit'em without much light but I figure they'll start blazin' away at each other once we start shootin'. With luck, they'll at least wound one another and we can finish'em off. I'm most worried about that old varmit. He's old but he's tough. Pretty fair shot, too, if rumors hold any truth."

Jake snorted and said, "You and Morgan sound like a couple of old women the way you talk about Averill. Maybe he was somethin' back in his day but he's gettin' pretty long in the tooth. I hope he's still movin' around when we go down to finish'em off. I wanta see the look on his face when I put a bullet in his heart."

Jake was about to say more when Pete put his finger to his lips and pointed toward the cattle. Jake looked down and saw Jared moving closer to where they were hidden as he made his rounds. They waited quietly as he moved past them and headed toward the far side of the herd. Once he was out of earshot, Pete said, "I know you think you're tougher'n any wildcat in these parts but you got to learn to be smart, too. Nathan Averill's forgotten more tricks than you and I know together. If we ain't careful, it'll be him puttin' a bullet in our hearts."

Jake scoffed at Pete's words and turned his horse away. Pete reached out and pulled the reins back so that Jake was facing him. "Pay attention! Heck was to send Christy for the sheriff about two hours after sundown. That's about the time now if I read the moon right. It'll take an hour to ride out here, maybe more if he's bein' cautious. He'll come in from the south. We gotta get Delaney to come down just below us so when we start shootin', the sheriff'll think it's Delaney. Our timin's got to be right."

"How we gonna do that," Jake said in a sarcastic tone, "ring the dinner bell?"

Pete reached over and thumped his brother on the forehead. "Ow," Jake grunted, "what's that for?"

Pete whispered hoarsely, "Eejit, you're lucky we gotta be quiet or I'd give you worse than that. I got a plan. When the time's right, I'll ride down the ridge here and call him over, tell him Morgan sent me to help out. I'll get him talkin' about what's been happenin' while he was guardin' the herd. When I see the sheriff ride into the valley, I'll give a whoop and you start shootin'. I'll get the drop on Delaney while he's tryin' to figure out what's goin' on. With a little luck, you might hit Nathan. We can get'em both before they have time to slap leather."

"I like it," Jake said. "Once you take Delaney down, you start shootin' at that old sheriff. If you and Morgan are right about him, he won't just waltz in here with a bullseye on his chest."

Pete started to say something more but he heard the sound of Jared's horse approaching. He leaned over and whispered, "From now on, no more talkin', we just need to be on guard. I'll give you the sign when I'm ready to go down the ridge."

Jared walked his horse down into the valley so he wouldn't be highlighted against the horizon in case things shaped up into the trap he was sensing. He thought he heard a noise over the rise of the hill but when he stopped, it was quiet. He listened over the pounding of his heart. After a minute, he decided it was nothing. He gently reined his horse to the right and went on down to the bottom of the draw to wait and watch. Darkness crept in, dimly illuminated by the moon. Jared looked up and laughed softly when he realized it was what they call a rustler's moon.

"Well, that's fittin'," he thought as he scanned the horizon for signs of trouble. He watched, his senses alert but in one part of his mind, he continued to reflect on his conversation with O'Bannon. The more he thought about it, the more he was convinced it didn't add up. He'd never heard about the O'Bannons getting hit by rustlers before. If Morgan's explanation that it was because they had so many hands was correct, it made no sense that he'd be sent out alone to deal with the rustlers.

He figured Bob Evans had ridden off pronto to report Jared's suspicions about the Sunday morning branding to Morgan. The timing of this supposed outlaw raid began to look shadier and shadier to him. He remembered Ned telling him of Morgan's devious scheme of using his position as quartermaster to steal from the Union army, his escape from Andersonville Prison and his leading a band of outlaws throughout North Texas after the war. It was clear to Jared there in the dim moonlight that any man who could pull off all of those feats was capable of setting a trap for a young cowhand.

Recalling what he knew about Morgan's experience in the war, it struck him that the timing of Morgan's marauding through North Texas and the murder of his parents was not just a coincidence. What had previously been a suspicion in the back of his mind suddenly became truth. A chill swept through him. He thought about a memory of a voice both soft and hard, and the coldest blue eyes he'd ever seen. Inside his head, it felt like a fog was lifting. All of a sudden, he was shaken from his reverie by hoof beats galloping in his direction. A voice hollered, "Jared, pardner, it's me, Pete. Don't shoot!"

The rider approached at a gallop and Jared assumed it was Pete O'Bannon. As he drew closer, he hollered out again, "A no-good rustler's comin' over the rise, let's go teach him a lesson!"

As Pete pulled his horse up, Jared heard a commotion over the rise that included pounding hoof beats and then several gunshots in rapid succession. Pete leaned across his saddle. "Don't freeze up on me, Delaney, we're wastin' time!"

As Jared spurred his horse, it crossed his mind that Pete seemed intent on allowing him to lead the way. He found this suspicious since it was Pete's family's ranch and cattle they were defending. As he galloped toward the gunshots, he leaned down low in the saddle and this move saved his life. In a heartbeat after he leaned down to the right of his horse's head, another shot rang out, this time from behind him. Instinctively, he reached for his pistol, swung his horse around in a sharp circle and pulled off a shot at Pete. With equal parts luck and skill, the bullet found its mark. Pete tumbled from his saddle. Jared galloped over the rise to see what was happening on the other side and when he topped the ridge, he saw two riderless horses. He quickly dismounted and keeping to the cover of the underbrush, made his way carefully to where the horses were milling around. He could see by the pale light of the moon that there were two bodies on the ground about fifteen feet apart. One lay still while the other was trying to rise with great difficulty. In the dim light, he could see it was Nathan Averill. "Nathan, it's me, Jared," he called out from behind a bush, "don't shoot!"

Nathan continued trying to get up but seemed to lose his strength and sink back to the ground. Jared approached cautiously. "Did they wing you?"

Nathan lay quietly until Jared was within a few feet of him, then said in a labored voice, "Jake shot me but it's the last thing he'll ever do. So . . . did you come to help me or finish the job?"

Jared took a step back and didn't speak for a moment. "I guess I had that comin'," he said. "I'm here to help you. Pete tried to bushwhack me and I knocked him down. I don't know if he's done for or not. I'd better get back over the hill to check or we may get ambushed again. I'll scoot on up to see, then come back for you."

Nathan nodded and said with some effort, "You do that. I'll try to collect myself. I'm hit in the left shoulder but I doubt it's gonna kill me."

Jared turned and walked quickly to the top of the ridge where he ducked down behind some bushes. He carefully made his way back to where he thought Pete would be laying up. He spotted his horse and crept over to him but saw no sign of Pete. He figured if Pete was alive and trying to get away, he was as dangerous as a wounded grizzly in the brush. He was pretty certain his bullet had struck Pete but he didn't know how badly he was hurt. He figured it would be difficult for Pete to move quietly if he was hit and decided his smartest move

271

would be none at all. He hunkered down in the brush, listening intently and scanning the ground for a shape that didn't fit the terrain. His efforts were rewarded in a moment when he heard the sounds of grunting and brush crunching. Very quietly, he circled to get ahead of the noise and as he crept back to that spot, he saw a shadowy shape. It was Pete with his pistol cocked looking back to where Jared had been previously. Quiet as a mountain lion, he snuck up on Pete and put the barrel of his pistol at the back of his head. "Lay it down slow and lift your hand away from it. You get in a hurry, it'll be the last thing you ever do."

For a moment, Pete hesitated. Jared exerted more pressure on the back of his head with his gun barrel. Pete did as he was told. Jared reached over and snatched the pistol up, then took a step back. Pete rolled over with a groan and said, "You're mighty lucky, Delaney. If your wild shot hadn't nicked me in the leg, I'd have had you." He coughed and moaned with pain. "You're a dead man anyway. Morgan'll be comin' with a vengeance any moment now and you'll be done for along with your old pardner, Averill."

Jared gave a snort of derision. "You're confused, Pete. Nathan's just over the rise there, alive. He's got a bullet wound but he's a tough old buzzard. I believe he'll be all right. The one who's done for is your no account younger brother. He's lyin' over there with a bullet through his heart."

Pete's face registered disbelief, then shock, followed by acceptance. "Morgan and I both told Jake he couldn't take Nathan unless he was real careful and quick but he didn't want to listen. That don't change nothin', though, you're still in a heap of trouble."

"I believe you've got it backwards, Pete, it's you who's in big trouble. I'm loadin' you up and takin' you into town where you can get started spendin' time behind bars. It's a view you should get used to . . . you'll be lookin' at'em for quite a spell."

He hauled Pete to his feet amidst much groaning and complaining. Jared could see his bullet had pierced the thick muscle of Pete's upper leg. It'd be painful but wouldn't prevent him from being transported back to town. He walked to his horse with Pete limping ahead of him. When he got there, he took his lariat and knotted it around Pete. He tugged Pete along with him to where Nathan lay and said, "Look what I brought for you, Nathan, someone to keep you company at that lonely old jail of yours."

Nathan chuckled, then groaned from the effort. In a moment, he said, "Maybe you'll reconsider the offer I made when you first came to Cimarron. I think I can make it on to my horse and back to town but someone's gonna have to deal with this mess. If it ain't you, I don't know who it's gonna be. I'm in need of a deputy in a real bad way right now."

Jared was quiet for a moment. "I probably should've accepted the offer when you first made it but I guess I wasn't convinced. I had to take a look at both sides." He took a deep breath, then grinned at the sheriff. "I'm convinced now. I reckon the answer is yes. Let's get you into the saddle, then Pete can decide if he wants to mount up or get drug through the brush back to Cimarron."

CHAPTER 24

The ride back to Cimarron was an ordeal.
Jared tied Pete's hands behind his back and
used his bandana to bandage his leg, then
helped him on his horse, all the while keeping his lariat knotted around his waist. He
tied the other end to a scrub oak while he
helped Nathan mount up. He hadn't realized how badly Nathan was wounded until
he gave him a boost into the saddle. At that
point, he saw he was still bleeding. The bullet had come in high and to the left so it
missed his heart and lungs but it'd passed
through his left shoulder, leaving him in
tremendous pain. The old lawman tried to
remain stoic but Jared could see how much
every movement cost him.

"I don't know if you can make it all the
way to town, Nathan, but I reckon we'd better get away from here pronto. Pete's right,
Morgan'll be ridin' in any time with some
hands to back him up. He wouldn't pass up

the chance to finish you off."

Nathan's face was a mask of pain. "Don't worry about me, I'll make it all right. This ain't the first time I've been shot. It hurts like the dickens but it'd be worse to stop and rest. I'm still losin' blood and that's what'll kill me, not the pain. The sooner we get back to town, the quicker doc can take a look at the mess Jake made of my shoulder."

Jared untied his lariat from the scrub oak, then walked over to where Pete was waiting. "We're gonna make this ride quick as we can with you ridin' in front of me. You try to make a break for it, I got you tied up snug. You'll pop off that horse like a cork out of a bottle. You understand me?"

Pete scowled at Jared. "You can't expect me to ride with a shot-up leg and my hands tied behind my back. What if I fall off?"

Jared looked at Pete with disgust. "You're lucky Nathan's wounded, too, or we'd be gallopin' back to Cimarron. You fall off, I'll drag you the rest of the way, so I suggest you hang on. Now, head on out. Set a good pace or I'll spank that horse of yours with my lariat to get him movin'."

Jared went back to his horse, mounted up and took his dallies, then urged his horse into a slow trot. Pete complained bitterly throughout the entire ride and several times Jared had to warn him to speed up. Nathan never said a word, although Jared heard him groan a time or two and he slumped forward to the point where Jared was afraid he might fall off. The trip took a couple of hours, nearly twice what it would normally take, and throughout, Jared listened anxiously for the sound of hoof beats signaling Morgan and his men overtaking them. After what seemed like a lifetime, they finally reined in at the hitching post in front of the sheriff's office on Main Street.

As Jared dismounted, Nathan called out weakly. "Get Pete in the lock-up right quick. The keys are in the top right hand corner of my desk. I got a hunch we'll be seein' Morgan real soon. I want his no-good brother locked up tighter than Dick's hat band when that happens. Once you get him in the cell, come help me down."

Jared pulled Pete none too gently off his horse. Pete glared at Jared and said, "Have your little fun right now, Delaney. You won't be laughin' when Morgan gets here."

Jared ignored Pete's words and tugged him into the sheriff's office. He located the keys and escorted him into a cell. He removed his lariat and untied Pete's hands, then walked out, locking the cell. He turned around to address Pete. "Your little brother is layin' up in the high country servin' himself up as dinner for the coyotes and you're locked up in a jail cell. This might not unfold the way you think. You may be dancin' to a different tune before you know it . . . maybe at the end of a rope." Jared turned on his heel and went out front to help Nathan off his horse and onto the cot in the front room.

Jared helped Nathan down off the wrong side of his horse so he could grab the saddle horn with his right hand as he dismounted. Even so, Nathan almost slipped as he swung his leg over and tried to step down.

"I ain't used to getting off that way," he said with a pained chuckle. "I just about fell on my face."

Jared tried to make light of the situation. "Don't worry, Nathan, I won't tell anyone about your clumsiness. I reckon they'd cut you a little slack anyway, your shoulder bein' busted up and all."

Jared put Nathan's right arm across his shoulder and half-walked, half-carried him into the office. As they got to the cot, Nathan said, "Here's what to do. I need the doc to get this bleedin' stopped but I need you here when Morgan arrives. Eleanor's place is close. Go tell her to get Doc Adams here quick as she can. Don't lollygag around, just tell her that and get back over here."

Jared looked like he would question Nathan, then shrugged. "You're right, that's the best plan. I'll get you situated and leave right away."

Nathan laid out on the cot with a groan. "I'm about as situated as I need to be, you get movin'!"

Jared walked out the door. When he got to the street, he broke into a trot toward the schoolhouse behind which Eleanor had her living quarters. His mind was a tangle of thoughts and emotions at the prospect of seeing Eleanor again but he realized there was no time to sort any of that out. Eleanor wouldn't be pleased to see him. He needed to immediately impress upon her that Nathan's life was at stake. He arrived at her door and began pounding on it.

Jared saw a light come on. A strong and familiar voice behind the door said, "Who is it? State your business!"

"It's Jared Delaney. We got big trouble. Nathan's been shot by Jake O'Bannon. He needs Doc Adams to come right away."

The door opened. Eleanor stood there with a lantern in one hand and a Colt pistol in the other. Her face was a mask of pain, confusion and concern. "Eleanor, we don't have time for all the questions you've got. Nathan's life is at stake! You need to get Doc. I need to get back to the jail right now. Morgan's on his way, hell-bent on bustin' his brother out. If I don't get back there, there'll be nobody to stop him."

Eleanor stared at him, confused and suspicious. He could almost see the wheels turn in her mind as she tried to make sense of his words. He could see in her eyes the moment she came to her decision. "Get back over there, I'll get Doc. And Jared," she said. "Be careful."

Their eyes met. Jared replied softly, "You be careful, too."

He turned and raced back to the sheriff's office. As he got closer, he slowed down and kept to the shadows, wary of an ambush. Within about fifty yards, he saw no people or horses and broke into a run again. He figured it wasn't likely Morgan would try to sneak up on them, knowing they were wounded and under-manned.

Jared closed the door behind him and looked over at the cot. Nathan's eyes were closed and Jared was afraid he'd passed out or worse. Before he'd taken two steps toward the cot, Nathan spoke. "Get the twelve gauge. Have your six-shooter ready when Morgan comes bargin' in. Stand behind my desk. If shootin' starts, use it for cover. Have that twelve gauge cocked and propped over your arm so all you have to do is raise and fire." Nathan's face was ghostly pale.

Jared quickly went to the gun case on the other side of the room where he found the shotgun and a box of shells. He loaded the shotgun and set his Colt revolver on the desk as Nathan had suggested. As an afterthought, he went back to the gun case where he found another Colt. He made sure it was loaded as he walked back over and put it on the desk with the other pistol.

"There may not be any gunplay or it may get done pretty quick," Jared said to Nathan, "but I'd feel more at ease with this extra pistol here, just in case."

Nathan didn't respond and Jared figured he was in too much pain and needed to conserve his strength. "Eleanor has gone for Doc Adams, they should be here soon. I pray they don't walk into the middle of a gun battle but I didn't know what else to do. If Doc don't take care of that bleedin', I'm gonna get promoted to sheriff before I'm even used to bein' a deputy."

Out of the corner of his eye, Jared saw the ghost of a smile flicker across Nathan's lips.

Neither of them spoke for what seemed like a long time but was, in reality, only minutes. Then Jared heard the noise of hoof beats coming from the north end of town.

"Sounds like we got company," Jared said quietly. "I don't know how many but it sounds like more than one or two."

The horses pulled up in front of the sheriff's office and they heard voices as the cowboys dismounted. Jared stood and laid the shotgun across his left arm, pointing it in the general direction of the door. He waited. Within seconds, the knob turned and the door swung slowly open. Nothing happened for a long moment, then Morgan walked deliberately into the room, followed by Bob Evans. Jared waited without a word, noting that the hands who'd accompanied Morgan had apparently been instructed to wait outside. He wondered if they might be surrounding the building or even planning to try to burn them out but he figured they wouldn't risk Pete's life until they knew where he was and what condition he was in.

Morgan looked coolly at Jared. "Evenin', Delaney. You look like you're expectin' trouble. Not a very friendly welcome for a citizen who's come to file a complaint about havin' his cattle rustled."

From back where the cells were, Pete hollered out, "Morgan, is that you? Get me outa here! That old sheriff shot Jake and they're tryin' to railroad me."

Jared looked O'Bannon in the eye. "Morgan, you might as well give up the game, I know what's been goin' on. You tried to set me and Nathan up to shoot each other with your false rustler attack and your brothers tried to finish the job by bushwhackin' us." Morgan started to argue but Jared talked over him. "Jake's lyin' dead up in the high country and Pete's in the jail. That's where he'll stay until we get the circuit judge over to conduct his trial for attempted murder. If you make trouble, you'll be interferin' with a deputy doin' his duty."

"So . . . you're a deputy now, are you?" Morgan looked at Jared and smirked. "Well, Mr. Deputy, looks like the old man over there isn't much help to you right now, is he? There's one of you and two of us plus the hands waiting outside." Morgan put his hands behind his back and walked a few paces away from where Jared stood. "I think what happened here is you got caught rustling my cattle. When Nathan and Pete brought you in, you broke free and killed the sheriff. Luckily, we got here in time to stop you." Morgan smiled his cruel smile.

"Unfortunately, you were killed in the

fracas. That's how this is shaping up in my mind."

Jared said, "Could be, Morgan, but you left out one important part. Before your men shot me, I took you down with both barrels of this twelve gauge. How does that sound to you?"

Morgan blinked, then regained his smirk. "Maybe you could and maybe you couldn't but if I don't get you, Bob will. There's one of you against the two of us."

From the open door behind them, Morgan heard the click of a hammer being cocked. A voice said, "Well, now, Mr. Morgan, maybe them odds are a little more even than you think. Raise your hands and keep'em as far as possible from your guns . . . unless you want to see how it feels to get blasted from both sides."

Morgan slowly raised his hands, as did Bob. He cautiously turned his head to look back over his shoulder. In the door holding a shotgun pointed square at the middle of his back was Miguel Mares.

"You're gonna be mighty sorry you stepped in the middle of this, Mares," Morgan snapped. "This is between me and that boy over there. You butted in, now you're gonna pay the price, too."

"Maybe so, Mr. Morgan, but I ain't gonna

pay it right now. You and that cabron next to you keep your hands up, walk out of this office, get on your horses and ride out of town. If you try to come back, you should know my sons are posted on rooftops with their rifles somewhere along Main Street, just itchin' to pay you back for all the times you and your ranch hands insulted them."

From in the back, Pete hollered out. "What's happenin', Morg?"

"Shut up, Pete," Morgan shouted in reply. He turned back to look at Jared. "You know this isn't over, Delaney. After all I've been through in my life to get where I am, if you think some wet-behind-the-ears saddle tramp is gonna ride into town and take me down, you're dumber than I thought. You got the drop on me now but that'll change in the future, believe me, mister."

Morgan turned to go. Bob Evans looked at Jared and gave a little shrug. "I kind a liked you, Delaney. You're a good hand. Maybe under different conditions, we coulda been friends."

Jared gave Evans a cold look and said, "Bob, there ain't no conditions exist in which we could be friends. You know the difference between right and wrong, yet you choose wrong. My friends don't do that."

Evans reacted as if Jared had slapped him

in the face. He started to reply but Morgan cut him off. "Come on, Bob, no time for idle talk, let's head back to the ranch."

Morgan walked toward the door and Evans followed. Miguel stepped back and to the side, keeping his shotgun pointed at Morgan. As he walked past, Morgan gave him a cold look. Jared and Miguel waited, holding their breath until they heard them ride away. Jared continued to listen, half expecting to hear rifle shots if Morgan changed his mind but apparently he had believed Miguel and decided to wait for a better opportunity.

Jared let out his breath in a rush. "Miguel, I'm always glad to see you but I can't recall a time when I've ever been more glad. How did you get past Morgan's men outside?"

Miguel chuckled. "They were all talkin' and laughin' like they were at a church social. They didn't even notice me when I snuck up the walkway. Miss Eleanor stopped by my place on her way to get the doc. She told me to get over here quick, that Nathan needed help." Miguel grinned at Jared. "It's good to finally see you on the right side, amigo."

Jared smiled back. "Maybe now I'll start gettin' good steaks again instead of ones that're tougher'n shoe leather."

Miguel laughed out loud at that but then turned serious. "What happened to Nathan? Is he gonna be all right?"

Jared looked grim and said, "That rascal Jake shot him. If doc don't get here fast, we may lose him. He was bleedin' pretty heavy and I ain't had time to try to stop it because of the trouble with Morgan."

As if on cue, Doc Adams stuck his head in the door. "Is the coast clear? Miss Eleanor told me Nathan'd been shot. She said there might be shootin'."

Jared said, "Come in quick, Doc, the trouble's over for now but Nathan needs help. He's shot in the shoulder and lost a lot of blood."

Doc walked toward Nathan's cot. Eleanor walked in the door after him. She said, "It looks like Miguel got here in time. We didn't hear any gunshots. What happened?"

Jared told Eleanor what happened, saying, "I was mighty glad Miguel showed up when he did. If he hadn't been here, Morgan might've made a play even though I had the drop on him. He acts like he can't be killed, like he's too mean or somethin'. Or maybe he thinks he's so good that I couldn't have taken him." Jared paused to reflect on that possibility. "Heck, I don't know, he might've been right about that. Anyway, Miguel was a sight for sore eyes!" Jared clapped Mares on the back. "It was a comfort to hear that your sons were in position to make sure they didn't double back on us."

Miguel grinned. "Si, it would have been grand for my sons to be in position, as you say, but unfortunately, there wasn't time." Miguel gave a short chuckle, then got a fiery look in his eyes. "They have endured too many insults from those cowboys and would most certainly enjoy the chance to pay them back. Perhaps they will have their chance pretty quick, que no?"

Jared looked incredulously at Miguel. "You're tellin' me you bluffed Morgan O'Bannon? That's rich! You sure had me believin' it so I guess it makes sense that Morgan did, too."

Miguel recovered his smile. "It was good to put one over on the patron after all the years of disrespect." The smile faded then and he said, "We can laugh now but you know what he said is true. This isn't over, not by a long shot. He'll be back, it's just a question of when."

Eleanor had been assisting Doc Adams with Nathan but she came over to where they were in time to hear Miguel's last statement. "Jared," she said, "Would you please fill me in on what's happened? It sounds like we need to be as informed and prepared as possible."

Jared said, "You and Miguel are both right. We've stirred up a hornet's nest. The O'Bannons are gonna come buzzin' around sooner rather than later. Pete's in the cell in back with a bullet wound in his leg. Doc'll need to look at it once he's done with Nathan." Both Eleanor's and Miguel's eyes widened in surprise at this news as Jared continued, "What Morgan's likely even more twisted up about is his little brother, Jake. He's lyin' dead up in the high country."

Eleanor gasped. "What happened?"

"Jake and Pete tried to set me and Nathan up to shoot each other," Jared continued. "They bushwhacked us as the deal was goin' down. Jake didn't count on Nathan's bein' so handy with a gun which led to his undoin'. Pete thought he would catch me unawares. He tried to get the drop on me."

Miguel smiled and said, "Since you are standing here and he's in the cell, it looks like he missed."

"I was able to turn it around though I ain't quite as handy with a six-shooter as Nathan is." Jared smiled in return at Miguel. "I just winged him. Morgan was tryin' to make it look like I was rustlin' cattle and when Nathan tried to stop me, we wound up killin' each other. Morgan would have a free path to takin' over all the ranches in the area."

Eleanor looked thoughtful. "That's diabolical but I think Morgan is capable of coming up with such a convoluted plot. Because of his own dark nature, he overlooked some details that derailed the plan."

Miguel cocked his head and asked, "What did he overlook?"

Eleanor continued. "Morgan knows Nathan is clever and not easily fooled but he probably thought he had all the angles figured and had the upper hand. What he expected Nathan would do . . . it's what Morgan would have done . . . is to assume the worst about Jared and believe he had turned cattle rustler."

Eleanor turned toward Jared. "It never occurred to Morgan that Nathan would keep believing in you. He knew you'd never be a party to such a thing."

Jared paused and looked down at his boots for a moment. He looked Eleanor in the eyes and said, "After how I acted, I wouldn't blame any of you for thinkin' the worst of me. But I guess Nathan was right. I'd begun to have questions." Jared took a deep breath. "Things Morgan and his crew were tellin' me didn't fit, like you all tried to tell me since I hit town. Maybe I'm thick but hit me over the head enough times, I finally see the light. I caught Pete, Jake, Bob Evans and some hands changin' brands on some cattle with their cinch rings and I was gonna face Morgan about it. I never got the chance, though, cause that's when he sent me off on a wild goose chase that was supposed to have an unhappy endin'."

Doc Adams came over to them and they turned their attention to him. "Nathan wants you to come over to the cot. He has some things to say and he doesn't want to have to holler or repeat himself. You got five minutes with him then he needs to rest quietly. His shoulder is pretty bunged up and he's lost quite a bit of blood. He's got some serious recovering to do."

They moved over where Nathan lay. He had a gray pallor that was alarming. Doc Adams noticed the looks on their faces and said, "He looks pretty bad . . . that's due to blood loss . . . but he'll probably make it. The bullet passed through so we didn't have to worry about taking it out. It went through the muscle but missed his shoulder socket and upper arm bone. He'll be laid up for awhile but the bleeding's stopped. With rest, he should heal up."

Nathan motioned with his good arm for them to come closer. As they gathered around, he spoke in a harsh whisper. "This thing'll come to a head fast, we gotta get ready. They may try to break Pete out before we notify the judge. We can't let that happen." Nathan took a painful breath and closed his eyes for a moment. "We need help keepin' him locked up and someone'll need to ride over to the circuit court in Taos to file the complaint. Ned and Lizbeth'll help us and maybe that hand of theirs." Nathan closed his eyes again and they waited. Jared could see his jaw muscles tighten as he fought through a wave of pain.

In a minute, he said, "Lizbeth came to town two days ago, told me what she thought Morgan was up to. She had it figured pretty good. It helped to put me on guard so I didn't fall into Morgan's trap, at least not all the way." Nathan gave a look that was somewhere between a grin and a grimace, saying, "With this shoulder messed up, reckon I didn't outfox'em completely."

Eleanor reached out to put her hand on Nathan's good arm and said, "How did they get you to go out to the herd tonight?"

Nathan looked at Jared, then back to Eleanor. "I got help from an unexpected source. Roberts sent that young woman from the saloon, Miss Quick, to spin a tale about how Jared was rustlin' the O'Bannon cattle." Nathan saw the pained expression on Eleanor's face and saw Jared look away. "She started in the way they told her but it didn't ring true. I asked her to be honest. They threatened her life but she told me the truth anyway, for which we're all indebted. She told me about Jake and Pete waiting to ambush me and Jared. I made a half-circle, came in from the east and caught Jake lookin' the wrong way. I had him covered but he went for his gun so I had to shoot him, which I regret. He was mean and ornery but I don't relish killin' a man, no matter what."

Miguel snorted and said, "If you'd put a bullet in him when you rode up, it would've saved some wear and tear on your shoulder."

Jared spoke up, "Miguel, we can't think like that or we're no better than the O'Bannons."

"Maybe so," Miguel said defiantly, "but you've only been here a short while. I've lived here all my life. The O'Bannons act like they're the ones who've lived here for hundreds of years and we're the newcomers. Like they're better than us because they're gringos and we're 'Meskins . . . pepper-bellies,' all those names they say with a sneer. Like they taught us the vaquero skills instead of the other way around." Miguel held his head up and said, "I don't want to be like them but I'm proud to stand against them and I will take some pleasure in bringing them down if we succeed."

Jared said, "I want to be able to hold my head up and not be ashamed of anything I do when we stand up to these scoundrels, that's all." He paused and looked Miguel in the eye. "I couldn't pick a finer man to stand beside than you, no matter how it turns out." Miguel reached out his hand and Jared took it. They gripped each other's hands firmly and nodded, no words being necessary.

Nathan cleared his throat. "There's a lot needs savin' but we don't have time. Miguel, ride out to Ned Kilpatrick's place, tell'em what happened. They need to be alert. Morgan may strike where we're not expectin'." The sheriff winced in pain and took a shallow breath, then continued snapping off orders. "Tell Ned to send his hand, Juan, to Taos to file charges with the circuit judge. See if they can spare a deputy or two to help us out." He stopped to take a breath again. "Jared, there's an old warrant in my desk, it'll show you how to write it up. Get it done, I'll sign it." With a pained smile, Nathan said, "Good thing Jake shot me in the left shoulder. At least I can still sign my name."

Jared rummaged through Nathan's desk until he found an old warrant and a pad of paper. He sat down at the desk to fill out the new warrant while Miguel accompanied Doc Adams back to the cell to examine Pete's wound. Pete howled like a scalded dog as the doctor cleaned and bandaged it, but with Miguel's shotgun trained on him, he made no move to try to escape. As Doc and Miguel returned up front, Jared finished filling out the warrant and brought it over to Nathan. He brought a book from Nathan's desk to put under the warrant and the quill pen for him to sign with as Nathan attempted to prop himself up. The effort brought a groan from Nathan and Eleanor rushed over to help him up, fluffing up the feather pillow on the cot to give him support. Nathan signed the warrant, then lay back with a sigh. "Signin' my name wore me plum out," Nathan said with a soft chuckle. "That's never happened before."

Jared said, "Doc was right, you need to get some rest. Miguel, could you send your sons over to help guard the jail? Once they're here, I'll walk Eleanor home and be right back. I don't think Morgan and his crew'll backtrack tonight but we'd better be prepared just the same."

Doc Adams, who'd been quiet up to then, said, "Jared, I guess you're in charge now. Nathan needs rest more than anything. I'll double check to make sure the bleeding's stopped but he needs to stay still and not re-open the wound. As long as it doesn't get infected, he should be up and around in a few weeks." Doc did a quick examination of Nathan's shoulder and took his leave.

Jared turned back to Miguel and Eleanor. "Doc's right, I'll have to take charge now, at least until Nathan recovers." He cleared his throat uncomfortably. "You know that doesn't mean I won't listen to your opinions, so don't be shy expressin' them."

Miguel laughed. "You really think Miss Eleanor would not share what she thought? That's not very likely. Me and my sons, we are with you but if what you say doesn't make sense, we will speak up. This is a life and death, there's no room for mistakes."

Jared nodded. "Sounds fair. I'll take all the help I can get, that's for sure. Right now, we need to move fast to get our defenses in place, then we need to get some rest. We don't know if Morgan will strike right away or take his time and make us sweat. We gotta be ready for both. We'll spell one another watchin' the jail so we can rest enough to stay alert." Jared paused and considered what else needed to be done. "Miguel, I know you got a café to run but I could use you here when you get back from Ned and Lizbeth's place."

Miguel nodded. "My wife can handle the kitchen and my daughters can wait on customers. My sons and I will take turns guarding the prisoner."

Eleanor spoke up. "Jared, I know this is a serious situation but I've got a school to run. I won't have this interfering with the children's education. When school is out, I'll do whatever I need to help out but the students are my first duty."

Jared looked uneasy. "I was hopin' you'd cancel school, both for your safety as well as the children's. I wouldn't put anything past Morgan, even hurlin' women and children."

"Using women and children as a bargaining chip isn't his style. He thinks he's invincible. I believe he'll come at you from the front. The school stays open." Eleanor spoke with an air of finality that brooked no argument.

Jared sighed. "I don't know if you're right

but I ain't sure you're wrong, neither. It'll be your call for now. If things change and I think you and the children are in danger, I'll have to insist."

Eleanor said, "All right. I'm not trying to be stubborn. Besides, if there's shooting, all the citizens of Cimarron will be in danger. If it comes to that, we'll be safer in the schoolhouse. Those adobe walls are thick."

"I guess that'll do for now," Jared said. He turned to Miguel, handing him the warrant. "Why don't you head out to Ned's now so we can get Juan on the road to Taos. The quicker he leaves, the less time Morgan'll have to set up an ambush. Tell him to take a fast horse, watch his back and vaya con Dios." Miguel said adios and left the jail.

Jared glanced at Nathan, who appeared to be sleeping. He turned back to Eleanor. "I could walk you back to your place," Jared said. "There's things I need to say to you, the first one bein' that I'm sorry for all the trouble and pain I've caused."

Eleanor shook her head. "We've got talking to do but now is not the time. You can't leave Nathan. We don't know what Morgan is up to." Eleanor looked at Jared for a long moment. A single tear rolled down her cheek. "Anyway, I'm not ready to talk yet. I know you're trying to make things right but your actions have been hurtful, not only to me but to others as well. It will take more than a simple apology to gain back all the trust you've lost."

Jared couldn't keep the hurt look off his face. He paused before responding. "Yesterday, I would've told you to forget about it. I hope I've changed. I told Bob Evans he'd never be my friend because my friends know right from wrong and choose to do what's right. Not just when it's convenient but every time, even when it's hard and no one else appreciates it. If I'm right, then I have to act the same to be worthy of my friends. I can't do what's right just to get approval, I've got to do it because I know it's right."

Eleanor brushed away her tear. "That doesn't make everything all right either, but it helps. I've never lost sight of the fact you're a good person, Jared. Whatever happens, I hope you remember what you just said."

Jared reached out to Eleanor but she shook her head. "No, let's just leave it there for now. We'll do our best to get through this ordeal and try to sort out what's still between us when the smoke clears. I'll go get some rest now so I can be awake when the school bell rings. After school is out, I'll stop by to check on Nathan and you."

CHAPTER 25

The next twenty-four hours were a blur to Jared as he shored up his defenses and marshaled his forces to be ready whenever Morgan made his move. After Eleanor left, he dozed fitfully for a couple of hours in Nathan's office chair, waking at sun rise with a crick in his neck. He checked on Nathan and found him sleeping, his color still somewhat gray and his breathing shallow. He wanted to help Nathan but didn't know what to do, so he left him alone. He walked outside the sheriff's office and breathed in the cool morning air. It filled his lungs and cleared his head. As he looked to his left up the street, he saw Miguel's son, Tomas, step out from a doorway where he'd been standing inconspicuously. Tomas touched the brim of his sombrero with the barrel of his rifle. Jared responded in kind. He looked the other direction down the street and saw Miguel's other son, Estevan, do the same thing. He nodded and felt a little less nervous knowing the young men were there.

There was a chill in the air, but he knew when the sun had been up for a few hours, it would give way to the warmth of the New Mexico spring. He thought it strange that at a time when the snows had melted and living things were blooming everywhere, such dark events were upon them. He felt he was at a crossroads in his life . . . he faced both the possibility of a violent death as well as the chance to redeem himself in the eyes of those who were truly important to him. Was this the end or the start of a new and better life? Having so much at stake heightened his fear and sharpened his resolve to not let the evil of Morgan O'Bannon rob him of the rewards that were within his reach. After another moment's reflection, he went back into the sheriff's office.

As he walked in, he glanced over at Nathan and saw that his eyes were open. In a soft and weakened voice, Nathan greeted him. "Mornin', Jared, looks like you been takin' in the mornin' light. How do things look?"

"We're still alive and kickin'." Jared smiled and said, "You ain't kickin' all that much, though."

Nathan returned his smile. "I'm weak as a new-born calf. Doubt I'll be doin' any kickin' for awhile. I do feel a bit better after gettin' some rest and the fact I'm hungry as a bear is prob'ly a good sign. You have to get some food for our prisoner anyway. Why don't you see what Anita can cook up for us at Miguel's place. She can have one of her daughters bring it over."

"Good idea," Jared said. "Will you be all right while I run over to get that goin'?"

"Now's prob'ly the best time for you to leave me alone," Nathan replied. "Once you get that rascal Pete fed, maybe you and I can think this thing out over tortillas and eggs. I know you've been considerin' it already. We need to get everything in line so we're ready when they come at us."

Jared nodded and left for Miguel Mares' café. Within minutes, he was back with a plate covered with a cloth napkin. "I brought Pete some beans and tortillas and a cup of coffee," Jared said. "I reckon he'll complain about the fare but I'll remind him he ain't stayin' at the St. James. Anita'll send somethin' more fillin' for us in a few minutes and we'll have that talk." Jared took Pete's breakfast into the back area. As he suspected, Pete complained bitterly.

"First you shoot an innocent man," Pete

whined, "and now you're tryin' to starve me. You'll be sorry for how you're treatin' me, Delaney."

Jared shoved the food through the slot in the cell door. "Pete, I don't care a lick whether you eat this or not. As for bein' sorry, I'll have to deal with what's comin' whether I feed you tortillas and beans or beefsteak, so that don't carry much weight with me in regard to plannin' your menu." Pete glared at Jared but then stood up, took the plate and coffee cup and sat back down to eat without another word. Jared went back into the front room and pulled his chair over by Nathan's cot.

"Sure as shootin'," Jared said, "Morgan's gonna come after us . . . where, how and when, I'm not sure about. We only have a few folks we can count on and we're gonna be stretched thin. I'd sure appreciate your thoughts."

Nathan said, "Grab that blanket from over there by the gun case and prop me up a bit more. I'd like to look you in the eye when we talk."

Jared tried to be careful as he helped Nathan move into a more upright position. Even so, Nathan couldn't stifle a groan of pain.

"It hurts when I move," Nathan said, "but I can mostly feel it in the muscles, not the shoulder joint. Doc told me if we can keep the dressing clean to avoid infection, I could be up and about in a few weeks. In the meantime, you're right, we're stretched thin. Maybe they can send help from Taos but I wouldn't count on it." Nathan grimaced as he shifted his position slightly, then continued. "Morgan *will* be unpredictable. He might come stormin' in here with fifteen cowboys blazin' away or he might make midnight raids on some of the ranches to try to draw us off. One of the first things we need to do is tell folks to pull in their herds as close as they can and to stay alert. I'd like to provide protection for everyone, but we can't. They're gonna have to fend for themselves. At least if they know what's happenin', they'll be better prepared."

"That makes sense," Jared said, "I'll ask Miguel to send his sons out later this mornin' once he gets back from speakin' with Ned and Lizbeth." As he mentioned the Kilpatrick's names, a troubled look crossed his face.

Nathan took note of the expression. "Jared, I know you're crosswise with Eleanor and Ned both and you'll have to settle up at some point. Right now, we gotta keep our minds in the middle, stay focused on defendin' ourselves and make sure justice is done. Eleanor and Ned understand that. Whatever unfinished business you got, they won't let it interfere with doin' the job facin' us. I don't expect you will either."

"You're right, we don't have time for talk . . . and if we don't take care of business, there'll be no chance later cause we'll all be dead." Jared twisted uncomfortably in his chair. "I'll say to them what I want to say to you now." Jared sat up straighter and looked Nathan in the eye. "I apologize for bein' a fool. It might take me some time to figure out what led me down the foolish path I took, but I'm truly sorry for the trouble I caused, bein' so pig-headed . . . not the least of which is you lyin' there with a bad shoulder."

Nathan smiled. "This shoulder ain't your fault, it's mine for gettin' old and slow. If you hadn't taken Pete down while me and Jake was shootin' at one another, we wouldn't be havin' this conversation. I accept your apology. I know your life's been complicated by losin' your parents at a young age. It makes it hard to know who to trust." Nathan paused and looked carefully at Jared before continuing. "The true test of what you're worth is whether you learn from your mistakes or just keep on makin' the same ones over. If I was to bet, I'd put my money on you changin'."

Jared looked at Nathan and said, "That means a lot to me, Nathan. I see things clearer now, but it helps havin' someone you respect to believe in you. I'll do my best to make sure you've made a smart bet."

Nathan nodded. "That's good enough for me. Far as I'm concerned, that's all we need to say." Nathan took a deep breath and said, "I got one more bit of unfinished business I need to get out of the way, then we can finish plannin'."

Jared looked puzzled and said, "What's on your mind?"

Nathan frowned and said, "I don't know any other way to do this but to ask you straight out . . . you realize it was Morgan who killed your parents, don't you?"

Jared nodded slowly before answering. "I wasn't sure until up on the ridge last night. It came to me like a fog was liftin'. I don't have a clear recollection, I just see bits and pieces in my mind. It makes too much sense to just be a coincidence since Morgan was maraudin' through that part of the country back then."

Nathan said, "It must've been awful for a

young boy. I'm not surprised the memories aren't clear. We all cut out painful things we don't want to dwell on, kind of like when your body shuts down so you don't feel the pain from an injury in its full force." Nathan grinned ruefully. "Speakin' of which, I wouldn't mind my shoulder shuttin' down about now." He shifted uncomfortably. "We don't need to speak about this again any time soon but I wanted to make sure you were aware of the truth. I wouldn't want it dawnin' on you right in the middle of a situation where you need a clear head."

"You got that right," Jared said. "Like yesterday . . . it seems like a week ago but I know it was just yesterday . . . when I drew down on that big cat." Jared remembered the thought flashing through his mind about the similarity between the eyes of the cat and those of the man in his dreams. "When it's life or death, you can't make it more complicated than it is or you'll wind up dead. I got some thinkin' to do but now ain't the time, that's for sure."

There was a soft knock at the door and Jared opened it to find Miguel's young daughter, Esperanza, with a box containing two plates of food. In Spanish, she told him she would be back with coffee in a moment. Smiling shyly as Jared took the box from her and thanked her, she turned and went back down the street to the café. Jared carried the box inside and said, "Soup's on."

They ate in silence with Nathan giving a good account of himself in spite of only having the use of one of his hands. Again, there was a soft knock and Esperanza was waiting with two mugs of steaming coffee when Jared opened it. He said, "Gracias, Esperanza," which drew another shy smile and a giggle before she headed back to the café.

For the next hour, they discussed and debated their strategy. They knew they could count on Ned and his hand, Juan, as well as Miguel and his sons, giving them a total of six able-bodied men counting Jared. Nathan proposed having two men patrol in town with the others riding out through the countryside scouting for trouble. They realized Ned or Juan would have to be on guard at the ranch and Miguel or one of his sons would need to keep a close eye on the restaurant, which limited them somewhat. Jared insisted that one man always remain at the jail with Nathan to keep an eye on Pete O'Bannon. Jared didn't say it but Nathan understood that the other eye would be watching out for him.

Nathan huffed and puffed about that.

"You don't have to watch over me like a new-born babe. Morgan ain't gonna ride in here in the middle of the day because he'll figure we'll be watchin'. He's more likely to create a diversion and try to sneak Pete out. We'll have to keep close watch on Heck Roberts, as well. He'll be Morgan's eyes and ears in town."

Jared said, "You're prob'ly right but I won't leave the jail unguarded. No offense, but you ain't exactly in tip top shape right now, Nathan. If Pete O'Bannon's gonna receive the justice he's got comin', we can't have anybody breakin' him out. There's gonna be a guard here at all times. You put me in charge of this outfit, let me *be* in charge." Jared finished speaking and set his jaw.

Nathan started to say something then paused and grinned. "I reckon that's why I offered you this job right on the spot when you first came to town. When you ain't makin' things too complicated, you cut right to the chase. You're right, I can't stand guard right now, though if this stretches out for a time, I plan on recoverin' so I can help. This has been buildin' to a head for years. If this is the finish, I sure don't want to miss it!"

Jared said, "A lot of folks'll have to give

their all to get this job done. You may wind up in the thick of things before it's over." Jared walked over to the cabinet where Nathan kept the guns. He turned and said, "If it weren't for you, Morgan and his outlaws would've taken over this part of the country years ago. When it comes down to it, nobody's gonna accuse you of slackin' off."

"All the same," Nathan replied grumpily, "I'd feel better if I had the use of both my arms."

Nathan hesitated and then said, "I know you were special friends with Miss Quick over at the Colfax Tavern and that didn't set well with Eleanor. It ain't my business and I wouldn't mention it but for one thing. If it weren't for her, we'd both be dead. She's deathly afraid of Heck Roberts but she told me the truth instead of that cock and bull story about you bein' a cattle rustler." Nathan's chin jutted out with determination. "Folks look down on those in her line of work but I'll tell you, she's got more guts than most men I know."

Jared nodded in agreement. "You're right, there's somethin' special about her."

"Here's the thing," Nathan said. "If he can, Heck'll hurt her. We owe it to her to check up on her well-bein'. Since we're keepin' an eye on Heck anyway, maybe you should walk on down to the Colfax and make a call on Mr. Roberts."

CHAPTER 26

Morgan was seething as he led his cowboys out of town that night. He was sorely tempted to turn around and storm the jail to free Pete and finish off Jared and the old sheriff. He was gripping the reins so tightly that his knuckles were white and his horse shied at the pressure he was applying with his knees. Exercising the steely self-control he'd developed over the years, he breathed deeply and calmed himself so he could think through the problem clearly. As much power as he wielded in this part of the country, he was aware that Nathan Averill had his share of friends in high places, too. There were too many people who had some idea of what was going on. If he engaged in a bloodbath, it could lead to an investigation that would make life far too complicated. He decided to bide his time and find a more oblique way of dealing with the problems at hand. Turning in the saddle to, he said to Bob

Evans, "You boys head on back to the ranch, I'm going back to have a word with Heck. I'll join up with you when I'm done. In the meantime, I don't want anyone doing anything out of the ordinary until I give the orders."

Bob looked as if he had questions but he saw the flint in his boss's eye and decided the best course would be to keep his mouth shut and do what he was told. He turned to the other hands and said, "Let's head on back, boys." Without another word, the cowboys rode off towards the O'Bannon spread.

Morgan turned his big bay and trotted back toward town. As he reached the outskirts, he slowed to a walk and looked around cautiously as he rode toward the Colfax Tavern. He didn't know if Miguel Mares was telling the truth about his sons laying an ambush but he didn't want to take any chances. Although it was late, there were still customers at the bar. Morgan tied his horse to the hitching post and walked around to the private entrance in back. Walking in, he went to the inner door which led to the bar area, opened it a crack and waited until Roberts walked down the bar to the vicinity of the door. When Heck got within earshot, Morgan said quietly, "Heck, we need to talk private . . . now."

Roberts was startled but regained his composure. "I'll get Leon to cover the bar and be right there." He went over to his assistant bartender and said, "I've got to do some work in the office, cover the bar for me." He walked into the office.

Without preamble, Morgan said, "We've got trouble. We need to come up with a new plan."

Heck looked puzzled. "Fill me in, Morgan, I'm a little lost. I thought we had this thing figured down to a T. Obviously, something's gone wrong."

Morgan shook his head grimly. "You can say that again. Jake's dead and Pete's in jail. Averill is wounded but still alive and Delaney is the new deputy sheriff. I thought the boys would get the drop on'em. They must've been tipped off because Averill was ready for the ambush." Morgan gave Roberts a hard look. "Maybe you can explain how they knew about the plan ahead of time."

It was Heck's turn to look grim. "Looks like Christy didn't follow her instructions," Heck said. "I was worried she might've fallen for that cowboy. I suspect she's the leak in our bucket. Guess I need to have a little talk with that young lady."

Morgan nodded and said pointedly, "I think you're right about the leak. I'm surprised you sent her to do the job if you had questions about her loyalty."

Heck looked indignant as he said, "Morgan, that girl knows to be afraid of me. I'd have bet good money she wouldn't double cross me. She knows what's in store for her if she did."

"You would have bet . . . and you would have lost!" Morgan bit off his words. "You do need to 'have a talk with her' as you so delicately put it but first, we've got to figure out how to deal with this mess. Much as I'd like, we can't just shoot everyone who's making a stand. It would raise too many questions and bring too much attention." Morgan had been sitting on the edge of his rolltop desk but he stood and began pacing as he pondered their situation. "We've got to find a way that results in the death of Nathan and his new deputy and makes it appear we're innocent bystanders." Morgan stopped pacing and turned to Roberts with a reptilian smile. "They'll expect us to strike back right away so we'll do the unexpected . . . we'll wait. In the meantime, we'll spread information that puts things in a different light. That's your job."

"How do you propose I do this?" Heck asked.

Morgan looked thoughtful for a second. "Tell your girls that rustlers hit our herd and Jake was killed in the raid. Tell them when Nathan came out to investigate, he turned on Pete, shot him in the leg and with the help of Delaney, brought him in to frame him. Say he's always had a grudge against the O'Bannons and this was his way of settling old scores." Morgan became more animated, almost as if he believed the story he was concocting. "Everyone knows about the bad blood between us and Nathan. It'll sew a seed of doubt when and if there's an investigation. Once your girls hear it, it'll be only a matter of hours before most of the townsfolk hear it."

A smile spread over Heck's face. He said, "I like it . . . and you're right, it'll spread like wildfire once the girls tell a few customers."

Morgan said, "Get to it, then. I'll go back to the ranch and figure out the next steps. We're not going to rush into this thing. We'll take our time and come at them from a different direction than they expect." Again, that small flicker of a smile touched his lips but not his eyes. "Kind of like the old days, huh? We'll make them pay." Morgan left by the back door and Heck headed up the stairs to settle with Miss Christy Quick. When he got to her room, he kicked the door open but she wasn't there. He went back downstairs to ask the other girls if they'd seen her. Despite his threats, no one would admit to seeing her. She was nowhere to be found.

Jared took a stroll around town to get a feel for what the townspeople knew and what their state of mind was. People who were out and about tended to avert their eyes when they passed him on the street. The few who greeted him were skittish. Apparently, word had already spread about what happened and folks were anticipating trouble. He would like to have reassured them but most folks mainly seemed interested in putting distance between themselves and him. He stopped in the fares café to get another cup of coffee for Nathan, which he figured he would drop off on his way down to the Colfax Tavern. Anita Mares hurried over to him and said, "Senor Jared, what's going to happen?"

Jared shook his head and said, "Anita, I don't know what's gonna happen but I do know we've all gotta be ready. I'm sorry your family got drug into this but I promise

I'll do my best to see us through it."

"I know you will," Anita replied, "Miguel, he thinks you are a good man." This surprised Jared and it must have shown on his face because Anita smiled gently and said, "It's possible to be confused and still be a good man, Senor Jared. When you are young, you don't always make the best choices, especially when it comes to the ladies. That doesn't mean you don't have a good heart."

Jared was touched. "Thanks, that means a lot to me. I'll do what I can to get this thing with the O'Bannons settled without shedding the blood of your family. I'm afraid it'll get dangerous before it's over, though."

Anita looked at him with determination. "Our family has taken all the insults we will stand for. This is as much our fight as it is yours . . . maybe more. We'll take our chances, same as you. It is time to make a stand and we will do our part."

Jared nodded and said, "You're right, it *is* time to make a stand." Jared took a deep breath and looked Anita in the eyes. "I'm with you."

Anita held his gaze for a moment, then with a twinkle in her eye, said, "And in return, I think I'll give you more coffee, que no?"

Jared chuckled and said, "I expect old Nathan could use another cup if you've got it to spare." As Anita turned to go get the coffee, Jared reached out and touched her shoulder. When she turned back around, he said, "Thank you, Senora." She nodded, turned and went back to the kitchen.

Jared took the coffee back to Nathan at the jail and headed to the Colfax Tavern. As he walked, he thought about what to say to Heck Roberts. He figured chances were good Heck already knew about what had happened so he saw no reason to beat around the bush. He figured it was time to show O'Bannon and his minions that the people of Cimarron were done being bullied. With that in mind, he walked into the tavern.

"Well, looky here, if it ain't the new deputy," Heck said with a sneer. "You know, Delaney, you make my head spin with the way you keep changing sides. Last I checked, you were employed by Mr. O'Bannon, but now I hear you've joined up with that washed up old sheriff."

Jared took his time walking the length of the bar to where Roberts stood, noticing that even though it was early, there were quite a few customers. Realizing something was happening, they fell silent. When he was even with Heck, he turned, looked him in the eye and spit on the bar. Roberts' jaw dropped and for a moment, he was speechless. In that moment, Jared spoke. "No more changin' sides, Heck, the lines are drawn. You and your boss have operated outside the law for a long time but that time's comin' to an end. You got crimes to answer for and believe me, you'll answer. And one more thing . . . if I find out you've done anything to hurt Christy, you'll wish you only had to answer to the law." Jared leaned forward over the bar until his face was inches from Roberts. "I'll take you straight down to hell."

Before Heck could respond, Jared turned on his heel and walked toward the tavern's swinging doors. As he walked, Roberts found his voice and sputtered, "You'll be sorry for the day you rode into this town, Delaney. Morgan O'Bannon will chew you up and spit you out! He could take you before he's had his morning coffee!"

Jared ignored Heck and could hear him shouting even as he walked down the street. He grinned to himself. It was a small victory to wipe that smug expression off Heck's face and see him lose his temper. He figured O'Bannon and his crew, unaccustomed to not getting their way, were temporarily thrown off balance by what had happened. Anything he could do to keep them off balance would buy time to muster support from the legal authorities in Taos. He prayed Miguel had made it out to the Kilpatrick's place and Juan Suazo was on his way to visit the circuit court judge. Once he heard from Miguel, he figured he'd head out to the Kilpatrick's and see where they stood.

As Jared walked back to the sheriff's office, he saw Miguel riding in from the north end of town. He waved, pointing in the direction of the jail and Miguel waved back in acknowledgement before heading his horse that way. Miguel had dismounted by the time Jared arrived. He turned to him with a worried look. "Suazo is on his way to Taos but I think you're gonna have to talk with Ned Kilpatrick. He's not sure he can trust you even though I told him things are different. His wife, she tried to tell him, too, but he wasn't much for listening."

Jared gave, Miguel a rueful smile. "That sounds like the Ned I know. The only person I know more stubborn than him is me. Reckon I'll have to have a man to man talk with him." Jared took off his hat and scratched his head. "I got a favor to ask,

Miguel."

Miguel tied his horse to the hitching post as he looked over his shoulder. "What you need me to do, amigo?"

"I told Nathan I wanted someone lookin' after the jail at all times," Jared said. "He understands that includes watchin' out for him since he ain't quite ready to look after himself. He don't like it but he understands it. I know you'll want to go check on things at the café and get somethin' to eat but I'm in a hurry to get straight with Ned. Would you send one of your sons to keep an eye on Nathan and our guest so I can head out to the Kilpatrick's place?"

"Si, I'll send Tomas over right away," Miguel said. "He's my oldest and he has a level head. Estevan thinks it would be a grand idea to get a rope and arrange a little necktie party for senor Pete. I'd better have a talk with him like the one you had with me. We're trying to enforce the law. I don't suppose we should go around breaking it, as tempting as it is."

Jared chuckled and said, "You're right but it's amusin' to think about the look on Pete's face if we walked in with a rope. I think the O'Bannons and Heck Roberts have gotten away with bullyin' folks for so long they don't know how to act when it ain't workin' out the way the planned. That could give us a little bit of an edge. Who knows, if we stick together, we may get some satisfaction out of this before it's all done."

Miguel nodded but said, "You're right about Pete and Heck Roberts but I think senor Morgan is different. He's used to having his way but I don't think he'll be buffaloed if it doesn't happen. He won't give up. He's like a snake waiting to strike, patient and quiet until the time is right, then before you know it, he's got you. We can't let our guard down for a minute."

"You're right, pardner," Jake said emphatically. "I've thought more than once Morgan was like a snake with those cold, dead eyes sizin' you up like you're a field mouse he's havin' for dinner. We gotta all pull our weight in the same direction. That's why I'd better get on the trail to Ned's place to get this straight between us."

Miguel said, "I'll send Tomas over right away." He walked away and Jared went inside to wait.

When Tomas came in, Jared gave him instructions, then went out, mounted up and headed out in the direction of the Kilpatrick spread. As he rode, he thought of what he wanted to say to Ned and Lizbeth but he also tried to remain vigilant for signs of an ambush. Nothing seemed off to him, no interruption of the sounds of nature that would suggest the presence of an intruder. As he listened to the birds twitter, he was again struck by the contrast between the beautiful spring day and the threat of danger he felt hanging in the air. He maintained a steady pace as he pondered this disparity and before he knew it, he came upon the Kilpatrick ranch house. He slowed to a walk as he approached the house to give Ned plenty of advance notice of his arrival.

As he dismounted, Lizbeth came hurrying out the front door and ran up to him, taking his hand and saying, "Oh, Jared, I'm so glad you came. Please come in, let's talk." Jared was heartened by her reception but he looked up on the porch as Ned came out. There was not a hint of friendliness on his face and he looked displeased at his wife's reaction to Jared's arrival.

On his way out, Jared had decided the best approach was a direct and honest one. It would either work or it wouldn't but there wasn't time to tiptoe around the topic. He walked over to Ned, extended his hand. He said, "Ned, I've made some foolish choices I'll regret all my life. For that, I'm sorry. I reckon you got things to say to me and I want you to know I'm man enough to hear'em. Right now, though, we got a dangerous situation hangin' over our heads. Nathan needs to know if he . . . and I . . . can count on you."

Ned seemed taken aback by Jared's immediate apology, as if he had expected something different. He shook his head in surprise. "I wasn't sure what to expect from you but I reckon you could've done worse. I do have questions but they can wait until we get this taken care of with the O'Bannons. And for what it's worth, you ain't the only one who made bad choices." He glanced at his wife with a crooked grin and said, "I've had help in seein' my behavior wasn't top shelf. I expect I owe you an apology as well." With that, he reached out, took Jared's hand firmly and shook it. "Let's talk about what you need us to do and save all the palaverin' for another time. Miguel was out here this mornin' and we've already sent Juan to Taos with the warrant." Ned's face clouded. "I told him to deliver it, bed his horse down at the livery and get some rest. If he gets started at daybreak tomorrow and there's no delays, he should make it back by suppertime. I got to admit I'm worried, though."

Jared nodded and said, "I'm thinkin' he

prob'ly got away before the O'Bannons had time to set up an ambush. I'm afraid they may try some trickery when he's on the way back, even though the deed will be done. After backin' down in the jail last night, my guess is Morgan'll want to send us a message he ain't afraid to use force whenever it suits him."

Ned said, "I figure it the same way, which is why I warned Juan to be on a sharp lookout, especially through Cimarron Canyon. After bein' shot up by them fellas once, Juan'll be extra cautious. We both know when the situation calls for it, that boy can flat-out ride. I bet if they chase him, he'll outrun'em."

Thinking back on happier times when he and Juan would have horse racing competitions, Jared smiled. "I never admitted it and I'd deny it if he was here now, but he could take me in a sprint and I'm a pretty fair rider myself. You couldn't have asked for a better hand for the job."

Lizbeth stepped up on the porch and said, "Seein' as how you don't appear likely to kill each other, let's go inside where we don't present such large targets. I'll make a fresh pot of coffee."

Ned and Jared followed Lizbeth inside and sat at the table where she served them coffee. Jared outlined the strategy he and Nathan had come up with and asked Ned and Lizbeth for their thoughts. Ned was of the opinion Morgan would try some subterfuge, perhaps attacking one of the outlying ranches to create a diversion to cover up an attempt to break Pete out of jail.

"Jared," he said with a worried frown, "He knows we been behind Nathan all the way and have tried to stand up to him. I'm afraid he's gonna target our place. I'll need to keep a sharp eye to make sure he doesn't destroy what we've worked so hard to build. I wish I could be in town to help but I don't see any other way but to stick close to home."

"I understand about protectin' what's yours," Jared replied. "That leaves us short-handed when it comes to protectin' the jail though. I reckon we'll have to ask all the ranchers to watch over their own land like you are." He shook his head in frustration. "We don't have the manpower to cover the countryside. I'm afraid the best we can do is hold on and wait for the judge to take action. That could take time but if we can get Pete to trial, we got an open and shut case."

Ned snorted at that. "Wait till Morgan gets that fancy pants lawyer, Catron, into the deal. I don't trust those fellas any farther than I can throw'em."

"You may be right," Jared said. "I'll be interested to hear from Juan what the judge's reaction to this warrant is. By all accounts, he's a fair man who don't seem to give in to that Santa Fe Ring." At the mention of the Santa Fe Ring, Jared made a face as if he'd just taken a swallow of curdled milk. "Still, I worry the longer this thing drags on, the greater the chance Morgan'll do more damage or find a way to slide out from under this."

Lizbeth spoke up. "That's why guardin' the jail is the most important job you've got. Not only do you need to keep Pete in custody, you've got to get Nathan healed up and keep him safe. He's the key witness. If it comes down to one man's word against another, he's a lawman with years of honorable service. The judge is likely to believe him. Morgan knows that . . . he'll make an attempt on Nathan's life."

They talked awhile longer about how to best protect Nathan and their prisoner. Ned agreed to send Juan out when he returned to warn the neighboring ranchers. Jared was struck by how natural it felt to be sitting around the kitchen table once again talking with Ned and Lizbeth. He realized the tension between them would return once the crisis passed. He knew all too well they'd need to deal with it head on when that time came but he was heartened to see how they were able to set it aside for the present. Finally, they'd said all that needed to be said to prepare for the troubles ahead. Jared stood up to leave.

Jared said. "I know we've got some talkin' to do yet in order to clear the air. I made some bone-headed mistakes because I refused to see what was in plain sight in front of me. For that, I'm sorry. You and Lizbeth are the closest thing to family I've had since my parents were killed, yet I couldn't bring myself to trust you when things got tough. I won't make that mistake again."

Standing to face Jared, Ned looked over at Lizbeth, who smiled at him. He looked back at Jared. "It's hard for a man to admit he's made mistakes, especially when he lets his pride get in the way. It's a measure of a man that he's big enough to admit he's been wrong." Ned looked down at his boots then back up at Jared. "The fault ain't all on your side, Jared. I coulda handled things different and who knows, maybe we wouldn't have had to go through all this heartache. Still, you can't change what's done. We'll just make the best of it. I'm willin' to let the past stay in the past. I'll give you another chance if you'll do likewise with me."

They shook hands. Jared turned to Lizbeth, who reached out and embraced him. "It's good to have you back in our home and in our hearts," she whispered. "When this is over, you've got a place here anytime."

Jared stepped back and looked at Lizbeth with a hint of moisture in his eyes. He shook his head, too overcome with emotion to say anything. He smiled and walked out the door. He headed back to town, not knowing what the future held but knowing some things that were wrong had been made right.

CHAPTER 27

Jared made it back to town without incident and relieved Tomas at the jail. Nathan was sitting up and had eaten a light lunch, which seemed to improve his spirits as well as his health. Jared figured Nathan came from hearty stock and might just recover in sufficient time to play an important role before this business was over.

"Still lollygaggin' around, huh?" Jared said playfully. "Good to see our county tax dollars hard at work."

"I reckon that's your cowboy way of tryin' to cheer me up but it ain't workin' so give it a rest." Nathan looked down his nose at Jared. "How'd your talk with Ned go?"

Jared laughed at Nathan's foul mood and proceeded to fill him in on his encounter with the Kilpatricks. Nathan looked relieved and encouraged by the report and they proceeded to talk once more about their limited options.

Over the next couple of days, Jared went about his duties as deputy, keeping an eye on Nathan and his prisoner when he wasn't making the rounds in town. He stopped in at the Tavern to check on Christy when he knew Heck was out to see if she was all right. Each time, he was told that no one had seen her since the night of the confrontation with the O'Bannons. He worried that something had happened to her but didn't have time to track her down and didn't know where to start anyway. He figured she'd have to take care of herself for better or for worse but vowed again that if Heck Roberts harmed her, he would settle up with him personally.

Two days following his trip to the Kilpatrick's ranch, Juan Suazo rode into town and came to see him at the jail. The encounter was awkward at first but Jared inquired about Maria and that broke the tension. Juan told him Ned had repeated what he said about Juan being the better rider and they quickly got back into their old rhythm of teasing each other.

Once they were a little more at ease, Jared asked Juan about his ride to Taos. He told Jared he'd made the trip without a hitch, although he feared he would encounter an ambush on the way back. He said when the judge received the warrant, he chuckled and said it looked like old Nathan had finally gotten the goods on the O'Bannons. Juan thought the judge seemed partial to Nathan, which was good news. The bad news was he was tied up with a trial and it would be several weeks before he could get to Cimarron. Even worse, they were short-handed and could spare no deputies to help out. They were on their own.

Jared figured Morgan had sources in Taos and had this information as well. It gave Morgan more time to sweat them but Jared was sure that sooner or later, Morgan would make a play. The problem was they couldn't let down their guard. It could happen today, tomorrow or next week and there was no way to predict it. That was the hand they'd been dealt so it was the hand Jared would play but it would make for some sleepless nights and long days with his nerves on edge.

It didn't help that his attempts to talk with Eleanor hadn't gone the way he'd hoped. She was polite but not encouraging. She was busy with the children at school and he had his own hands full with guarding the jail and keeping alert for signs that Morgan was making a move. The third time he asked to speak with her, she came straight out and told him she wasn't ready to talk about the future. She reminded him of the night Nathan had been shot when they'd agreed they needed to survive this ordeal before trying to sort out what might still exist between them. She said she still felt that way and his continuing to push wouldn't help. Jared's heart sank when he heard this but he figured the best thing he could do was nothing. He resigned himself to focusing on the tasks at hand and did his best to be friendly and polite when he saw Eleanor, without coming on too strong. In spite of himself, however, each time he made his rounds, he went by the school so he could lay eyes on her even if they didn't speak. The days went by and turned into a week.

Jared didn't know how he'd gotten back up into the mountains but there he was, facing the largest mountain lion he'd ever seen. All he had was his pistol although he knew he needed a rifle to bring down a cat this size. He trembled in the clutches of his fear and looked around for someplace to go or some way out but saw nothing. The big cat gathered itself, staring at Jared with its cold eyes flashing in the light of the quarter moon. As he looked into the cat's eyes, he could've sworn he heard it speak to him though he knew that made no sense. He heard a voice saying, "It's time you made a stand, boy." Then he awoke with a chill running down his spine.

CHAPTER 28

"How long are you gonna make that young cowboy sweat, Morgan?" Heck Roberts inquired. "It's already been over a week. It's amusing to watch him make his rounds . . . he looks more nervous with every day that goes by, but sooner or later, the judge'll get over here from Taos. We have to get things tidied up by then, I figure."

Morgan smiled a thin smile. "Don't worry about the judge, Heck, I've got eyes and ears over in Taos. I'll know he's coming right after he knows, believe me. In the meantime, this waiting game isn't just for our amusement. Keep people on edge long enough, they get antsy and make mistakes. The boy is getting close to that stage now. When the time is right, I'll strike in a way he's not expecting and we'll finish this thing off. In the meantime, you continue to reconnoiter in town and report like you've been doing."

"Whatever you say, Morgan," Heck

replied. "I'm concerned with how fast that old sheriff is healing up, though. He might be the wild card in the deck."

"Nathan Averill is an old man and he's wounded bad," Morgan snorted derisively. "I give him his due, he was tough in his time but that's passed. Once Delaney's out of the picture, we'll take care of the sheriff with little trouble, I promise you. Now get back to town and keep watching. I'll let you know when we make our move." Morgan waved his hand to dismiss Roberts. "In the meantime, you need to locate Christy. I don't know how you let her vanish but I'm not pleased. That's one more loose end we need to tidy up."

Heck looked grim and said with some annoyance, "I don't know where she is but she can't have just vanished. She didn't take the stage, I know that. I can't believe anyone would've been fool enough to give her a horse. She's got to be hiding around town. I'll find her sooner or later and she'll be plenty sorry when I do." Roberts walked out, mounted up and headed back to town.

"You sure you should be movin' around like this, Nathan?" Jared inquired nervously. "It's only been ten days since you got shot. I don't want you to re-open that wound and take a chance on it gettin' infected."

Nathan shook his head in wry amusement. "You're like an old woman fussin' over me. I told you before, when I lay around, I stiffen up and the pain's worse. Movin' keeps me loose and Doc says it helps with the healin'. Between you and Eleanor, I'm gonna have to get well pretty quick or you'll both nurse me to death!"

Jared knew Eleanor made frequent visits to the jail after school hours but she timed them for when he was out making his rounds. He was disappointed she felt she had to avoid him but comforted that she was checking in on Nathan. Whatever their differences, he knew they shared affection and admiration for the crusty old sheriff. The more time Jared spent around him, the more his respect for the old lawman grew.

"Reckon you're right," Jared said reluctantly. "I just don't want you to take a turn for the worse. We might need your help before it's all over."

"Speakin' of that," Nathan said, "Let's talk about what we know and what we think we know. You realize Morgan's tryin' to spook you by makin' you wait and sweat don't you?"

Jared nodded. "I know . . . sometimes knowin' don't help. Walkin' past the Colfax

Tavern yesterday, I heard a loud noise. I almost shot a cowboy whoopin' it up after a few drinks. I'm like a long-tailed cat in a room full of rockin' chairs, ready to jump."

Nathan chuckled at the image but then turned serious. "Morgan can drag this out another week at the most before he makes a move. He ain't the only one's got sources in Taos and my sources got access to a telegraph to keep me informed. I hear the judge'll get his trial wrapped up within the week. Once it's done, it'll take him a day or two to gather what he needs to head over and begin preparations for a trial."

"That gives us an idea of when the judge will be headed our way but I ain't sure it tells us much about when Morgan's gonna move," Jared said.

Nathan continued to walk slowly and deliberately around the office. "You're right, so we got to be alert at all times. We know Morgan needs me and you dead before the judge gets here, we just don't know how he plans to do the deed. I'm worried with us bein' spread so thin. If he tries a diversion by attackin' one of the ranches, you'll have to go. If that's how it goes down, I'll have to be ready for a sneak attack here."

"If it comes to that," Jared said, "Miguel and his sons'll have to get down here lickety-split. In a few more days, you may be healthy enough that if I hear of an attack, I can light a shuck out of here and you can fetch Miguel." Jared frowned. "I worry that Morgan will make a move on the school. It would take a black-hearted devil to do somethin' like that but Morgan fits that bill."

Nathan nodded soberly and said, "I'm afraid you're right. I knew Morgan before he went to war. He was wild and rowdy but there was some measure of humanity in him. Once he came back, he'd changed and that humanity was gone. People don't mean much to him other than as pawns in his personal chess game. I wouldn't put it past him to use Eleanor and the children to his advantage. We'll have to cover that along with everything else."

"It's like one a them jigsaw puzzles with some pieces missin'," Jared mused. "Makes it hard to fill in the whole picture."

"That's about right," Nathan nodded. "As for me gettin' healthy, if things keep on the way they're goin', I could handle a pistol and move around a bit within a couple more days. It's lucky Jake hit me in the left shoulder since I handle my Colt with my right. To tell you the truth, the pain ain't nearly as bad now as the itchin'. Doc says that's part of the healin' but I could sure do without it!"

Jared laughed at Nathan's predicament and they joshed back and forth a bit, then Jared left to make his rounds. This went on for the next four days, with Jared and Nathan trying to keep loose as the tension mounted. Jared stayed in contact with Miguel and his sons, having them spell him at the jail when he went to check the outlying ranches. He stopped by the Kilpatrick's place twice during that time and it did his heart good to see that he'd been welcomed back into the family without reservation. Ned was a little stiff when he went out the first time but they got to talking about cattle and Ned's plans for the future if all this unpleasantness worked out in their favor and pretty soon, they were back on level ground with each other. Lizbeth would have fed him until he popped if he'd let her but he kept his visits short because he had a lot of ground to cover.

These visits, along with his time with Nathan, kept him from going loco as he waited for the other boot to drop. At times, he found himself worrying about what might happen between him and Eleanor but he tried to force himself not to think about that because he knew any distractions could prove fatal. He also knew Morgan and his crew were scheming all the while and that was a constant source of annoyance in the same way Nathan's itch bothered him. He wished there was some way to be a fly on the wall to learn what they were up to but he knew there was no way to get close enough. That left it up to guesswork and though he wasn't pleased about that, it was all he had. He knew Morgan had spent his life plotting against others and coming up with strategies to gain the upper hand but he figured Nathan was pretty crafty as well. He just hoped when the time came for a showdown, they had guessed correctly. Time crawled by and his nerves wore thin.

CHAPTER 29

"You wanted to see me, boss?" Bob Evans said to Morgan O'Bannon.

Morgan turned from the fireplace in the big hacienda where he'd been looking at the military sabre and quartermaster's bars above the mantle. Without preamble, he said, "Tomorrow night's it. I heard the judge will make the trip from Taos three days from now and we need to have this taken care of before then. Send one of the hands to tell Heck and get the rest of the boys ready." Morgan turned back toward the mantle and resumed his study of his mementos from the war.

Evans hesitated. Morgan, sensing he was still there, said, "Was something I said not clear?"

Evans cleared his throat and said hesitantly, "This is more than I signed on for, Mr. O'Bannon. I'm just a cowhand . . . I didn't mind changin' a few brands and scarin' a few Meskins but once we cross this line, there ain't no goin' back. Ain't there no other way to handle it?"

Morgan stared at Evans with his icy blue eyes for a long couple of seconds. "Bob, decide right now if you're in or out. If you're out, you'd better hightail it far away from here faster than I can reach my rifle. When I'm done with this business, I'll hunt you down and kill you. Is that clear enough for you?"

Evans turned white and for a moment, couldn't speak. When he found his voice, he stammered, "Uh, yes sir, Mr. O'Bannon. I'll get right on it." He hurried out the door.

When the sun came creeping through the window of the back room of the jailhouse the next morning, Jared shook himself awake and sat up slowly. He felt uneasy, like he often did when he'd been dreaming but he couldn't remember having one. As he pulled on his boots, he chuckled softly at himself, realizing there were plenty of things happening during the daytime that could make him uneasy. He sure didn't need childish nightmares to do the job. He walked into the front room to see if Nathan was awake.

Nathan was sitting in the chair at his desk

when Jared walked in. "Mornin'," he said. "Bet you're worn out this mornin'."

Jared looked at him with puzzlement on his face and asked, "What are you talkin' about Nathan?"

Nathan smiled and said, "Sounded like you spent the whole night fightin' outlaws. You called out in your sleep. I was worried you were gonna fall off your cot, tossin' around so hard. Did you whup'em?"

Jared smiled ruefully and said, "I'm still here, it must've turned out all right. I reckon I worked pretty hard, though, cause I got a powerful hunger this mornin'. I'll walk down to Miguel's and get us a couple of platefuls of that fine breakfast they serve."

Nathan got up from his chair and said, "I'll go, I can use the walk to get the stiffness out. I'll have Tomas or Estevan carry the vittles back and we can plan for the day. I figure somethin'll happen today or tomorrow. We'd best be ready."

After Nathan left, Jared went back to the cell to check on Pete. After the first two days, when he'd been loud and cocky, Pete had fallen into a sullen silence most of the time. As Jared approached the cell, Pete rolled over on his bunk and sat up, staring venomously at him but saying nothing.

Jared couldn't resist pestering Pete a bit.

"Well, Pete, it's comin' up on two weeks and look where you still are. The Judge is headin' over in a day or two to get the wheels of justice a'rollin'. What about that?"

Pete continued to stare at him for a moment, then smiled. "If you think there's gonna be a trial, cowboy, you're even dumber than I thought. Morgan's judge and jury. He's gonna pass sentence on you and that old sheriff. By the time that Taos judge gets to town, the case'll be closed."

Jared shook his head. "Pete, I gotta hand it to you, you don't give up on an idea very easy. I guess you've never known anything different so you can't imagine how it could turn out any other way. I'm here to tell you, though, this'll be different, mark my words."

Pete smirked at Jared and said, "Keep tellin' yourself that, Delaney, it just makes it easier for Morgan. If you had any sense, you'd get on your horse and ride away." Pete leaned back on the cot and propped his boots up. "You ain't got no sense, though. You'll just have to learn your lesson and pay the price."

"I learned my lesson, Pete," Jared said firmly. "By not takin' a stand, I was payin' way too high of a price. I figured it out though and nothin' you say'll change my mind. You're a snake and I don't listen to snakes. I look out for their fangs and shoot'em when I have to but I don't pay attention to their hissin'. Tell it to the wall here in your cell, maybe it'll listen." Jared turned on his heel and walked out to the office.

Behind him, Pete was hollering, "You wait, Delaney, you'll see I'm right. Just you wait." He went on for a few more minutes, then Jared heard him kick the pail in the cell and lie back down on his bunk.

Nathan and Tomas walked in as Pete was hollering. They gave Jared a questioning look and he laughed. "Pete woke up in a foul humor. Reckon he don't like his accommodations."

Nathan chuckled and said, "He won't have to worry about it much longer. When Judge Thomas gets here, I think he'll get a change of scenery pretty quick. Once he gets to the penitentiary in Santa Fe, I expect he'll start missin' his old hangout."

The three men had a good laugh at Pete's expense, then Jared said to Tomas, "Would you keep an eye on our friend while Nathan and I take a little walk?" Turning to Nathan, he asked, "You are up to a little more walkin' ain't you, pardner?"

Nathan nodded. "I'm feelin' pretty spry for an old codger with a bum shoulder. I can take a turn around town without fallin' on my face."

Nathan and Jared left Tomas and walked north on Main Street in the direction of the Colfax Tavern. They went a ways without speaking. Finally, Jared turned toward Nathan and said, "I reckon it'll happen today or tonight. We know Judge Thomas will head this way in a couple of days. Morgan's gonna need a day to take care of business and a day to clean up the mess. Do you agree?"

Nathan nodded and said, "Yep, that's about how I had it figured, too. I expect Morgan'll make his play in the dark, that's what his kind do. We got a quarter moon now and that's his time . . . the rustler's moon. I still don't have a good sense of whether he's gonna come at us straight or pull some trickery to spread us out. What's your take?"

Jared shook his head and said, "My gut says he'll come at us head on to salve his wounded pride from Miguel getting the drop on him in the jail house. If he does, he'll come after dark so we won't be able to tell right off how many men he has. He's not likely to burn us out cause we got Pete inside."

Nathan laughed and said, "See, you been

thinkin' Pete was good for nothin'. Turns out he's our protection against a fire. Maybe we shoulda been feedin' him beefsteak after all."

Jared grinned at Nathan's attempt to lighten the mood and continued, "If nothin's happened by sundown, let's have Miguel and his boys join us so we can have a welcomin' party ready for Morgan. I'd put Tomas and Estevan up on the roof, with me and Miguel in the front room and you in the back keepin' an eye on our prisoner."

Nathan looked Jared up and down. "That makes sense though it don't escape me that you're shufflin' me off into the back so I'm not in the way."

Jared looked Nathan in the eye and said, "I suppose you could look at it that way. I was thinkin' you'd be our last, best chance if the rest of us went down. Only one at a time can come through the door back to the cell. With a couple of pistols, I reckon you could discourage'em from comin' through after a couple of men go down. With luck, one of'em might be Morgan. Whatever else happens, I'd be satisfied with that."

Nathan stared back at Jared for a moment, then grinned and said, "Well, it's good to have a plan!" What he failed to mention is that things rarely go according to plan.

As the sun began to set behind the mountains, Nathan got up and grabbed his hat. "I believe I'll walk down to Miguel's and get some grub," Nathan said. "I'll send Tomas down here right away so there'll be two of you here. When I'm done, I'll come on back with Miguel and Estevan."

Jared said, "You might consider bringin' some grub back with you along with some coffee. If I get shot tonight, I don't want to die with an empty stomach."

Nathan chuckled and said, "If you get shot tonight, what difference will it make?"

Jared grinned and said, "Makes a difference to me. Are you gonna bring me some food or not, old man?"

"If it means that much to you," Nathan said with a shake of his head, "I'll accommodate you. I won't be long." He walked out and a couple of minutes later, Tomas came in, nodded to Jared and had a seat over by Nathan's desk.

After their discussion that afternoon, Jared and Nathan had set their artillery in strategic spots around the office. Jared double-checked the loads on the pistols and made sure there were boxes of ammunition within reach of each weapon. It wasn't likely they'd have a chance to reload during a gun battle, but better to have'em and not need'em than need'em and not have'em. The afternoon light was fading and Tomas began to light the lanterns in the office. All of a sudden, Jared heard hoof beats approaching from the north. He grabbed a shotgun and raced to a window, cautiously glancing outside. He couldn't see much in the gathering gloom but it sounded like one rider in a big hurry rather than a group. As the rider got closer, to his amazement and confusion, he saw it was Lizbeth Kilpatrick. She leapt off her horse and as he opened the door, she practically fell inside. Sobbing, she collapsed in his arms.

Jared held her tight as he spoke. "Lizbeth, calm down, tell me what's goin' on." She pulled away from him and tried to speak but he couldn't understand what she was saying because she was sobbing so hard.

"Take a deep breath and try again," Jared said with patience that he didn't feel. "I can tell somethin' bad has happened."

Her eyes began to focus and she took a couple of deep breaths. Then she spoke, her voice cracking with emotion. "They shot Ned. Oh, God, Jared, Morgan shot Ned!" For a moment, Jared thought she was going to lose control again but she shut her eyes tight and gripped the edge of Nathan's roll-top desk until her knuckles turned white. After a moment, she regained control and was able to continue. "There's no time to explain everything. You got to get to the ranch and save Juan and Maria. I'm afraid Ned is dead, they wouldn't let me check on him. They made me ride in to tell you, so I don't know." Lizbeth sagged as if the air had gone out of her from telling her story.

Jared reached out and put his arm around her shoulder, walking her over to the cot where Nathan had laid up while he was recuperating. He said, "Lie down and rest, I'll take care of this." He turned to Tomas and said, "Fetch your father and Senor Nathan right away. Tell'em I headed to the Kilpatrick's to face Morgan O'Bannon. I'd bet they'll try to break Pete out when I'm gone. Get back here quick as a lightnin' bolt!" Without a word, Tomas ran out the front door of the sheriff's office.

Jared strapped on his gun belt and grabbed a rifle from Nathan's desk. He went to the door, then turned back to Lizbeth and said, "I'll take care of this, I promise. If Ned's alive, I'll try to save him. If he's gone, I'll take a measure of vengeance on that bastard, Morgan. It won't bring Ned back but it's what he'd want me to do." Without waiting for a reply, he ran to his horse, mounted up and spurred his way to a gallop out of town.

It had happened at dusk. Ned and Lizbeth had just sat down to supper when they heard a commotion from the section just south of the ranch house. The cattle began bawling and Ned could hear the sound of cowboys whooping like they do when they're pushing a herd to get moving. Looking at Lizbeth with a mixture of alarm and anger, he said, "It's started. Get in the back of the house. I'll get my gun. You stay put no matter what." Lizbeth sat stunned for a moment as Ned grabbed his rifle and ran onto the porch. She heard hoof beats, a voice and then she heard something that chilled her to the bone . . . a gunshot. She sat for another moment, paralyzed with fear, then forced herself up and raced out the door. To her horror, she saw her husband lying on the porch bleeding from a gunshot wound to his body. Morgan O'Bannon sat on his big bay with a pistol still smoking in his hand.

Lizbeth started to run to Ned's side when Morgan barked a command. "Stop right there, woman! One more step, I'll put a bullet in you, too."

She stopped but turned to him defiantly. "If he's dead, go ahead and put a bullet in me. I don't want to live without him." She looked helplessly at Ned. "What kind of man are you, Morgan? You shoot down innocent folks with no more thought than if they was dumb animals."

He gave her his chilling smirk. "That's really all you are to me, Mrs. Kilpatrick, just dumb animals that happened to get in my way. You're like varmits that cause me minor problems . . . so I get rid of you like I would any other varmit. Before I get rid of you, though, I have a job for you and you'd better be quick about it."

"What makes you think I'd do any job for you?" Lizbeth asked with scorn.

"Oh, you'll do this one," O'Bannon said, "You still think there's a chance I can be stopped. I want you to ride into town as fast as your horse can carry you. Tell that young cowboy I'm waiting for him." Morgan's voice rose and his eyes flashed. "Tell him we've got unfinished business and I'm going to finish it tonight. Can you tell him that, Mrs. Kilpatrick?"

Lizbeth looked at him a moment longer then without a word, she went to the barn, saddled a horse and rode quickly in the direction of Cimarron.

CHAPTER 30

Within minutes after Jared rode off, Tomas ran back into the office. He shut the door and turned to Lizbeth, saying, "My father and brother will be right here, Senora. Can I get you something to ease your pain?"

As Tomas uttered the words, the door flung open behind him. He saw a look of horror in Lizbeth's eyes and started to turn but he heard a voice say, "Hold it right there, pepper belly. So much as twitch and you're a dead Meskin. Raise your hands, turn around and get down on your knees . . . slow!"

Tomas did as he was told. As he turned, he saw Heck Roberts and Bob Evans standing at the door with their pistols cocked and aimed right at him. Evans laughed. "Looks like we get a bonus tonight, Heck. We spring Pete and there'll be one less Meskin in town when we're done. Where's the keys, you bean-eatin' rascal?"

Tomas nodded toward the sheriff's desk. He said, "The drawer on the right, senor."

Heck ran over to the desk and grabbed the keys. He turned to Evans and said, "I'll get Pete, keep this youngster covered."

Bob nodded and looked at Tomas with loathing. "I'll cover him, all right, and when we're done, I'll send him to hell."

As Heck went in the back to get Pete, Lizbeth sat up on the cot. "How'd you come to have such hatred in your heart, Mr. Evans? That boy's never done nothin' to harm you. Go about your dirty business breakin' Pete out of jail if you must but why do you need to kill an innocent man?"

Evans looked over at her and said, "Lady, you don't know what you're talkin' about. These Meskins act like just because they been here for hundreds of years livin' in their mud huts, we should bow and scrape and treat'em like royalty." He was flushed with self-righteous indignation. "This land belongs to the cattlemen because we're strong enough to take it. Them that gets in the way'll have to live or die with it."

Heck came out with a limping Pete O'Bannon and grabbed a pistol and gun belt off the desk, handing it to him. "Look, Pete, that's mighty thoughtful of Delaney, leaving a weapon for you."

Pete strapped on the pistol and said, "All right, fellas, let's get outa here quick."

Evans said, "Not so fast, Pete, I gotta finish cleanin' up the mess in here first." He stepped forward towards Tomas and put his pistol up to his temple. "You pepper bellies are all church-goers, ain't you? Maybe you oughta say your prayers now cause you're not long for this world."

He cocked his gun and was just beginning to exert pressure on the trigger when the door crashed open. A tremendous shotgun blast threw Evans halfway across the room. Miguel and Estevan burst into the sheriff's office and turned their guns on Heck and Pete. Miguel cut loose with the other barrel of his shotgun while Heck and Pete made a play for their weapons. As they drew, Miguel reached for his pistol and in the blink of an eye, the four men were blazing away at one another with their Colt .45s. Roberts was the first to go down, followed soon after by Pete, but not before he rounded Estevan in the leg. The shooting stopped and momentarily, an eerie silence prevailed, soon interrupted by Estevan's groans. The air was heavy with smoke and the acrid smell of black powder. Lizbeth struggled to clear her mind as she attempted to see through the haze. Slowly, the smoke filtered out the front door which had remained open when Miguel and Estevan burst in. As the fog lifted, she could see Evans, Heck and Pete. They were all lying dead on the floor. It was over.

A moment later, Nathan came puffing through the front door, his gun drawn. Seeing it was over, he holstered his pistol. "Sorry I couldn't get here quicker," he said breathlessly. "I still ain't movin' at full speed. Somebody want to fill me in?"

Lizbeth said, "There's no time, Nathan. Morgan came to the ranch at suppertime and shot Ned down in cold blood. He sent me to fetch Jared . . . said somethin' about unfinished business he meant to finish tonight. I believe he means to ambush him." She shuddered. "Nathan, that man is evil to the bone."

Nathan stood up straighter. He turned to Miguel who was tending to his older son's wound, tying his bandana above the wound to staunch the bleeding. Tomas sat at the desk, visibly shaking in the aftermath of his brush with death. "Lizbeth's right, we got to do somethin' right now or it'll be too late. Get these bodies cleared out of here, then someone's got to help Jared."

CHAPTER 31

When Jared galloped out of town, he was enraged at the news that his friend had been gunned down. As the darkness set in, he realized if he didn't slow down, he risked riding into an arroyo where his horse could break a leg or worse. He slowed to a lope and proceeded as quickly as he dared. It took some time to get to the Kilpatrick's ranch and when he rode up to the ranch house, he didn't see anyone. This surprised him because he expected to see Ned's body on the porch. He dismounted and cautiously approached the door.

"Don't move, gringo," he heard a voice say from inside. For a second, he was afraid his efforts to stop Morgan would be over before they got started but then he realized the voice belonged to Juan Suazo.

"Juan, it's me, Jared," he said quietly. "Don't shoot yet, amigo, until you make sure it's really me."

There was a pause, then he heard a familiar chuckle from inside the house, "I should have known it was you because it took you so long to ride here from town. I would have gotten here much faster."

Jared laughed. "For once, I ain't gonna argue with you, compadre. Can I come in?"

Juan opened the door and said, "Come in, we need to do something for Senor Ned. He's hurt bad."

When Jared stepped into the living area, he saw Ned lying on the couch, either unconscious or dead. Jared turned to Juan and said, "We shouldn't move him anymore, looks like he's hit pretty hard. Someone's gonna have to fetch Doc Adams and I've got my hands full trackin' Morgan. Any ideas?"

Over to the side of the room, Jared heard the sound of a match being struck. The lantern flared. In the light, he saw Maria, who set the lantern down and walked over to Jared and her husband. "I'll get the doctor."

Juan said, "Maria, I can't let you do that, we don't know where O'Bannon's men are. It's too dangerous."

Maria turned to her husband with her eyes blazing and said, "Don't you tell me what's too dangerous, Juan Suazo, or what I can or can't do! Ned and Lizbeth are like my family. I will not stand by and let Senor Ned die. Besides," she said, turning to Jared with a grin, "I can ride faster than either of you. I just never said so because I didn't want to hurt your pride."

Jared turned to Juan and shrugged his shoulders. "I ain't gonna argue with her, pardner," he said. "We gotta do somethin' or Ned's gonna die. It's your call."

Juan looked at Maria, then back at Jared. He also shrugged and said, "I don't know what else to do." He smiled sheepishly and added, "She's right, you know. She is faster than both of us."

Maria turned and walked to the door. She stopped, turned back and went to her husband, embracing him. She murmured something in Spanish in his ear, then went outside, saddled her horse and rode off.

Jared stood beside Juan as they listened to Maria's horse pound away. He said, "Time's slippin' away, Juan, I need to head out after Morgan. Maria's gonna make it, you'll see. Keep Ned still and see if you can stem the bleedin'. And keep a sharp eye out for Morgan's men, there's no tellin', they might double back. If they come, shoot first and ask questions later."

Juan reached out his hand to Jared and

said, "You are my amigo, I guess I'll have to trust you. I don't like staying here and doing nothing but I don't know what else to do. Vaya con Dios." Jared shook Juan's hand and went out to mount up.

Knowing he couldn't track Morgan in the dark, Jared tried to guess where he'd most likely head. He knew Morgan was setting a trap . . . he was as much the hunted as the hunter. Briefly, the old feeling of being paralyzed by fear took ahold of him. He forced himself to think about his loved ones . . . his family now . . . and with an iron will, he focused on the problem at hand. Considering Morgan's options, he reckoned he'd go to his ranch. That was the land he was most familiar with and would provide him the best opportunity to ambush Jared. He wasn't sure but he had to make a decision and that was his best guess. He made his choice and spurred his horse, casting his lot in that direction.

Riding as fast as he dared for about a half hour, he came down into a small valley and saw a rider top the next rise and head down the other side . . . O'Bannon! He felt a stab of uncertainty which was immediately replaced with resolve fueled by righteous anger. The man thought he could kill innocent people and never pay the piper. Well, he was about to find out different! He spurred his horse after him.

The light of the quarter moon was barely enough to see the trail, especially with dust swirling around him. As he galloped through the darkness, he had an eerie sensation he'd been through this before, but he had no time for reflection. It was all he could do to remain in the saddle. At the top of the rise, he saw another hill in front of him, even higher than the one over which he'd just ridden. There was no sign of O'Bannon.

He slowed his horse and tried to pick up signs of a trail. Suddenly, he felt like he'd been hit in the shoulder with a railroad tie. A split second later, he heard the sound of the shot. As he fell off his horse, the thought occurred to him that it was strange the way you felt the impact of the bullet before you heard the shot. He landed hard, which stunned him further. He lay there trying to clear the cobwebs from his brain and take stock of the damage. The pain in his right shoulder was agonizing and it was all he could do not to scream. Once again, he called up the faces of his loved ones in his mind. Slowly, the wave of pain receded, allowing him to think clearly. From the sound of the shot, he figured the wound was the result of a pistol rather than the Winchester rifle he knew O'Bannon carried in his scabbard. Small consolation . . . his right arm was useless. He tried rolling to his left so he could reach his pistol with his left hand and nearly passed out from the pain. Jared knew if he lost consciousness, he was done for. O'Bannon would be searching for his fallen body. His only hope was to rest a minute, then muster the strength to grab his Colt with his good left hand. Before he could make the move, he heard footsteps approaching from up the rise. He looked up and there stood Morgan O'Bannon, silhouetted by the light of the rustler's moon, just as he had been that night twelve years before.

"We've got us quite a situation, here, don't we?" said O'Bannon in a voice that cut through Jared like a knife. "I predicted things might get interesting for us years ago when I killed your Ma and Pa. I thought it might come down to something like this. Remember, sonny, me looking down at you trembling under the mesquite bushes?"

"I didn't remember for a long time," Jared spit at O'Bannon, "but it came back to me recently. I recall what a gutless, bushwhackin' outlaw you were then and still are. It don't take much of a man to prey on simple farmers."

"That's pretty amusing coming from a man who let himself get outwitted and outgunned. If we're judging manhood, you come out on the short end of that stick." O'Bannon let out a chilling laugh. "I could have killed you when you were just a pup but I didn't. You're not much more than a pup now, are you? The difference is, now I'm bored with you. Say your prayers, sonny, cause the next bullet's going right in your brain."

Jared's mind raced, grasping for his next move. In a heartbeat, he realized he had no more moves. As the realization sunk in, he thought of Eleanor and the future they'd never share. As painful as his wounded shoulder was, that thought was far more agonizing. Then the pain passed and he felt a sense of calm come over him. It occurred to him that for a time, at least, she had truly loved him. There was no better measure of his worth than that.

He looked up at O'Bannon and said in a calm, even voice, "Morgan, you ain't the better man, just the better shot. You got twisted up over the years, figured bein' strong gave you the right to bully folks. I went through some confusion myself, actin' like right and wrong was hidin' in the gray of the moonshadow instead of bein' laid out right in front of me plain as day."

Morgan lowered his pistol and looked down with a smirk, knowing he was helpless. "I'll let you have your last words before I end your pitiful life."

Jared couldn't suppress a groan because of the fiery pain in his shoulder. He took a breath and continued. "Some real decent folks helped me see the light of day. You may kill me, but as I leave this world, I know I've chosen what's right. That makes me the better man, no matter what kind of a cold-blooded killer you are. Go ahead, do what you're gonna do, but mark this . . . we both know in our hearts what's right and wrong. Whether you ever tell another soul, we know who the better man is."

O'Bannon was stung by Jared's words. His voice had an edge to it as he answered. "Pretty fancy speech but it won't save your hide. It's knowledge I can live with and you can die with. You're trying to buy time, anyway, and the fact is, you've run out of time." O'Bannon raised his pistol and aimed at Jared's head. "This game's over for you, Delaney."

Jared heard the report of the Colt, but felt no impact of the bullet, which he found strange. He'd closed his eyes, but after the shot, he heard a body fall and looked up to see Morgan O'Bannon on his knees before him with a puzzled, faraway look in his eyes. He held his left hand out toward Jared, then without a word, fell face down in the dirt. Jared shook his head, trying to clear away the dust that seemed to be as much inside his head as around it. He heard a noise off to his right and looked in that direction. Nathan Averill stepped out from behind a small pinon tree with his pistol in his hand.

"My God, Nathan, what . . ." Jared sputtered. As the sheriff walked quickly over to his side, Jared said, "Where in the world did you come from?"

"When you tore out after O'Bannon, I figured I'd better follow in case it came down to somethin' like this. I don't move too fast, but sometimes racin' into things ain't necessarily the best way to proceed, as it looks like you discovered." Nathan uttered a mirthless chuckle. "I figured Morgan would set up the ambush on his ranch so I came here directly. Let's take a look to see how bad you're hit."

Jared shook his head angrily. "Never mind that! I'm hit pretty good but I ain't gonna die right away. How long were you standin' there listenin'?"

With a little half-smile on his face, Nathan

said, "Long enough to hear what you said. For what it's worth, I think you're right."

Jared half rose up, which elicited a gasp of pain. When he recovered, he said in an outraged voice, "You mean to tell me you were standin' there watchin' Morgan point his Colt revolver at me, knowin' he might pull the trigger at any time and you were just listenin'! Didn't it occur to you if you waited too long, I'd be dead?"

The sheriff looked at Jared and said, "It did occur to me. It also occurred to me that I owed you the opportunity to face your demon and spit in his eye. I figured that was more important, even if it was the last thing you did on earth, than me rescuin' you like you were that young kid years ago. I ain't your daddy and you're a grown man. You needed to act like one. You did, and that's that. If you got any complaints, I guess you can shoot me if you feel like it."

Jared shook his head in exasperation. "So I suppose I should be thankin' you for almost lettin' me get shot?"

Nathan chuckled with a little more humor this time and said, "Well, somethin' like that, I reckon."

As he lay there, Jared began to chuckle as well, which hurt like hell. "We're a pair, ain't we, Nathan? Yes, thank you for savin' my life and lettin' me make my stand, even though I had to do it lyin' flat on my back. I'm a pretty imposin' deputy, ain't I?" Jared laughed again, which again brought forth a groan. He said, "You know, you never did bring me my grub this evenin'. I guess I went and got myself shot on an empty stomach after all."

The sheriff kneeled down and said, "Let's try to get the bleedin' stopped, then I'll get a fire goin'. We'll camp here for the night. I'll ride into town in the mornin' and get some help to get you back home.

CHAPTER 32

The next morning, Nathan prepared to head back into town. They'd spent time during the night talking in the faint light of the rustler's moon about what had happened, trying to fit the pieces together. Jared told about Lizbeth's arrival at the office with the terrible news about the shooting which led to Jared's rapid departure. Nathan filled in the rest of the story of Heck Roberts and Bob Evans barging in to break out Pete, and of Tomas's narrow escape from getting a bullet in the brain. Morgan had orchestrated a plan designed to lure Jared out to be ambushed while Heck and Bob murdered Nathan and anyone else left guarding the jail. Luckily, he'd underestimated his foes.

In the light of the dawn, Jared shook his head. "I don't feel any sorrow about Heck Roberts. In fact, if he's harmed Christy, I was gonna send him to meet his maker myself. I do regret about Bob Evans, though. He was a good cowhand but he just seemed to have grown bitter and bent. He turned his head when it came to lookin' at what Morgan was doin'. I got the notion he didn't feel right about it but it didn't stop him from bein' a part of it. I guess those choices come back to haunt you, don't they?"

Nathan looked at Jared for a moment and then they both grinned as Jared realized that he could have been describing himself not too long ago. Nathan said, "Yeah, your choices always come back to you, good or bad. Bob was a grown man. The reasons he made his choices don't much matter, he still had to live with'em . . . and die with'em."

Jared nodded and replied, "You got that right. Now you ought to head on down and get someone to fetch me. You went and shot all the outlaws, I reckon there's not as big a rush to get me back to town as there was the night you got shot." Jared paused for a moment as pain washed over him. "That bein' the case, I'd just as soon ride in a wagon as try to stay on my horse. Have'em bring along some blankets to ease the bumps."

"Wantin' to ride in style, now, are you?" Nathan asked. "We can prob'ly arrange some paddin' for you. I'll get to town quick as I can. I still ain't movin' at full speed myself."

Jared said, "That was plain enough last night when you took so long before you shot Morgan. I'm still not sure quite what to think about that."

Nathan smiled and said, "I was quick enough . . . you're the one's lyin' there complainin', ain't you?"

Jared smiled back and said, "When you put it that way, I see your point." He turned serious and said, "I wonder how Ned's gettin' along? I didn't get a good look at him last night but from what I could see, he looked to be in pretty bad shape. When you send the wagon, send news about that deal."

Nathan nodded and said, "I'll send Estevan, he can fill you in. I hope the news is good but I got a bad feelin'. I don't know what Lizbeth'll do if Ned dies. She could run that place with the right help but I don't know if she'd have the starch to do it without Ned beside her."

With a downcast expression, Jared said, "I hate to think about that. She and Ned were better to me than anyone's been since I lost my folks and I sure didn't repay'em properly. Lizbeth was like a big sister in some ways and sorta like a mother in other ways. I don't know what in the world I could do to help but I'd give anything if I could to make things right."

Nathan shook his head slowly. "Sometimes we can't make things right, we can just be there to help the ones left behind get through. If it comes to it, you can do that much."

Jared didn't know what else to say so he just nodded and lay back on his blanket to rest. Nathan checked his shoulder once more to make sure the bleeding hadn't started back up, then mounted up and headed in to town. Jared settled in as best he could, knowing it would be well after noon before a wagon could get back to pick him up.

It was mid-afternoon before Estevan Mares arrived with the wagon. He had no news of Ned's health which was part of the reason he hadn't arrived sooner. Nathan wanted to consult with Doc Adams about the safety of moving Jared but the doctor hadn't made it back to town by mid-morning and Nathan didn't want to delay any longer. The ride was bumpy and although Estevan had thrown some blankets in the back, they didn't do a great deal to cushion the jolting over the rough terrain. By the time Estevan pulled up to the front of the Sheriff's office,

Jared was in a great deal of pain and his wound was leaking blood. Tomas and his brother helped Jared inside where they laid him down on the cot on which Nathan had recuperated.

Nathan came in behind the Mares sons carrying a stool and some clean cloths. As he sat down to apply a compress to Jared's wound, he said, "No one's heard anything about Ned. Doc hasn't come back yet and we can't spare anyone to ride out and check. I'll get you cleaned up and as comfortable as I can but doc's got to take a look at you. I reckon the bones ain't shattered or you'd be howlin' a lot louder but he still needs to examine you to make sure the bullet passed on through."

Jared nodded but was too weak to say anything. Nathan cleaned him up, which was a painful process, then left him to rest while he went over to his desk and began writing up an account of the events that had taken place.

"I ain't gonna hover over you like you did me," Nathan said with a grin. "Besides, with Judge Thomas due here tomorrow, I'd better have this all down in writin' so he can look over it before he starts askin' questions. I've known him for years. He's a good man but he'll sure have questions cause he's gonna have to answer a bunch himself when he gets back to Taos." Nathan's grin widened. "I expect old Tom Catron will be fit to be tied. He ain't use to his land-grabbin' schemes not workin' out."

Nathan got to work at his desk and Jared slept fitfully. Several hours later, at dusk, he awoke and saw that he was alone. He dozed again and then his eyes opened when he heard the door. Nathan walked in and said, "You've got some company if you're up to it."

Jared nodded weakly and looked over to the open door. He saw Eleanor walk in, followed by Christy Quick. He blinked, shook his head and found himself speechless. He tried to speak once, then twice, then he shook his head again. Finally, he found his voice and said, "I got so many questions I don't know which one to ask first. Can somebody explain to me what's goin' on?"

The young ladies looked at each other and smiled slightly. Christy nodded to Eleanor, deferring to her. After a moment, Eleanor spoke. "Miss Quick wanted to thank you for your kindness and let you see she's all right. On the night she warned Nathan about the ambush, she came to me for help."

At that point, Christy joined the conversation and said, "I knew if I went back to the tavern, Heck'd kill me." Noting the startled look on Jared's face, she said, "Miss Eleanor don't approve of my life but she ain't like most of the high-fallutin' ladies in town, lookin' down their noses at me. I figured if anyone'd be willin' to help, it'd be her. I didn't know where else to turn."

"Miss Quick explained how she'd told Nathan what Morgan was doing," Eleanor said. "I felt I had to do something to help her. She took a tremendous chance exposing their plot. It took a great deal of courage. I couldn't just leave her to the mercy . . . or should I say, the lack of mercy . . . of a man like Roberts. I took her to Reverend Richardson and he went to get Father Antonio. The two of them came up with the idea of hiding her in the sanctuary. They've been bringing her food and water on the sly since then."

Christy chuckled and said, "Church was the last place Heck would've thought of to look for me nor would he expect the town's ministers to be the ones to help me. He didn't think too highly of the 'servants of God,' as he called'em but they sure gave me a helpin' hand when I needed it. Them and Miss Eleanor," she added gratefully.

Jared lay there in stunned silence trying to get his thoughts together. Finally, he said,

"Christy, I'm mighty glad to see you're alive and it's me who should be thankin' you. If you hadn't done what you did, we'd all prob'ly be dead now." Jared paused. "Did Nathan tell y'all everything that happened?" he asked uneasily.

Christy and Eleanor both nodded and Eleanor said, "Nathan filled us in on most of what happened. I'm sorry all this business had to end in bloodshed but I don't see how it could've gone any other way. I'm just glad it ended with you and Nathan alive."

Jared blushed, not knowing how much of his final showdown Eleanor was aware. He said, "I'm glad to be alive, too, though not at full strength." He nodded toward Nathan. "You prob'ly know, I owe my life to old Mr. Averill over there."

Eleanor looked from one to the other and said, "Nathan was a little vague on the details. He just said the two of you made a pretty good team. Maybe one of these days when you're feeling stronger, we can get the full story."

Jared looked gratefully at Nathan who said, "Maybe so, we'll wait and see." Nathan looked over to Eleanor and Christy. With a look of mischief, he said, "Why doesn't 'old Mr. Averill' accompany Miss Quick over to the Colfax Tavern to gather her things. I reckon it's safe now for her to do that." He turned to Jared and said, "I believe Eleanor had a few more things to discuss with you in private."

Eleanor walked Nathan and Christy to the door, closing it behind them. She hesitated for a moment then turned to face Jared, her eyes full of pain. "We agreed we'd wait until this business was over before we talked about us," she said. "I suppose it's close enough to over that we can have that talk now . . . that is, if you feel strong enough to do it."

Jared cleared his throat and replied, "I ain't in the best of shape as you can see but I've been waitin' to speak with you for weeks, I sure don't want to put it off any longer." Jared shook his head again in amazement. "I'm still tryin' to get over seein' Christy alive and well. I'm surprised to hear she came to you for help . . . although I reckon it makes a lot of sense. You're the most decent and honest person I've ever met. If I needed help, you're the one I'd turn to."

Eleanor looked away for a moment, then turned back to Jared. "I appreciate that but you need to know it wasn't easy for me to help her, not after everything that's happened. Most of it wasn't her fault, though and I can't say I'd have done any better if I were in her shoes. She's got spirit . . . there's something decent about her in spite of the rough life she's lived."

"You're right about all of that," Jared said. "What happened was my fault alone from the git go. I know I made a lot of mistakes. If I don't stand up and face the music for the choices I've made . . . good or bad . . . I ain't the kind of man I want to be and all this trouble will have been for nothin'."

Jared saw a tear brim over from Eleanor's eye and roll down her cheek. He wanted so badly to go over and take her in his arms to comfort her but all he could do was lay there helplessly. She looked at his face, sensing both his intention and his frustration. She smiled wistfully through her tears and said, "I know, it's hard. Funny, isn't it, how you'll most likely heal from your bullet wound quicker than the two of us will heal from the pain we've caused each other."

"I know I've caused you pain," Jared said emphatically, "but you haven't done anything to me. I don't blame you for backin' off like you did. I just wish I'd of come to my senses sooner. I can't be cryin' over spilt milk, though, I just got to get to work cleanin' it up."

With another wistful smile, Eleanor said, "Well, I guess that's what this talk is for, isn't it . . . to start cleaning up the mess we've made. I don't know any other way to do this but to ask you directly. Do you want to be with me or Miss Quick?"

"That's easy to answer," Jared said. Then he hesitated. "Well, no, it ain't. It's simple and clear but it ain't easy. I went to Christy for comfort after I'd turned my life all topsy-turvy. Along the way, I became fond of her. She does have spunk and underneath that rough outside, she's a good woman . . . but she's not you. I've learned when you make a hard choice, folks may not like what you decide. I don't want to be hurtful to her but in my heart, I know it's you I love. You can turn around and walk out of my life forever but it don't change how I feel. There it is, that's my answer."

Eleanor looked Jared straight in the eyes and in addition to the pain he'd seen earlier, he also saw her strength. "You're right, there's no easy way through this. I'm not going to walk out of your life but understand . . . it won't be easy. You made some painful mistakes and while I forgive you, I'm not able to just forget what happened."

Jared nodded and said, "I understand and

I'll try not to expect things just to go back to the way they were before all this happened. All I want is a chance to prove I've changed."

"I'll give you that chance," Eleanor said. "I'd say you've earned it for what you've done to help Nathan and everyone in Colfax County shake free from the O'Bannons' grip."

Jared shook his head. "Nathan gets most of the credit, Eleanor. I just tried to help him out the best I could. When push came to shove, he stepped up and saved my bacon. I don't reckon he told you but if it weren't for him, I'd be a dead man."

Eleanor said, "Nathan Averill told me you were the bravest man he's ever known. No offense but when Nathan tells me something, I usually believe him."

Jared didn't know what to say so he lay there quietly. Eleanor said, "When I think about it, I disagree that you've changed." Jared started to protest but she waved her hand to shush him and continued. "I think you're the same good man you were when you first rode into Cimarron. I just think you've been through some tough times and as a result, you've grown into a better man now. That's the way life works. The tough times define us . . . we either get stronger and learn from them or they warp us and damage our souls. That's the difference between you and Morgan O'Bannon, right there in a nutshell. You're a better man today than you were when you came to Cimarron and I believe you'll be an even better man tomorrow. That's why I love you."

Jared lay there quietly for a moment then asked, "Well, what do we do now?"

Eleanor laughed. "I expect you should go back to sleep so you can heal up. No one's heard from Doc yet but I know Nathan wants him to look at you as soon as he's back." As she said that, they both realized they still didn't know the fate of Ned Kilpatrick. Eleanor said, "I'll let you know as soon as I hear anything." She came over, kissed him on the forehead and left the sheriff's office.

Sometime later in the night, a noise startled Jared awake. He looked up and saw Nathan come in followed by Doc Adams. He couldn't bring himself to ask the question but as they lit the lantern, both men saw it in his eyes. Doc said, "There's no news yet, Jared. When I left the ranch, Ned was still unconscious. He was shot through a lung and he's lost a lot of blood. There's not much we can do for him but keep his wounds clean. That and pray, if you're so inclined."

Doc examined Jared's wound, cleaned it and applied a new dressing. He told Jared to drink as much water as he could hold and eat something regularly whether he was hungry or not. "Your body needs food and water to heal," Doc said. "It's no time to be picky about what tastes good or how hungry you are. The better you take care of yourself, the sooner you'll be up and around. Now, I'm gonna go back to my office, have a shot of that whiskey I keep in my desk drawer for emergencies, and go to bed." Doc pulled out his handkerchief and wearily wiped his forehead. "I tell you, I'm mighty tired of patchin' up gunshot wounds. I'll check on you tomorrow morning." He walked out of the sheriff's office.

After Doc left, Nathan hemmed and hawed a bit, then came out and asked Jared straight up what had happened between him and Eleanor. Jared said, "Mighty nosey, ain't you, pryin' into a fella's personal business."

Nathan looked at him for a minute, not sure if he was joshing or not. "Yeah, I'm nosey, it comes with bein' a lawman. Now, tell me what happened fore I arrest you."

Jared chuckled and said, "Well, since you put it that way, I guess I'll tell you." Turning serious and said, "I reckon you could say we cleared the air and know where we stand. She knows I love her and I know I hurt her real bad. She's still got feelin's for me but it's gonna take some time to heal and sort through all this mess. At least she knows she stands at the head of the line with me . . . not that there's a real long line!"

It was Nathan's turn to chuckle. "I'm guessin' the other lady in line was Miss Quick who, by the way, is a mighty spunky lass herself."

"I agree," Jared said. "Under different circumstances, I'd be inclined to try to make an honest woman out of her. This ain't 'different circumstances,' though. It's what it is. I hope I ain't hurt her feelin's too bad but I can't help the way I feel about Eleanor."

"Miss Quick's an intelligent woman," Nathan said. "She'll understand the situation and recover pretty quick . . . just like her name. I wonder what she's gonna do now, though. I suspect she's had her fill of the sportin' life but I don't know what other choices she's got here in this rough country." Nathan shrugged. "I know life's hard but it won't be right if that young lady don't get some sort of second chance. I can't think of anyone who's earned it more." Nathan and Jared talked for a few more minutes but Nathan could see that Jared was weak, so he left to let him get some sleep.

The four days following the showdown were like a fog for Jared. He drifted in and out of sleep and experienced a great deal of pain in his shoulder. Doc Adams dropped by twice a day to make sure his wound was clean and his dressing was fresh. The other frequent visitor was Eleanor, who came by before school and then late in the afternoons. They didn't really talk much about their relationship, she just filled him in on the daily shenanigans of the students and bits of news and gossip. It was amazing how quickly things returned to normal. By the afternoon of the fourth day, Jared was beginning to feel the itching that Nathan had described and while it nearly drove him to distraction, it was an encouraging sign.

The afternoon of the fourth day, Eleanor came in for her visit and told him she had some news. "Good or bad?" he asked.

Eleanor smiled playfully and said, "Why good news, silly. We've had more than our share of bad news lately." Jared waited expectantly for her to continue and after a moment, she did. "I'll be taking on an assistant at the school starting next week. She'll learn from me how to be a teacher just as I did from Hattie. Isn't that exciting?"

Jared nodded as enthusiastically as he could and said, "That's great news, Eleanor! I always thought you had your hands full, especially since more families are sendin' their children there. I expect it's a tribute to the fine job you do. Do I know the lucky young lady who'll be under your wing?"

Eleanor grinned wickedly and said, "Why yes, I'd say you know her pretty well although there are things you don't know about her."

Jared was confused. "You got my curiosity up now. Who in the world are you talkin' about?"

"Why, I'm talking about Christy, Jared," Eleanor said with a smile. "Who'd you think I meant? By the way, one of the things you don't know about her is that her name is Christine Johnson. She came out here from St. Louis, too."

Jared, who had been sitting up on the cot, lay back down on his pillow and just shook his head. "Don't that beat all," he said. "What'll you think of next? I reckon that's gonna make somebody sweat a bit . . . most likely me. The two of you'll prob'ly have a hoot at my expense."

Eleanor nodded smugly and said, "You're right about that. To tell you the truth, we'd gotten to be friends over the last several weeks while she was hiding out. Since everything came to a head and the threat was gone, we began talking about the future. Christy doesn't want to continue with the life she was leading and as it turns out, she had some schooling as a child. She can read and write some and she's willing to learn more. She's worried about the 'high-fallutin' ladies, as she calls them but between Nathan and myself, I think we can nip any gossip in the bud. It won't hurt matters that both Reverend Richardson and Father Antonio are two of her biggest supporters."

They talked some more about what was happening in town and what people were saying about the shootouts with the O'Bannons, then Eleanor left to prepare her lesson for the next day. Doc came by to check Jared's wound and declared that it looked good. As he had the previous days, he told Jared that there was nothing new to report on Ned Kilpatrick. He'd been unconscious since the night he was shot and while he was still breathing, he was not responding to anything Doc had tried. "It doesn't look good," Doc said. "The longer he stays unconscious, the worse his chances are."

CHAPTER 33

The morning of the sixth day following the showdown with the O'Bannons, Jared finished his breakfast and got up to walk around the office a bit. He felt wobbly but Doc had insisted he needed to walk around to build up his strength. After a few minutes, he was exhausted and went over to rest on the cot he'd been occupying for nearly a week.

He was dozing off when the door opened. He looked up and saw Lizbeth Kilpatrick standing at the entrance. One look told him the awful news. He was speechless in the face of her grief. She walked over to the cot, pulled up a chair and sat down. He held out his hand and she took it, holding it loosely on her lap. She sat with tears rolling down her cheeks for several moments, not saying a word. Finally, she said, "He's gone, Jared. I went in to see if I could wake him early this morning and he wasn't breathin'.

I guess he passed some time during the night. He never made a sound and he never woke up."

Jared tried to speak but his voice didn't seem to work. Finally, he was able to say, "Lizbeth, I don't have words to say how bad I feel. If I could've taken the bullet for him, I would have." He wanted to say more but couldn't think of anything that didn't sound useless so he just squeezed her hand.

Lizbeth looked at Jared and said, "I know, Jared. I'm sorry he didn't wake up before the end so I could tell him what you and Nathan did. He'd have been proud of you and satisfied that the O'Bannons got what was comin' to'em."

"I know they did," Jared said despondently, "but that don't seem nearly as important now. This ain't how it's supposed to end."

Lizbeth bowed her head and sobbed gently for several minutes before looking up again. "I've been thinkin' that for the past six days . . . it's not supposed to end this way. I began to suspect Ned wasn't gonna make it and I didn't know how I'd go on without him. It's the toughest thing I've ever faced and you know what I thought about?" Jared shook his head. "I thought that always before when I had a problem, I talked it out with my best friend, Ned. This time, I couldn't do that . . . or at least that's what I thought."

Jared looked puzzled and asked, "What do you mean?"

Lizbeth looked up at the ceiling, then into Jared's eyes. "I realized me and Ned knew what the other was goin' to say before they said it . . . heck, sometimes even before they knew they were going to say it. So I asked myself, what would Ned say to me?"

Jared stayed quiet, looking intently at Lizbeth. Finally, he said, "What do you figure he'd say?"

Lizbeth said, "I know exactly what he'd say. He'd say, 'honey, life's hard but it goes on.' With the O'Bannons out of the picture, there's a fightin' chance of makin' the ranch a success. If I want to honor his memory, that's the greatest honor I can think of. Ned would tell me, 'You still got a ranch to run.'"

Jared thought about what Lizbeth had said. "You know, I think you're right. I think that's exactly what Ned would've said. It reminds me of somethin' I was discussin' with someone the other day. I said it was simple and clear but it wasn't easy. I reckon the same's true about this. It may be the hardest thing you ever tackle but it's clear what you should do."

Lizbeth looked gratefully at Jared and said, "I knew you'd understand, that's why you're the first person I wanted to tell about Ned's passin'. There's more, though and you need to hear it."

Jared's puzzlement showed on his face as he asked, "What do you mean, there's more?"

Lizbeth said, "You know what's invoked in runnin' a ranch and you know I'll need help. Juan's a good hand but I'll need more help than just one good cowboy. You know what you said about Ned's bein' like a brother to you? You were like a brother to him, too, even the part where after you argue, you're both so pig-headed you won't speak for months. Ned would want you to run the ranch with me, that's what. He'd want me to take you on as a partner, fifty-fifty."

Jared was stunned and couldn't speak for a minute. Finally, he said, "I don't know what to say, Lizbeth. Are you offerin' me partnership in your ranch?"

Lizbeth said, "That's exactly what I'm offerin' . . . what Ned and I are offerin'. Will you consider it?"

"I keep sayin' I don't know what to say, then I rattle off at the mouth without makin' a lick of sense, but I still ain't sure what to say." Jared looked around the room as if the answers were to be found written on the walls. He turned his head back to Lizbeth. "I'm tryin' to get on my feet and make up for the terrible pain I caused Eleanor. I hadn't even given much thought to how I was gonna make a livin' though I'll have to think of somethin' pretty soon. I just don't know." Jared realized that he had once again rattled on and not come to a firm conclusion but he felt at a loss. A thought crossed his mind. "Lizbeth, what would people in town think if I moved in with a newly-widowed woman? I'd never want to do somethin' that'd put you in a bad light with folks."

Lizbeth got a look of wry amusement on her face. "I'd be flattered if anyone thought a young pup like you'd be interested in a dried-out old ranch wife like me." Jared started to protest but she waved her hand dismissively. "I'm just teasin'. To tell you the truth, I hadn't given that part much thought. Seems to me you might be comin' out to the ranch with a wife of your own soon enough. I reckon that'd take care of the problem."

Jared said, "I hope you're right but there's no sure way to tell what'll happen between Eleanor and me. That's just one more thing

I'm rasslin' with in my mind."

Lizbeth said, "I know I'm comin' at you with a lot at once. You just found out Ned was gone and now I'm offerin' half ownership in a ranch. I understand you need to think about it. Just don't take forever to decide."

Jared looked at Lizbeth and a half-smile formed on his lips. "I've done some growin' up since I first rode into Cimarron. I don't know my answer today but I won't straddle the fence for long. That's a fine and generous offer. I appreciate it more than I can say. Somehow, it seems right about it bein' what Ned would want, too. I can see him grinnin' and waitin' to see what I say . . ." Jared choked up at this point and couldn't go on.

Lizbeth rose. "I've complicated things enough for one mornin'. You need your rest. I'll let Reverend Richardson know Ned's gone." A tear trickled down Lizbeth's cheek. "Ned wasn't a church-goin' man. He always said he spent most Sabbaths in God's church . . . that's what he called it . . . out with nature on horseback. I don't reckon he'd mind if the Reverend came out and said a few words over his grave, though.

Jared sat upright again. "Let me know when. If I can make the trip, I'll be there."

"Thanks, Jared. I can't tell you how much it means to me." Lizbeth got up and went to the door. She turned, like she wanted to say something more, then just waved and walked out.

Jared lay there, stunned at the news of Ned's death and Lizbeth's offer, his mind muddled. It was still that way later when the door opened and Nathan walked in.

Nathan looked at Jared. "I saw Lizbeth, she told me what happened. She also told me she'd offered you half the ranch. That's some offer."

Jared said, "That it is. I'll consider it but I can't help feelin' my place is in town, near Eleanor. I don't know how I can make things right with her if I'm out chasin' cattle all week long."

Nathan said, "Things have a way of takin' a natural course. It'll be a spell before you're ready to be horseback. You got time to ponder it. I know someone who'll want to have her say anyway. You're gonna have to do some talkin' with her, I reckon. Who knows, she might just take to the notion of bein' a ranch wife."

Jared nodded. "You're right, we'll have to work this out together." Jared laughed. "You're right about another thing for sure. Eleanor's always gonna have her say!"

Nathan joined Jared's laughter and said, "Look on the bright side, son. She's a great one to have on your side. You sure don't want her against you!"

"You're right about that, too. Fact of the matter, you got a habit of bein' right about most things, it just took me awhile to figure that out." Jared turned serious. "I got another tough choice, don't I? Well, like I told Lizbeth, I've grown up considerable since I first rode into Cimarron. I need to give this some thought but I'll make my decision soon as I'm ready, then set out to make it work."

Nathan looked at Jared and said, "I expect you will. Get some rest. I'll go make my rounds."

Jared suddenly felt very tired. He made his way back to the cot and lay down, thinking about all the possibilities facing him. After a time, he drifted off to sleep.

In the dream, Jared was standing looking up at a boulder. There, crouched on top ready to attack, was the same enormous mountain lion he'd seen before in his dreams. Although he was keenly aware of the danger, for some reason, he didn't feel afraid. He stared into the big cat's eyes and it stared back, its tail twitching. They stayed locked in that stare for what seemed like an eternity to Jared. Then the cat relaxed and came out of its threatening crouch. It cocked its head, blinked, then turned and trotted off into the underbrush. Somehow, Jared knew it was gone for good.

ABOUT THE AUTHOR

Jim Jones lives in Corrales, New Mexico, and is a songwriter and performer of western music. He is also a licensed psychotherapist who has worked with individuals coping with post-traumatic stress disorder, a condition that, while not formally identified in the Old West, certainly existed. He has never rustled cattle.

CPSIA information can be obtained
at www.ICGtesting.com
Printed in the USA
FFOW05n1231030815